Dedicated to my lovely wife Kathy, my little dog child Cody, family, fans, and friends, here and abroad.

NEVER CRY

WOLF

LEE J. MINTER

"It is, what it is, no matter how fine the drapery."

~ Mintboogie ~

CONTENTS

INTRODUCTION

Five minutes in and five minutes out, that was the golden rule and how we did things, and this bank job would be no different. I was working with a crew of five other ex-convicts, including myself, which was simple math add it up, which made us six strong.

We had been casing this bank *Harper Creek Bank & Trust* for some time now in a small nondescript town inside of South Dakota. Keenly but discreetly watching the comings and goings of the bank manager and its employees, whereas we probably knew their routines better than them by now.

When they clock in when they clock out when they go to lunch, take a piss break, a crap break, a cigarette break, scratch their asses when they itch, and nobody is looking, you get the picture.

We knew the drop-offs and the pick-ups at this branch like we were the ones driving the Armor truck and handling the cash.

See, that was the problem with these small-town banks; they got into the comfortable habit of being routine. Yeah, they tried to mix it up now and then and change up the program. But if you were like me and watch them closely enough, you could tell there were only so many variations at their disposal, and hell to me, they might as well have been all the same.

Five minutes in and five minutes out. That was the golden rule.

I was not working with a bunch of Einstein's. Still, the plan was simple enough, get the money and get our sweet asses out of dodge, and hit the nearest backwoods high-way before Sheriff Rosco P. Coltrane and Deputy Doodah made the bank's alarm response in time.

The only thing I wanted them to catch is the smoke from our asses, as we got the fuck out of their apple pie ass town with their money and the shit we had stolen from the safe deposit boxes. But you know what they say about the best-laid plans? If something can go wrong, most likely it will; it is not a matter of if, but when? And like I said, I was not working with a bunch of *MIT grads*. Oh!' by the way, my name is Needy Sellars, and I am the leader of this crew, of this band of misfits.

And this is how it all went down before we – well, let me begin the story from when we enter the bank, shall I? And what was supposed to be a routine easy cash grab became this...

* * *

"Let's go; we don't have much time!" Needy yelled at one of her crew members that went by the nickname Freak. "I got this, just relax!" Freak shouted back as he emptied the rest of the contents from the safe deposit box into the bag. The bank manager and his teller looked on in shock with hands raised in the air at the brazen and heavily armed masked bank robbers. It became apparent to them that the one that was shouting the most orders that appeared to be of female orientation was the boss of this heist.

"Four minutes, we are right at the edge! Move your asses, you slow pricks!" Needy said as she glanced at her watch's timer that was counting down from five minutes.

One of the gunmen pointed a shotgun at the manager and the teller. "Both of you down on the floor now!" He ordered.

Both of them dropped quickly to the floor with their hands behind their heads, anticipating execution and praying that it would come quick and painless.

"Okay, let's rock and roll!" Needy said.

"Wait, did you hear that?" Dez asked.

Needy listen, it was a faint sound, but she could still hear the sound of someone crying in the building.

She put the nozzle of the assault rifle to the back of the manager's head. "Asshole, I thought you said y'all two were the only ones here?"

"Please, please, I never said that." He whimpered.

Needy nudged the nozzle deeper into the back of his head. "Who else is in here?" she asked.

"Sandy, she is in the employees' restroom! Please do not kill me," he answered nervously.

Needy eyes shot across the bank's layout. "Sandy? Where is the fucking restroom?"

The bank manager pointed in the direction of the restroom nervously.

Needy signaled to another one of her crew members, a big muscular guy, called Brick to check it out. They were now four minutes and thirty seconds into the job and knew soon it would be time to bail out.

Brick checked the restroom door; it's locked; as he knocked on the door for a response, he could hear someone crying from behind it.

"Come out, the shitter Sandy, or we are going to have to empty your fellow employee's brains all over this nice shiny floor."

"Now you don't want that, do you?" he teased.

Brick heard the sound of the door unlocking and stepped back with his weapon pointed at it as the door slowly opened. Sandy stepped out, hands raised in the air, sobbing.

"Please don't kill me; I have a family," she said.

"Don't we all," replied Brick as he shoved her to the front of the bank.

"Now, get your ass over there with the rest of them." He menacingly shouted at her.

The teller nervously made her way over to her fellow employees sprawled out on the floor with their hands behind their heads, but just before she was about to assume the same position, Needy stopped her and patted her down. As she was patting Sandy down, a cell phone stuffed in the bank teller's skirt waistband fell out onto the floor.

Needy looked at Sandy and already knew by the look of anguish on the teller's face what she had done.

She gave her watch another glance; they were now down to four minutes and forty-five seconds on the clock.

Her hyped-up crew looks on, ready to pump anything that moves wrong full of armor-piercing bullets.

"Boss, we gotta go," said one of her crew through a black ski mask like the others pulled down over her face, whereas only her eyes and mouth were visible.

Her name was Hallie, and although she was of slight build, she was just as ruthless as the other members of Needy's outlaw crew.

"The fucking pin now!" shouted out Needy as she picked the cellphone up off the floor.

Sandy rattled and blurted out the phone's pin code quickly. "086133."

Needy keyed in the sequence of numbers just as quickly and unlocked the phone.

Her eyes widened as she looked at the last call, dialed - 911.

"The police are on their way; we gotta go now!" She yelled out to her crew.

"You fucking bitch!" Hallie said, right before she raised her Sig Sauer to Sandy's head.

"On the floor now!" She ordered her pushing her gun into the back of the frightened teller's head.

"I am sorry, please don't kill me," Sandy said, shaking and pleading for her life again, as she nervously complied with Hallie's order while feeling the cold barrel pressed against her skull.

"I ought to blow your fucking brains out right now for calling the Po-Po," Hallie said coldly.

"That's not a good idea," A voice that was closer to her that she had been consciously aware of answered back. It was Needy's voice, and she meant business. Her and the Heckler & Koch Mp7 she carried. Hallie drew her weapon back from off of Sandy's head as she laughed at the fresh stream of urine running down the terrified woman's leg from underneath her skirt.

"I make you wet, huh?" Hallie asked with a grin on her face to Sandy, who was now sobbing but relieved to feel the cold steel no longer pressed against her skull.

Needy looked around at her crew. "I am only going to say this one more time; let's get the fuck outta here now!"

The sirens from police cars wailed not too far in the distance as Needy and her crew made their way quickly to a waiting van driven by another team member, a getaway driver whom they referred to as Scooter.

"Let's go, go, go!" Needy shouted out as she and her crew began getting inside the van to make a clean getaway and get the hell out of dodge. The sheriff 's patrol vehicles rolled up on them before the last bank robber Dez was inside the getaway van. The sheriff and his men exited their cars quickly with their service weapons drawn, shouted demands at them that they had no intentions of complying with, orders that fell on deaf ears.

"Police stop!" Dez raised his weapon at the sound of that command as he looked dead center at whom he referred to as pigs with their guns pointed towards him. He hated cops, and God knew they had no love for him either, with the lengthy criminal record he had earned starting as a young offender right on into his adulthood.

Dez's mindset was society's rules were for suckers and those who lack the balls to say fuck them. And today, as he raised his weapon and locked in on a pig taking cover behind his pig car, he felt no different about the matter.

A rapid succession of shots rang out from Dez's AR-15, causing Sheriff Alvarez and his deputies to take cover behind their vehicles as the armor-piercing bullets violently tore through the sheet metal in their cars.

The sheriff and his deputies return fire surprisingly to Needy and her crew with equal firepower.

Dez screamed out in pain as one of their bullets tore through his shoulder, almost causing him to drop his weapon.

Needy quickly grabbed him by the arm, pulling the rest of him in the vehicle.

"Fucking go, go, go!" she repeated.

"I got this!" Scooter shouted back as he listened to the sound of bullets bouncing off their bulletproof reinforced vehicle.

Scooter blew through a red light at a four-way intersection on one of the town's main roads. In their attempt to avoid hitting him, an oncoming driver quickly swerved and collided with a light pole.

With the noise of sirens wailing behind them, their van finally hit the main intersection roadway at 100 mph. Needy as she looked out the back of the one-way tinted windows in the van, she could see another patrol vehicle had now joined the pursuit and was hot and heavy on their asses also.

"Fuck," she murmured to herself; she knew she had to figure out a way to shake them and shake them quick.

"Are you okay?" she asks Dez, who was now applying direct pressure to his bloody shoulder.

"I'll live, more than I can say about those assholes behind us," he said, grimacing.

"We are bank robbers, not cop killers," Needy said.

"I doubt if they got that impression, nor do they care," Dez said.

"Fuck, get your shit together Dez, all of you!"

"Get us out of this mess; Scooter shake these assholes off our tail," Needy ordered.

"Got it, boss," replied Scooter accelerating.

Hallie was monitoring the police scanner in their van.

"They are about to drop spikes up ahead of the road," she said.

"Brick, give them some fireworks to drop them off our ass in the back!"

"No problem."

Brick flipped one of the back-door windows open on its hinges, stuck the barrel of his AR-15 out of it, and let loose at the patrol cars behind him, grinning as he watched them strategically swerve to avoid being hit by the lethal gunfire. As he continuously fired at them, the hot shells from his rifle ejected from his weapon's side port, hitting the van's floor with a pinging sound.

"That's right, get them muthafuckers!" Dez said, through a half-ass grin on his face as he fought back the pain emanating from the gunshot wound he had sustained.

He still had one good arm and hand to use, he thought as he unholstered a Sig Sauer P365 from his hip and opened up the second back van window. Dez begins popping off shots in the direction of the police vehicles that were still hot on their trail but had intentionally dropped back because of the direct line of fire coming their way.

Scooter notices the flashing of the railroad crossing lights and the sound of a train approaching up ahead immediately as the train gate arms begin to descend slowly.

"No fucking way, bust it!" Needy shouted out as they both could hear, and every occupant in the van the blaring sound of the train now blowing its warning horns as it quickly approached. Hundreds of tons of steel rushing towards them at no less than fifty obliterating miles per hour.

The train's conductor hit the horns again; he could see a vehicle up ahead jumping the tracks, but his train was too close and approaching too fast to stop or hit the brakes. He blew the train warning horns again, an ear-piercing shrilling noise emitted from the train horns, but the black van kept going.

"Fuck me!" the conductor said as he watched the black van smash through the railroad gate arms, splintering them as it shot across the track just mere seconds before disintegrating the gate arms into oblivion as he sped past the lucky bastards! Also missing them by seconds.

"Goddammit!" shouted Shannon as she brought the SUV to a screeching halt so close to the train she could feel the SUV shake as the train passed.

The other two patrol vehicles quickly came to a squealing halt behind her.

Alvarez, who was shotgunning, watched as the train flew by them, just missing the van by a few feet.

"Are you okay," he asked his deputy.

Deputy Shannon patted her vest underneath her jacket. "I'm okay, Chief, and you?"

Alvarez nodded his head that he was okay as well.

"Those crazy sonsofbitches must be out of their minds to have taken a chance like that," he said.

"Desperate people do desperate things," Shannon said.

"You think?" Alvarez answered back, pissed off that their pursuit had now come to a grinding halt.

As the train and the freight it was carrying passed by the broken railroad gate; arms slowly went back up.

"We got spikes up ahead; hopefully, they will not get that far ahead of us," Shannon said optimistically.

"I don't know, Shannon; something tells me these are not your average assholes."

"All units ahead, be on the lookout for a black Ford Econoline headed in your direction towards Potter's Creek," said Alvarez into the radio's mic.

"Gotcha, Chief," said a voice back through the radio.

"Chief."

"What?" said Alvarez.

"Average assholes or not; they pick the wrong town to rob will get 'em," Shannon said.

"I like your spirit corporal," Alvarez said, but in his mind, he had calculated that it had taken the train almost ten minutes or more to clear. With that amount of time between them and the bank robbers for all he knew, they could be in bum fuck Egypt by now touring the site of the great pyramids, he concluded.

"That's a 10-4 Chief; we got them stingers up ahead," answered a voice back over the police radio.

"Holy Shit! You lucky sonofabitch," Needy said as she grabbed Scooter's chin and planted a kiss on the side of his face.

"I knew we could make it," Scooter said, grinning as he gripped the steering wheel tightly.

"I know but don't ever do that shit again," Needy said, winking her eye at him.

"We got spike strips up ahead," Hallie reminded her boss as she monitored the police transmissions on their van's built-in scanner.

Needy looked over to the side of a dirt road off the main intersection up ahead.

"Turn down that road to the left," she instructed.

Scooter made a sharp turn to the left down the dirt road off the main highway; the van tires kicked up dirt and dust as it sped down the isolated stretch of unpaved road.

"Where in the hell are we going?" Hallie asked.

"Relax, we got to stay off the grid until things cool down," answered Needy.

"Now listen up, everyone. We are going to find a spot out here to hide the van and ourselves until the coast is clear, and then we are going to get the hell out of this town after it gets dark."

"Sounds good, because I am sure every Joe Cop within a fifty-mile radius is taking a doughnut sabbatical to catch us so that they make Officer of the month?" said Dez.

Freak laughed. "Good One," he said, as he patted Dez on his good shoulder, Dez grimaced through the pain.

"Let me take a look at it," Needy said, kneeling in front of Dez.

Dez removes the sticky bloody rag from his shoulder.

Needy carefully inspected the wound from front and back.

" Good, the bullet looks like it went straight through," she said.

"Freak give Dez a sip of that Jack in that bag and get 'em patch up," Needy said, pointing to a large black duffel bag over in the corner of the van.

"I' I' boss," Freak said.

"That's what I am talking about," Dez said, as he snatches the open bottle out of Freak's hand, taking a long swig, spilling some of the whiskey on his chin.

Freak snatches the bottle back out of his hand. "Calm down, Cowboy; I need some leftovers for that nasty wound."

Freak poured some of the liquor over Dez's gunshot wound to sterilize it as Dez clenched his teeth in pain from the burning sensation of the whiskey. He then handed Dez back the bottle of Jack Daniels as he began the task of sewing the wound up with a large needle and thread.

As the needle penetrated Dez's flesh, he flinched. "Shit! Easy will 'ya I thought you were a medic in the army."

Freak grinned. "I was, but I never said I was a good one."

"Fuck," Dez said, taking another swig from the bottle.

"Just don't bleed all over my van back there, Cowboy," Scooter shouted back, grinning.

"Fuck you and this heavy-handed bastard," Dez said, wiping the whiskey with the back of his hand off his mouth.

"Goddammit! That hurt," Dez shouted out.

"My bag, it must be my heavy-ass hands," Freak said, with a grin on his face.

Brick had remained quiet all this time as he sat on guard in the back of the van staring out the pop-up window for any sign of movement behind them.

It appeared that they had lost the cops, at least for now, he thought.

He was the biggest one in stature out of the crew at six-foot-three and almost two-hundred-pounds, all muscle. In high school and college, a standout linebacker whom NFL prospects were unfortunately sidelined when he suffered a devastating knee injury in college. Unable to play at the level he once did, he turned to drugs and alcohol to suppress his world that appeared to be crumbling around him. And to top it all off, Brick graduated from college with a degree that was about as useless as nipples on a crow; with a now-pregnant girlfriend and an addiction to painkillers and a family to support, he soon sought out easy and not so easy ways to make a quick buck. His girlfriend Jasmine was now his wife and mother of their five-year-old daughter Ashley. Not only two of the most important people in the world to him. But two of the most influential people in the world to him, whereas he now had to conceal the truth that he was a professional bank robber.

Drops of cold rain now began to beat down on the van; two minutes later, it was a downpour as the van tires sloshed through the muddy back roads, making travel now even more difficult.

"Seems like someone up there just answer our prayers," Brick said as he caught some of the raindrops on his tongue that shot through the open window.

"All done, Cowboy," Freak said as he cut off the stitches.

"Good, you sew like my Grandmother," Dez said.

"Stop bleeding all over my van's floor back there!" Scooter shouted back at Dez.

"Fuck you, asshole," Dez shouted back at Scooter defiantly.

What is that up ahead? Needy said to Scooter as she shotgunned upfront.

Scooter leaned forward in the driver's seat. "It looks like a Cabin... was the last word Scooter was able to get out of his mouth before the ground beneath the van gave way, and the van went headfirst into a five feet ditch with an explosion throwing everyone and everything that was not secured around like rag dolls.

Both front airbags activated, upon impact, exploding in the driver and front passenger faces.

The van was now upright at an angle on its rear wheels, five feet deep in a muddy embankment; the hissing sound of the airbags deflating reverberated off the inside cabin of the van.

"What the fuck just happen?" Scooter said, still dazed by the airbag.

"I think we just went into a sink-hole?" Needy said, gathering her bearings while wiping the white powder dust from the airbag off her face and clothes.

"Is everyone okay back there?" Needy shouted back in the van.

Hallie rubbed the back of her neck as she looked around at her other team members.

"As soon as we get off the top of each other's asses back here," she said.

Brick kicked the back doors open to the van and began exiting out the rear opening; the rest of the crew followed, except Needy and Scooter, who exited out the van side doors.

"What the fuck is this?" Scooter asked as he got out, ankle-deep in mud.

"Can we get the van the fuck out of this drop-off?" Needy said, pissed.

"Eighteen feet van, five feet-ditch, not without a tow," Scooter answered back.

"Fuck!" Needy blurted out, shaking her head sideways in disbelief and frustration.

"Get everything we need out of the van, and let's go pay our new house guest a visit down the road," she ordered.

Hallie jumped back down in the ditch with them and began assisting with getting the backpacks of money and equipment back up to Freak, Dez, and Brick, that was at the top of the ditch.

"Dez, I need you to get your ass on sentry in case someone attempts to sneak up on us," Needy said.

"No problem, boss."

"About twenty-five yards should do."

"Gotcha," he said.

Scooter walked over to Needy and whispered in her ear.

"This does not look like no sink-hole to me."

Needy shook her head sideways again as she assessed the situation that they were now in and faced.

"I know," she said.

CHAPTER ONE

N eedy knew that it was only a matter of time before the sheriff and his posse realized that they had given them the slip and double backtrack on this dirt road and discovered their van with its ass up, trapped in this ditch. The sooner they got this van out and concealed, the better she thought.

She had decided that only she and Hallie would approach the homeowners or occupants of the cabin home, seeking help under the pretense that they were both lost and needed help with their broken-down car. They both wore soft caps and dark sunglasses to obscure their identities.

As they both approached the nicely constructed cabin home, Needy instantly noticed an old tow truck in the driveway next to a station wagon. The gods had not abandoned them yet, she thought with a smile.

Hallie's eyes lit up as a smile came across her face. "Do you see what I fucking see," she said?

"Yeah, it appears our luck has turned; just play it cool."

Needy knocked on the cabin door. Immediately triggering a reaction from a dog that was inside that began barking. She could tell by the sound of its voice; it was not a Chihuahua for sure. Hallie looked at her apprehensively.

"Hush boy, Coming," she heard what sounded like a woman's voice from behind the door in conjunction with the dog's barking.

The door creaked open.

"Good afternoon, can I help you?"

Needy was right; It was a woman's voice. She was an attractive older woman of slim build in her late sixties with a tousled pixie cut of silver hair that framed an elegant but friendly face with piercing blue eyes.

Needy and Hallie eyes both went to the large German Shepherd that the woman held back by its collar.

"Oh, don't mind, Max. He's harmless, just a little skittish amongst strangers," the woman assured them.

Max let out a slight growl as he eyeballed the strangers as if co-signing his owner's statement.

"Yes, hello, I am sorry to be a bother. But my sister Daisy and I are lost, and we just had a car accident not too far from here," Needy said.

"My dear, was anyone hurt?"

"No, everyone's fine; it was just my sister and me. We drove into a hole in the ground."

"Those damn holes will do it all the time," said the cabin lady.

"Yep, that's what I told my ex," Hallie, aka Daisy, said.

The cabin lady looked at Hallie apprehensively.

"I like your sister, Daisy. She's quick-witted."

Hallie managed a smile. Where in the fuck did that name Daisy come from out of Needy's head, she wondered? Why not Delilah, Diana, or Destiny? She thought. Well, maybe not Destiny, she concluded.

"Anyway, it seems we can't get a signal out here on our cellphones, and I was wondering if you have a landline we can use?"

"I am sorry to hear that. Yes, please come on in," the cabin lady said.

"Max, go over there and sit," she said.

The dog obeyed its owner's command and took a post over by the fireplace on a large road, but still close enough to keep a steady eye on the two strangers.

Needy and Hallie slowly stepped inside the cabin, both with their hands unknown to the cabin lady on their concealed semi-automatics just in case it was a welcoming committee behind the door or Max got skittish.

As they enter the cabin, Needy cautiously scopes the place out. Much to her relief, there was no welcoming committee or surprises as she took in the cabin's spacious and accommodating surroundings.

"Nice and cozy cabin you got here," she said.

"Thanks, me, my husband John, and our son think so as well."

"By the way, my name is Deena."

"Excuse me," Hallie said.

"Deena,"

"Of course, nice to meet you, Deena," Hallie said.

"Yes, nice to meet you, Deena, and sorry for putting you out," Needy interjected.

"No worries, speaking of towing, my husband John has an old wrecker out there. I am sure he'll be glad to help you gals out when he gets back."

"How long will that be?" asked Needy.

"Maybe twenty or thirty minutes, give or take a few," Deena answered in a sing-song voice.

Needy looked over at Hallie. She did not trust this old bitch, but she had no reason to believe she was lying either.

Hallie silently answered her glance with a nod of her head.

Needy gave her a fake smile. "I guess we can wait until then," she said.

"Good, would you gals prefer coffee or tea?"

"Tea is fine, thank you," Needy said.

"Cream and sugar ladies?"

"Whatever floats your boat Deena," Hallie said.

Needy cut Hallie a sharp corrective look.

Hallie gave Deena another fake smile.

"So witty," Deena said as she made her way to the kitchen.

When Needy felt that Deena was no longer within earshot, she firmly addressed Hallie's flippant remark.

"Don't fuck with the old lady; she is our ticket out of here!" Needy said bluntly.

"Okay, man, chill. I was just having fun," Hallie responded.

"Bitch, you fucking chill and get your shit straight, you understand?" Hallie said, with a tone in her voice that signals to Hallie, she was willing to take this to another level if need be.

"Sorry, boss," Hallie said reluctantly, swallowing her bravado.

"That's better," Needy concurred.

Their new host soon returns with a tray with a small teapot on it, cookies, and some teacups.

"Please make yourself comfortable, ladies," Deena said, nodding towards a nearby sofa.

"You're too kind, thanks," Hallie said superficially, feeling Needy eyes scrutinizing her as she spoke.

Needy noticed that as Deena poured the tea in the cups slowly, some of it never made it in the cup but splashed on the outside. Needy also noticed how Deena had moved around the house in front of them. Slowly and methodically, almost as if she were counting her paces.

"Beautiful day outside, isn't it?" she asked Deena as she took the cup of tea from her and blew into the cup of hot tea to cool it off some.

"It is, isn't it?" Deena answered as she sat across from them in a lounge chair after setting the tray of hospitalities on a cocktail table in front of them.

Needy slowly waved her hand across her face before she responded again to Deena. And just as she had anticipated the old lady, although she was looking dead-on in her direction, she never responded to her gesture.

"John should be back shortly," she reminded them as she sipped on her tea.

As Hallie bit into the cookie biscuit, her mouth dropped open as she observed what Needy had possibly just discovered; why come she had not noticed it? She thought. To be sure, Hallie emulated Needy's gesture and waved her hand in front of her face while looking straight at Deena.

And just as she had done with Needy, their new host never responded. A smile crept across Hallie's face at the affirmation of their discovery.

"I know John is going to be mad at me for telling you gals this, but you seem like nice people," Deena said.

"Tell us what?" Needy said.

"Well, he told me never to tell anyone when I am home alone for my safety. You know there are nasty people out there who would like nothing more but to take advantage of an old lady, especially one home alone. "

"I understand, Deena, and If that is what your husband John told you, then you don't have to tell us anything."

"Are you gals nice people?" Deena said, catching the both of them off guard with her bluntness.

"We…we try to be," Needy said.

"In case you didn't notice, I am legally blind," Deena said.

"Wow, we had no idea," Needy lied.

"Yeah, honey, I can barely see a damn thing, that's including y'all pretty faces."

"Well, thanks, but I can assure you yours is just as pretty," Needy said.

Deena waved her hand in the air with a flick of her wrist. "Oh, this old mug, you're too kind," she said.

"No, she's right; you have the brightest blue eyes I have ever seen," said Hallie, aka Daisy.

Max started barking as he heard the sound of a truck from outside pulling up into the driveway; Deena was the second one to hear it approaching.

"I think my husband John is back," she said.

"What, I didn't hear anything," Hallie said.

"Dear, my eyes may have gone, but my hearing is impeccable," Deena said as she set her teacup down back on the tray.

Max sprung up from the rest position and strutted towards the door, tail wagging, and greeted his other owner with several strong barks.

Deena greeted her husband John, a tall, good-looking older man with a head full of salt and pepper hair at the door, as he brushes the droplets of rain off his flannel shirt.

"It's wetter than a possum's ass out there," he said.

"Hey boy," John said, as he petted their dog, Max, on the top of his head.

"Hey there?" he said, surprised, as his eyes went towards Needy and Hallie sitting in his living room.

"John, these two lovely gals Daisy and…" Deena paused, now remembering the other woman had never introduced herself, or had she just forgot?

"Sarah," Needy said, filling in the gap.

" Yes, and Sarah broke down not too far from here and was wondering if we could give them a hand," she finished.

John looked over at the two women skeptically.

"Is that right," he said bluntly.

"Yeah, that's about right," Needy, aka Sarah, said, all the while sizing him up.

"Where were you ladies headed? If you don't mind me asking?" John inquired, still eyeballing the two of them suspiciously.

"To Sioux Falls, we got friends we are visiting up there, but we got stuck in a ditch when we went off-road to take a piss break." Hallie intercepted.

"Is that right," John said, repeating himself for maybe the third time.

"Yep, that's about right," Needy said, remembering the weight of the concealed pistol that was locked and loaded just in case the old fool needed more convincing.

John stroked his mustache that was a mixture of the same salt and pepper colors as the hair on his head before he spoke again.

"That one sure has a mouth on her," he said, pointing over at Hallie.

"She sure does; she reminded me of myself when I was younger," Deena said, then laughing.

Hallie listens attentively as her hand moves slowly but closer to the gun that she concealed as well, as she waited for that one wrong question to come out of Deena's husband John's mouth that could quickly turn this situation into a hostage situation or maybe more.

John laughed. "Yeah, I guess she does, Ladies we will be glad to help you out. All I need to do is get the old wrecker started back up and will have you back on the road in no time."

"You guys are a lifesaver," Needy said as another man entered the cabin who looked like a younger version of John in his thirties. His eyes also went straight to Needy and Hallie. But they could see the look on his face was more of curiosity than suspicion, unlike his father's.

"Mom, you didn't tell me we were expecting guests?" He said as he kissed his mother on her cheek.

"This is our son Jason," Deena said.

Hallie eyeballed the handsome and younger version of John with a half-assed grin on her face.

"Nice to meet you, Jason," she said, flirting with her eyes.

Needy just nodded her head in agreement, still focusing on the mission ahead, which was getting their van out the ditch and their asses back on the road.

These two were extremely easy on the eyes, Jason thought, and not like the Broom Hilda types he was used to seeing around these parts of the woods.

"My pleasure," he said back, still trying to figure out what the hell brought these two beauties out to his parent's cabin.

His father provided that information before his mind wandered any further.

"Jason, these two nice young ladies got stranded in a ditch not too far from here while trying to view the wildlife, and we are going to get them back on the road," John said, winking his eye at them.

"Is that right," he said, sounding a lot like his father to Needy right now.

"Yeah, that's about right," she said again.

"It looks like the rain is letting up," Deena said as she stood in front of one of the multiple cabin bay windows taking small sips out of her cup of hot tea.

"Looks like it," John said.

"I'll go warm up the old wrecker, Pops," Jason said.

"Do you mind if I come with you?" Hallie asked.

Jason looked over at her and smiled. "Not at all."

"Don't worry, like I said, will have you folks back on the road in a jiffy," John reiterated.

For some reason, a Jiffy did not sound relatively quick enough for Needy right now, as she assessed how she was going to handle their newfound friends in case something went wrong. And although she did not want any harm to come to any of them, she knew if push came to shove, she would not hesitate to use whatever force necessary to put the situation back in her favor if required to save the life of her niece, Hannah. Her niece had the misfortune of being diagnosed with leukemia one year ago, and her medical care was not cheap. The bank robberies that Needy had committed but been in charge of were making sure her niece could continue to afford the high cost of medical care to sustain her life. And that she would one day see her niece Hannah healthy again and able to attend her high school graduation one day with the rest of her friends and peers her age.

Needy's sister Alice, Hannah's Mom, knew she had done and continued to do all she could for her niece. Through getting a second and third loan on her home, fundraising, and borrowing money, she could never probably pay it back. To make sure her daughter Hannah got the medical care she needed.

But Needy watched as those resources eventually began to run dry. Disappear just like her niece's father, Gary, had many years ago, from his daughter's life when she had needed him the most when any child needed their parents the most. Needy's perception was she never liked that sorry assed prick and had told her sister in so many words why. She never got a strong feeling that he was a steady rock in his daughter's life. Needy perceived him as more like a pebble at the bottom of a pond that was only good for frog shit or being occasionally picked up by a kid and tossed across the water to skip but failing miserably in its execution. Plopping and sinking back to the surface as if to say, "Sorry, but your expectations of me were much too high, now I must take my rightful place at the bottom of this pond, shamefully amongst the muck and frog shit which I belong."

But her sister Alice was like most women Needy had known; she was in love with a man who had no clue how to be a real man when the situation got too harsh and hot for them to handle. Men whose usual inclinations were to bail and run like pussies away from the women and children they confessed to love and take up with some other misguided victims who had visions of sugar and lollipops dancing in their head.

But just in case Gary decided to come back, Needy had an extra set of balls to lend him if he needed to strap on a pair.

Needy's thoughts went back to the enormous financial responsibility that she and her sister were no longer able to meet for Hannah's medical care. No longer if she had not decided to take from the same institutions that she felt had been taking from people like her all her life. Sure, at one time, she had done the nine to five and played by all the rules that society told her a law-abiding citizen was supposed to comply with within this world. But she soon realized all that reasonable effort, in the end, did not help her out at all when it came time to try to obtain financial help from legal sources to help her niece fight a disease that was now trying to take her young life. And that is when Needy had decided that she was tired of asking and begging assholes for help. She would find a way to help her niece do or die or come hell or high water.

Fuck the system! She concluded. As she slowly and discreetly put together a crew of other like-minded individuals. When Needy was finished, her bank robbery career began, and the new Needy Seller's was born. She buried her old self out of necessity that the latest upgrade of herself, good or bad, survive her chosen path.

At this moment, Needy felt she was surviving fine, and her ill-gotten gains were making sure that her niece received some of the best medical care that money could buy. Not that she gave a fuck that people look at it that way.

Needy's thoughts were now broken by the old tow truck's sound starting up outside with a loud throaty grumble.

That was her cue to leave and hope the old lady forgot she was there.

"Deena, we gotta get going now; thank you much for all your hospitality," she said.

"The pleasure was all mine, dear; we don't get much company up here in these parts, take care of yourself and that sister of yours," Deena said.

"I will," Needy said.

As Needy exited the cabin and began her descent down the cabin stairs, Deena called out to her. "Sarah, Sarah."

Needy finally turned around when she heard the fake name called out the second time.

"Yes," she said, looking at the old lady quizzically.

"Funny you don't seem like a Sarah," Deena said.

Needy smirked, "Yeah, that's what my last girlfriend said."

Deena smiled and waved goodbye as she watched Sarah or whatever her name was, she thought, walked over to her sister and the old wrecker and her boys.

That is what Deena liked to call John and her son, "Her boys."

"Jason, can you come here for a second," she screamed out at her son.

Her son Jason excused himself from Hallie's attention and walked over to see what his mom wanted? " Hey, what's up?" He asked.

"I don't trust those two bitches there; watch your father's back," she said curtly.

Deena could tell by the look on Jason's face, her words had caught her son off guard and understandably so, as he looked at her baffled.

"I will, mom, but why don't you…"

"Hey Jason, let's go," his father John yelled out, interrupting him before he could finish his question.

"Look, son. I may be blind, but that doesn't mean I am dumb," Deena said.

"Don't worry, mom. I will," he finally said.

"Let's go, Jason!" his father yelled out again.

Deena looked over at Needy and Hallie to see if they were watching them. They were not. She moved in closer to her son and passed him a small lunch bag.

"Here are some sandwiches in case y'all get hungry," she made sure to say loud enough in case the two women were listening or watching and suspected something was amiss.

Jason unzipped the lunch bag and looked inside at the .45 Desert Eagle.

"Just in case," she said.

Deena smiled again over at Needy and Hallie, waving in their direction, but it was all for show.

Just like they had been sizing her up, but unknown to them, she had been sizing them up as well.

And one thing she was sure about after talking with them both the first one, as she had first thought, did not seem like a Sarah and her sister if she was? Sure, was no daisy or any blooming bud for that matter.

But she could be wrong; she thought as she made her way back into the cabin and its warmth.

Deena walked over to a large radio sitting on top of a vanity table and turned it on.

A news reporter's voice came booming out of the radio's speakers. *"Police are looking for five brazen bank robbers that hit Harper Creek Bank & Trust in Lincoln County earlier today. The suspects were involved in a violent shootout with local police and are reported to be driving a black Econoline van with tinted windows and out-of-state plates."*

CHAPTER TWO

The cold rain had now let up as the old wrecker made its way clumsily down to where Needy and her crew's van had got stranded in the ditch. Needy rode with John in the tow truck, followed by his son Jason and Hallie from behind in a sport utility vehicle.

Needy immediately noticed that it was no sign of life around as they pulled up to the area where their vehicle had taken a plunge in the sink-hole. It was apparent that the rest of her crew had made sure that they had made it their business to disappear from the scene so as not to draw suspicion.

As she and John exited the old wrecker, although oblivious to John, she could still sense their presence close by, even watching; after all, they were her crew, and she had trained them.

"Goddamn, that's a helluva bear trap!" Jason said out loud as he approached the van ass up and immobilized in the five-foot-deep sink-hole.

Needy looked down at the now white van in the sink-hole and smiled. Good job, she thought to herself, on the job her crew had done, removing the temporary black transport wrap from off the van. The police would be looking for a black Econoline van, not this white one, she reasoned, that's stuck in this fucking hole in the ground.

John begins preparing the winch to the wrecker to pull the van out of the ditch while his son Jason was hooking up some straps to the van's undercarriage to aid in the task. Once the straps were secure, John activated the winch and gently pulled the vehicle out of the ditch as the winch made a grinding humming noise.

When the vehicle was finally back on a flat surface, Needy could now assess the damage better. It was not as bad as she thought, but not good either.

The airbags that had deployed would need cutting out, and she noticed that the front tire on the driver's side was flat. It had probably got punctured, she assumed by something in the ditch.

John inspected the vehicle and looked underneath the body of the van, checking for structural damage. The rain that had been coming down had been a blessing for these two travelers, he thought. To his assessment, the rain had softened the soil, cushioning the vehicle as it went into the sink-hole, so it was more like a slide in the sink-hole than falling straight in head first, ass up.

"I don't see that much damage, except those balloons sticking out your steering wheel and dash and this here front tire," said John, as he wipes his forehead off with the back of his hand. He bent down, rechecked the front tire, grabbed it from the side, and began shaking it, from side to side, as it noticeably wobbles.

"Wait, wait, wait… shit! I spoke too soon ladies, sorry for the bad news, but you all got yourselves a broken tire rod."

"Shit!" Needy said softly to herself. This new revelation was not good, and she knew it! The longer she and her crew stayed around these parts, the more they put themselves at risk of being discovered and caught.

"Good news, though I think I can fix her once we get her back to the cabin," John said.

"Really?" Needy said.

"Yep, but it might take an hour or so before I can get y'all back on the road."

"Excuse me," Jason said as he flipped open his cellphone and read an incoming text.

"Harper Creek Sheriff Department: Black Econoline van with possible stolen license plates, was involved in a bank robbery at 9:45 am, Harper Creek Bank & Trust, suspects are armed and considered extremely dangerous, if this vehicle spotted in your area do not approach, contact Harper Creek sheriff's office immediately."

Jason closed the cellphone and put it back in his pocket.

"Wow, hey pop's, you're not going to believe this one," he said.

"Believe what?" John said, as he now made sure the van was secure and ready to be towed on the old hook & chain wrecker.

"I just received an alert on my phone that there was a bank robbery this morning in Harper Creek, and there is a BOLO on an Econoline van, driven by the suspects."

Needy froze as she quickly glanced over at Hallie that tuned in on her Que, which was, "Get ready because things now might go to hell in a handbasket real fast." Hallie kept her hand inconspicuously close to her concealed hardware just in case.

"Econoline van?" John said as he stopped what he was doing and looked over at Needy.

Hallie's hand was now on her weapon.

Jason laughed at his Dad's reaction. "Don't worry, Pop's the Econoline van they're looking for is black," he said.

"Wait, you didn't think these two are bank robbers, did ya?" Jason asked, teasing his father.

Hallie laughed. "I hope not. Our mother would be turning over in her grave," she answered.

"Of course not, and my condolences to y'all lost," John said empathetically.

"Same here," his son Jason interjected.

"Thanks, she just recently passed away this year, and that is the main reason for our road trip just to get away from it all," Needy elaborated.

"Oh' no need to explain," John answers.

Something on the van's bumper caught Jason's eye as he walked over silently to identify what it was? He lifted a piece of black wrap clinging onto the bumper off of it, inspecting it in his hand. What the hell was it? He thought as he played with the filmy material in his hand. He looked over suspiciously at the women standing over by his Dad, whom they only knew as Sarah and Daisy. His mother's voice suddenly enters his head, "I don't trust those bitches, and neither should you," she said. He looked back down at the filmy material and back at the white van as he slowly removed the .45 from his pocket.

That is when he felt the barrel of something cold and hard pressed up against the back of his head.

"I wouldn't do that if I were you," Dez said sternly.

Dez disarmed Jason and walked him over to where Needy, Hallie, and his father were standing.

"What in the hell is going on here?" John screamed out! As he saw his son taken hostage and escorted with a gun pointed to the back of his head.

"Junior, figure it out," Dez said, as he raised the .45 Desert eagle he had confiscated from Jason in one hand while still keeping his weapon aim at the back of his now captive handsome head of hair that would be one bloody mess if he made the wrong move.

"You the sonofabitch that robbed that bank?" John said.

Hallie walked over to a frightened Jason and kissed him on the side of his cheek.

"You're not as dumb as you look after all," she said, with a smirk on her face.

"Fuck you!" Jason said.

Hallie grabbed Jason tightly by his buttocks, squeezing them as she held her gun underneath his chin.

"Maybe later, if I am in the mood for some pencil dick," she said.

Jason brushed her hand away and off his ass. She and Dez laughed at his reaction.

"What the hell is going on here?" John asked again.

"Easy Pop's," Needy said as she raised her gun at the old man.

She waved the semi-automatic in the direction of his son. "Get your ass over there next to Jr.," she commanded.

John hurriedly made his way over to his son with his hands raised in the air.

Needy stuck two of her fingers in her mouth and let out a loud dog whistle to the rest of her crew.

They watched in fear as the rest of her armed crew slowly emerged out in the opening and from behind where they were concealed. Strangers to them that had been watching them all this time in the shadows of darkness.

"Look, we don't want any trouble, folks. Just take our vehicles and go." His son suggested as his eyes darted nervously over Needy's gunmen.

What? So, you and your daddy can call the cops as soon as we get eyeshot, out of the sight of you two Yankee Doodle Dandies."

"I don't think so," said Needy.

Hallie laughed and cracked a wide shit-eating grin at her boss's comment; the rest of the team followed.

Needy tapped the tip of the barrel of her gun against her forehead. The gig was now up, she thought. Needy had to figure this now out and where to go from here. Because now what was supposed to be a simple bank heist had become kidnapping as well until she could think their way out of this debacle, she thought.

"No, we are going to stick to the original plan. We are going to tow the van back to that cozy log cabin you have and fix it, and then we will be on our merry fucking way," Needy informed John and his son.

"That's fine as long as no harm comes to my wife and my son; I'll do whatever you ask," John stated.

Needy smiled. "Good, as long as you keep that attitude, we shouldn't have a problem," she said.

She nodded at Brick. "Check these boys for more weapons before we leave; we don't need any more surprises."

Brick slung his weapon over his shoulder, walked over to both men, and began patting them down for any hidden or concealed weapons. He pulled out a large hunting blade that was in a sheath carried and worn by John.

"Look what we have here," he said, grinning as he held the enormous and deadly knife up.

Needy did not even blink. "Like I said, no freaking surprises," she reiterated.

"These two are clean, boss," Brick said after he finished the pat-down.

"Secure both of them and let's get the hell out of this area," Needy instructed.

Brick nodded his head in acknowledgment of Needy's orders and began zip-tying the men's wrist behind their backs. After he was finished with this task, Needy instructed John to ride in the wrecker with Dez, driven by Scooter and his son in the truck with her, Brick, Hallie, and Scooter. Jason was positioned between Hallie and Brick in the backseat so that they could keep a watchful eye on him.

"Cozy huh, lover?" Hallie said with a grin on her face to Jason.

"Yeah, very," he said glumly.

Jason looked Brick up and down out of the side of his eye, trying to size him up, wondering if he could take the big brute. He could see the man was all muscle and probably a steroid freak! "Not a chance in hell," the voice of reasoning told him. But then he never listened to that voice much anyway.

Brick could sense Jason's eyes on him, and he felt he knew what Jason was thinking, one false move by him, and he would not hesitate for a second to put a bullet through Jason's skull and have lunch afterward.

CHAPTER THREE

Dragos kept a watchful eye on the prisoner that they now held in custody at their compound, a castle nestled in the Carpathian Mountains of Sinaia, Romania. She was a rare import from the United States that had arrived four years ago, that he and the sect had agreed to keep under their control and in custody, as a favor for an antiquities' dealer he knew in name only as Solo Chase. This human he thought must be held in high regard by Marcellus, his sect's leader, for them even to consider such an arrangement.

The prisoner's accommodations were more like a large bedroom from the inside than a typical small cell but fortified with Titanium bars. Dragos stood guard outside of her cell, peering in on the prisoner who now set at a small desk with her backside towards him in the dim shadows, long black hair cascaded down the middle of it past her shoulders.

It appeared to him that she was writing something on a pad, a journal, perhaps? He did not know, nor did he care.

"I see that you're keeping yourself busy?" he said.

She turned around to answer him as she slowly emerged from and out of the shadows of her cell. Dragos could see that she was naked down to her waist as he admired her long, lean curvaceous body. Her eyes locked on to him, and that is when he caught the "Tapetum lucidum" night vision and reflectiveness of her pupils, only to confirm to him the only human thing about her was deceptively her appearance.

"I could think of better ways to spend my time night-walker," she said.

Dragos' eyes went from her supple breast to the white linen blouse she held in her hands as she approached closer.

She followed the guard's eyes and slipped the linen blouse over her head slowly, covering herself, but Dragos could still see that her nipples were erect through the material. He ran his blood-red tongue across his lips slowly and flirtatiously. She was a beastie that he would not mind spilling his demon seed in, he thought, although it was against his sect's fraternal order to copulate with her breed.

"I bet you could, Luna," he said, cracking a smile as Luna noticed that his dark eyes seemed to light up.

Something was stirring up in this one, Luna thought, and she was willing to take it as far as she could to get what she wanted.

As she liked to call them, most of the nightwalkers (guards) were not this friendly or social towards her and treated her with the compassion that you would bestow upon a feral dog you neither liked nor cared for that was around. The only comfort its presence brought you is the assurance that you could put it down if it bit you and got out of line.

Luna knew she had been that feral dog. She had been humiliated and used for the past four years as a tracker to hunt down the opposition and members of the Blood Order that had betrayed Marcellus sect. Yes, she hated vampires, but worse, she hated being on a dog leash and a vampire at the fucking beginning of its reins.

Now she had one of these bloodsuckers in front of her. "Dragos" who was jonesing for a taste of wolf pussy. After Luna discovered the nightwalkers had been doping her food to control her ability to transform at will. She decided to feed her food to the rats equal in size to their feline friends running around inside her cell and the dark corridors and tunnels of the sects castle.

Luna's mind went back to the leering nightwalker in front of her that glared at her salaciously. She had not eaten in a week and did her best to hide this fact from her captors. And although she felt weak from lack of sustenance, she felt strangely intense at the same time. She wondered if she could do it? She wonders if she could change on her own and rip every bloodsucker's head that walked this castle head clean off their fucking shoulders and eat the remaining of them alive.

Dragos reached through the bars, placed his pale hand on top of Luna's with its long black fingernails, and ran his razor-sharp nails across the top of her hand, slightly drawing blood.

"How long has it been since you been with a man?" He asked with a smirk on his face.

"I don't know? You see one around," she answered back.

Dragos grinned wider, revealing his thick red tongue and a healthy set of vampiric canines encased in black gums.

"A real fucking bitch, huh?" he said.

"You wanna find out?" Luna said as she removed Dragos's hand off of hers and put it around her throat. As she felt his grip tighten, she felt herself getting wet at the same time.

"I thought you'd never ask nicely," Dragos said, as he spun Luna around violently as he gripped her hair and raised her skirt with the other hand and ripped her panties off. Luna's buttocks are now pressed up against the cell's bars as she felt Dragos enter her, and gently he was not. He begins wildly grunting and pumping until he finally exploded his demon seed inside of her, his black pupils turned a crimson red in his orgasmic climax.

He slipped out of Luna more gently then; he eased in her as he gathered himself. But for Luna, his manhood or lack of it felt as cold as the blood running through his vampire's veins, and she knew when she was finally finished with him that she would not be the only one short shafted tonight.

"That was better than I thought it would be," Dragos said with a grin on his face.

"Yeah, once you go Wolfee, you never go Toothy," Luna quipped.

Dragos paused and looked at Luna with a confused look on his face. Then he busted out in laughter.

"I get it! I get It! You're a very funny bitch, Luna," he said.

Luna looked over at Dragos Heckler & Koch MP5 that he set aside against the wall outside her cell.

"I am glad one of us is pleased," Luna said bluntly.

Dragos pulled Luna closer to him thru the bars. "I will give it to you the way you like it, next time, baby! I promise."

"Doggystyle all day!" he yelled out as he began humping the air and barking at the same time.

"Fuck you!" Luna said.

"Just joke, just joking! Like you," Dragos said apologetically.

Dragos then pulled Luna in closer again and began passionately kissing her on the mouth. Luna reciprocated at first, and when he eased his fat red reptilian tongue inside of her mouth, she grabbed his tongue with her teeth and ripped it rights out of his mouth in one quick jerk! Dragos jumped back in shock as blood gushed out of his mouth.

Luna stepped back from the cell door and spat his tongue out on the floor, and began laughing.

Dragos' words now came out unintelligible to her as he tried to speak, but the look in his crimson eyes told Luna all she had to know, he wanted to kill her! He knew that she was being doped up and could not change into a Lycan at will. But he did not care about a fair fight as he unlocked her cell doors. He just wanted to drain all the blood out of her body before he ripped her apart.

The lock clicked as he unlocked the cell door and slowly entered; his eyes widened at the sound of something growling in the recesses of the darkness of the cell. Something large and powerful. Dragos screams reverberated off the cell walls as Luna ripped the vampire apart limb by bloody limb.

* * *

Luna picked up Dragos's H&K assault weapon that was leaning against the wall. It would come in handy on her way out of this compound, she reasoned. She felt the presence of the large black cat with the emerald eyes that watched her every move silently in the dark.

She looked over inside her cell. Dragos's headset on her vanity stand with his severed genitals shoved in his mouth, courtesy of the promise she had made to herself earlier. The cat walked over to Luna and rubbed up against her leg, and purred.

"Yeah, I agree. Drago was a bit of a pussy," Luna said to the cat.

The cat meowed as if it understood what Luna had just said.

"Yes, now Tommie, show me the way out of this hell-hole, will ya, and I promise I'll buy you the biggest fish sandwich you have ever eaten."

The black cat took off down the underground tunnel of the castle. As Luna followed, she knew one thing for sure she was on her way towards her freedom or her death, but in her mind definitively, so was any vampire that stood in her way. An alarm soon sounded as screams and gunshots now echoed throughout the dark tunnels.

CHAPTER FOUR

T he rain that had remained at bay just long enough for them to get the van hitched up on the tow had now returned with a vengeance as the wrecker and the SUV now occupied by new guests returned to John's and his wife's cabin.

The cold rain beat them in the faces like tiny wet needles as Needy, and her crew quickly exited both vehicles with their new captives in tow and under close watch and with plans for his wife Deena to soon join their flock.

"Let's get out of this damn rain and don't try anything slick," Needy warned, as she nudged John in his back with the barrel of her gun.

The other crew members hung back out of sight as Needy and Hallie slowly approached the cabin with John and his son to not draw suspicion to John's wife, Deena. They also had tactical and safety reasons in mind. In case an ambush was waiting for them behind that cabin door like Alvarez and his posse.

Needy knew her mind always had to be sharp and one step ahead of the law. If not, she knew that one misstep could cost her crew their freedom but most of all their lives.

They had got themselves in a pickle, she concluded, but she was determined to get them out of the jar. Not only for their benefit but most of all, Hannah's.

"Get out of this rain!" Deena shouted out to them as she met them at the doorway. Max barked and shot past her and ran out to greet her husband and son.

"Good boy," John said as he patted Max on his head.

Needy smiled at the dog and gave John another nudge to his back with her gun, just to make sure he had not forgotten who was in charge or in case he decided to do a foolish thing like warn his wife before they made their way inside the cabin.

Her present state of mind was, she did not want to kill any innocents if she could avoid it. But at the same time, she never took that equation entirely off the table either.

Lucky for Needy, the sensation of cold steel pressed up against John's back was all the persuasion he needed to cooperate with her and her crew.

Deena could sense something in the air as John, and the rest of them entered the cabin. The smell of the two strangers from earlier hit her senses.

"What's wrong, John? Is everything okay?" Deena asked, concerned as she grabbed hold of one of John's arms.

Needy and Hallie watched him closely as he answered.

"Yeah, we had to tow their van back because it had a broken tire rod, but I should be able to get them back on the road once I have it fixed," he answers, his voice somewhat shaky.

"Okay! well, get out of those wet clothes and let me fix you guys something hot to drink."

"Thanks, Deena, you're too kind," Needy said.

Hallie looked over at Jason and silently mouthed the word sit to him.

"What now?" He asked as he reluctantly sat down as ordered.

"Get y'all goddamn hands up and don't move!" Deena shouted out as she emerged from the kitchen with a shotgun.

Needy and Hallie's eyes went wide as they turned in her direction.

"John and Jason, get over here now!" Deena said as she waved the shotgun back and forth in one hundred eighty-degree axes.

"We both know you can't see a goddamn thing, you old bitch! You need to put that rifle down now!" Hallie said with her weapon drawn.

Deena followed the sound of her voice and pointed the shotgun directly at her, and smiled. "Maybe not bitch, but you're less than ten meters from me. Would you like to risk an ear or nose to find out?" She said confidently.

"I don't understand what's going on? Everyone just needs to relax." Needy said as she slowly eased out her weapon from inside her waist.

"You know damn well what's going on. I may be blind, but I'm not dumb. You two are as close to being sisters as I am to being the Pope," Deena said before she heard a familiar click behind her head. The click of something equally powerful as what she was wielding.

"Put the shotgun down, Pope!" A deep voice ordered from behind. As she felt the pressure of their weapon's muzzle pressed to the back of her head.

Like she had said, she may have been blind, but she was not dumb. Deena quickly complied and lowered her shotgun.

Needy cracked a smile. " Deena, in case you ain't figured it out, that's not my brother."

"Fuck you!" Deena said as she reluctantly surrendered her weapon over to Brick.

"You might want to start locking your windows," he said with a grin on his face as he took her weapon.

The cat was now out of the bag, metaphorically. There was no need to play any more games; Needy thought as she signaled to Hallie non-verbally with a nudge towards the front door to let the rest of their crew inside.

Dez, Freak, and Scooter now entered the cabin, wet and cold.

"I was beginning to think you people didn't have any hospitality," Freak said as he shook the water out of his stringy hair. Then proceeded to wipe the rain off his face with a rag from his pocket.

Although he was much taller, Freak reminded John of the infamous killer and cult leader Charles Manson. But this Manson called Freak he observed was not the shot caller. That status or honor from what he perceived went to the woman who introduced herself as Sarah.

Scooter looked to him like one of those new-agers that he saw down at one of those hippie shops in town. Dez and Brick he sized up was this band of misfits' muscle but not the brains either, he concluded.

Hallie, aka Daisy, looked over at John and gave him a menacing look before addressing him. "What in the hell are you looking at, Pops?"

"Nothing," he answered flatly.

"That's what I thought," she said, trying to intimidate John.

But John had long got her number. He had pinned her as unpredictable, aggressive, and someone that wanted to be boss of Sarah's gang of merry men of misfits. He wondered if he or they could play on those defaults if needed to keep them alive.

"Chill!" Needy said to Hallie before she turns her attention to John.

"John, I need you to get your ass out there and start working on our van. We don't want to overstay our welcome if you know what I mean," she said.

"Brick, you go with him," she orders.

"Sure," Brick complied, giving Needy the thumbs up.

All Freak's attention had been on John's wife Deena; as he watched her closely, he stroked the outside of his upper lip with his tongue. She was not bad for an older lady, he concluded and wondered if she still had a tight little ass underneath all those clothes she was wearing? He could tell that she was one of those older women that had kept herself up. And he was sure that old John was probably not sticking it to her as she deserved. No worries, he thought. He was here now and happy to take up the slack and get her juices flowing again.

Needy looked over at Freak and caught wind of him staring at Deena, Shit! It made her uncomfortable. She had no doubt Deena could feel his eyes upon her and felt the same uneasiness. "Freak, you okay?" she asked, breaking his trance-like stare down.

"Yep' she's a pretty one," he said, referring to Deena lustfully.

"Asshole, that's my Mother you are talking about!" Jason said, speaking up.

"Oh, how sweet; Freak is in love," Hallie said, then giggling mischievously.

Needy was not amused or entertained by either of their antics and quickly let them know as she both cut into them. "You two need to cut the monkey shit and keep your mind on the business at hand!" she said firmly.

The smile quickly disappeared from Hallie's face, and Freak nodded his head in agreement with what his boss just demanded.

Dez laughed. "You one twisted fuck, bro."

Freak looked over at Deena, but this time did not maintain his gaze and quickly looked away. "Just an observational statement," he answered.

Hallie looked over at Deena and frowned her face up. "I don't think that old biddy is all that."

"Fuck you bitch!" Deena replied.

"And she's got a nasty mouth for an old geezer, and that's my observational statement," Hallie said.

"She ain't all that old; she still got some good juice in her," Freak replied, as his tongue strokes his upper lip again.

Jason had heard enough and again came to his mother's defense at risk to his safety, maybe hers. " If you touch my mom, I will kill you, you fucking freak!" he shouted out angrily.

"At least he got the name right," Scooter said, grinning.

Needy picked up a glass flower vase and hurled it towards Freak's head. If he had not seen it coming and quickly ducked, she would not have missed her target by a few inches as the vase exploded against the wall into pieces.

"Shit, Needy!" he yelled out her name by mistake as he brushed some of the shattered glass out of his hair.

"What the fuck did you just say?" Needy asked.

"Nothing, boss," Freak answered nervously. Hopeful that their hostages missed a slip of the tongue in the drama that had just ensued.

Needy eyes narrowed as she spoke slowly. "The next projectile will not miss and be a glass vase; you understand, asshole?"

Freak knew, like the others, Needy was not a person to be fucked with or crossed, and he knew that she meant every word that she had just spoken as he nodded his head in agreement. But that nodding of the head was not good enough for her. She wanted to hear it from him verbally.

"Do you understand?" she asked again firmly.

"Yes, yes, I understand," Freak answered back.

"Now, since we got an understanding, I need you to post your horny ass outside and guard the perimeter," Needy said.

"It's cold as shit out there, and it's raining," Freak said.

"I am not going to ask twice," Needy replied sternly.

Freak did not say another word and knew it was best to comply and not further challenge Needy's authority as he made his way to the door and outside. A wide grin came across Scooter's face as he watched Freak being punk by

Needy. That grin would only last so long because Needy did not play favorites amongst her crew.

"What are you laughing at, Scooter? Get your ass in that kitchen and whip us up something to eat shithead," she said.

Dez let out a hearty chuckle at his boss remark. "And put that apron on that I like while you at it pickles," he teased Scooter.

"Fuck you," Scooter replied, throwing up his middle fingers.

"The hell he is the only one that is going to make meals in my kitchen is me," Deena said in an unwavering tone of voice that took Needy and her crew by surprise.

"What? Some people can see but can't cook worth of shit!" she said as she made her way to the kitchen.

"I gotta admit she does have a valid point there," Needy said.

Deena stood up. "I don't like what the hell is going on here. But if some good sandwiches and soup will keep all of you from hurting my family, I don't have a problem with whipping you up something."

"Thank you; I promise no harm will come to you or your family," Needy assured.

"You don't have a problem with assistance in your kitchen," Needy asked.

"Would it matter if I did?" Deena asked.

"No, it would not," Needy answers bluntly.

Needy addressed Scooter again. "Make sure all the sharp utensils are accountable for after our host is done whipping us up some chow. I wouldn't want any of them stuck in our backs."

"Gotcha, boss," Scooter replied.

Hallie looked over at Jason, sitting on the sofa quietly. He was eye candy to her, well-built and handsome. And probably could fuck like a rabbit, she thought once she got him in the sack. Other than his looks, he was usually not her type and too square for her eccentric taste. But she was horny and could envision him eating her pie out as she gave him a mouthful of muff in his pretty little mouth.

"Can I get you anything, baby?" she asked sweetly with only a hint of poison in her voice.

Jason looked over at her with a scowl on his face. "First, I am not your baby, but yeah, I gotta piss like a racehorse," he said, still upset about Freak's comment about his mother. He was glad his Dad had not been present because he probably would have lost it and tried to put his entire foot and leg up Freak's ass.

"Still playing hard to get and a bit bitchy, I understand," Hallie said, with a smirk on her face.

"But with them hands tied behind your back, looks like you are going to need an extra pair of hands to take your wanker out for you," she said flirtatiously.

"Dez, can you give him a hand?" Hallie asked. "Sure," Dez said, grinning.

" Never mind, I'll hold it," Jason said.

Hallie started laughing. " I am just fucking with you, Jason. Let's go empty that bladder. I don't want you pissing all over your mama and daddy's good furniture."

"Don't take too long," Needy said as she watched Hallie and Jason exit the cabin for the outhouse.

Needy looked at her watch on her wrist; how long had they now been in this County? An hour maybe more. She knew that the longer they stayed in this area, the higher their risk was getting caught and discovered. Not counting the fact that the sun would be setting soon and darkness would follow, making getting the hell out of this area even more complicated, she thought. But once again, a bigger question ate at her consciousness as maggots do on rotting flesh. And that was what the hell they were going to do with the Deena Clan once John fixed their van? Yes, she had promised them that no harm would come to them if they do as she ordered. But she still wrestled with the fact she would be able to keep that promise if everything went to hell in a handbasket as it did back at the bank in a New York minute.

"Goddamn, you do make some good sandwiches' lady," Scooter said, breaking her train of thought as he voraciously bit into the sandwich in his hand.

Deena entered the dining room area where they had now gathered at the table with a platter of robust-looking sandwiches with all the fixtures.

"All knives accounted for?" Needy asked Scooter.

"She was a perfect angel," Scooter answers.

Needy took a sandwich off the platter and looked over at Deena, who had now joined the rest of them at the dining table. Perfect angel, huh? She thought. There was only one person she knew of who deserved that title in her world, and none of the company at this table came close. Needy took a bite of the sandwich. Scooter was right; not bad at all.

CHAPTER FIVE

The behemoth of a man sat down on a huge boulder nearby, hidden by trees and twigs, to listen to the surrounding woods' sounds. For a long time now, he did not know who he was? What he was, or where he was? But something inside of him told him that he could not be amongst other human beings. His primal instinct said to him that this was necessary for him to survive. Nature and its environment around him had become a part of him. In contrast, he had also become a part of it as he wandered and survived evasively for years now in the wild.

His sense of sight, smell, and hearing had all heightened to extraordinary degrees for a human being in this process. He lived off the scraps that others left behind when he could not steal from their campsites. Sometimes, when that option was not available, his predator instincts allowed him to capture and kill whatever he had to survive in the harsh and unforgiving environment of the wild.

He was a wild man by all appearances, and he knew it after catching a shocking reflection of himself years ago in a nearby lake. But he knew he was not a Bigfoot. Because Bigfoot would not be wearing human clothes, would he?

He thought. The only human being that he was comfortable having contact with or had knowledge of his existence was an old lady who stayed miles away in a cabin with her husband. She had befriended him when she caught him wandering around her home, fed him, and gave him clothing. He was surprised at first that she did not seem shocked at all by his appearance. Only later, when he waved those big hands of his in front of her face, he discovered that she could not see, which explained to him her earlier non-reaction. But the more he got to know her, as he made it a habit only to show up when she was by herself and even gain her trust where she gave him chores to do around and outside of the cabin. He had summed up she was not like the rest of the humans that he intensely despised and could not trust.

She had introduced herself as Deena, but he called her Dee for short. And when she asked him what his name was, the only thing that he could remember was El, so that was the name that she referred to him by after their acquaintance. She was like a mother to him, but nothing like his biological mother. El did remember that he hated his mother, but unfortunately, no matter how hard he tried. He could not remember why? Was she dead or alive? He did not know that either, nor did he care. As far as he was concerned, Dee was his new mother, and he would do anything necessary within his power to protect her if need be.

He watched earlier from a distance as the vehicles pulled up and the strange people exited the cars with the guns pointed towards the two men he recognized as Dee's husband and the other her son Jason.

El watched closely as the other strangers emerged from different woodland areas that he had never seen before and made their way towards Mother Dee's cabin.

A rage now came over him, an emotion that he had not experienced in a long time. His eyes turned bloodshot red as he squeezed hard on a baseball-sized rock he had been holding in that hand. A cracking noise begins. When he opened his hand, the stone had disintegrated into pebbles and dust that he let fall casually to the ground.

Flashbacks came back to him of a giant beast grabbing hold of his throat as the creature, and he descended to the cold watery grave below them after it had knocked him off a cliff. He could feel the beast's teeth sinking into his shoulder blade as he fought for his life in those icy waters, then everything went black.

He does not remember how he got to the cliff that night and why he was there. And what the thing was that attacked him. All he remembered is waking up wet, cold, hurt, and wanting to hide from the world. Because he knew something was out to get him, whether it was humans or not. He felt his ability to survive now depended on his ability to remain anonymous until he could remember again who he was? But now, he had another matter that needed his attention. Mother Dee needed him, and it had been a long time since he had paid her and her cabin a visit. El pulled out a seven-inch knife that he had stolen from a campsite a while back ago. His eyes lit up and something stirred inside him every time El held the knife in his hand. He noticed blood from a recent kill on the blade as he admired its craftsmanship. El licked the blood off with his tongue and stuck the knife back into a sheath that was attached to his belt. He noticed that it was now starting to get dark, which was okay with him. He was comfortable with the darkness and operating within its shadows, because like all other animals that hunted at night. He was nocturnal by nature and a killer by birth.

* * *

After securing the necessary funds and paperwork, she needed through her connections back in the United States and some in Romania. Luna walked towards boarding Gate A at the Bucharest Henri Coanda Airport in disguise; she looked around the airport to see if she was being followed by any of the vampire clan from the compound that she had recently fought and killed her way out of fearlessly. She was acutely aware that after fighting her way to freedom and leaving a trail of dead vampire bodies in her wake. That Marcellus probably now had an all-points bulletin and bounty out on her head at any cost. He was a ruthless vampire sect leader, and what better way to prove his worth to the committee if he could offer her head on a blood platter, she reckoned after she had defeated and eradicated some of his best foot soldiers.

"Welcome to Lufthansa Airlines," said the Airline attendant cordially.

Luna handed the attendant her boarding pass as she looked behind her one last time for Marcellus's agents. She would deal with him and his sect at a later date, she had concluded. Her focus now was the score she had to settle back in the United States with the sonsofbitches that had shipped her in an ACME container like Wile E. Coyote to bum fuck Romania to be a service dog to a bunch of fucking bloodsuckers and nightwalkers in the Carpathian Mountains.

CHAPTER SIX

am exited a nondescript duplex belonging to the Langelli family on Chicago's Southside into the cool chilly air, which was a welcome relief from the nightmare that she had experienced inside a home that she had no doubt the devil had just visited. Two local Catholic priests, Father Merrick and Father Saldonaldo followed her outside of the house after performing a ritual exorcism on a ten-year-old girl named Marie Langelli inside the home with her immediate family members present. The two men of faith had been battling the demon that had possessed the child for months and had finally been able to free the young girl from the bondage of the demonic spirit that had attempted vigorously to destroy Maria and her family during the entire process.

It was a bitter victory for both men, but a triumph nevertheless that they both knew would leave the Langelli family with long-lasting scars, both physical and mental. Unlike the movies, they knew that there were real lives they were dealing with whom eternal souls were at stake. The unseen world was just as factual as the seen world as far as they both were concerned. The demonic entity that had chosen to inhabit and take over the body of a precious ten-year-old girl was a testimonial to that fact and the other battles that they had both fought since being authorized to perform the rite of exorcism in these spiritual battles over life and death.

They had given Sam unprecedented access through their diocese to witness and record these months-long rituals not for sensualism but as a record of testimony to educate the public on the rites of exorcisms behind closed doors. It was a task that Sam had not taken lightly either as an investigative journalist for her newspaper, The Night Turner Tribune.

For some reason, Sam's throat felt scorched. She reached in her purse and took out a small bottle of water, and took a sip of it to cool her throat. It worked.

"How are you doing, Sam?" Father Saldonaldo asked.

"Fine, Father. Thanks for asking," Sam replied.

Father Saldonaldo was an affable catholic priest of Cuban descent with a head of salt and pepper hair on a softly chiseled face on a tall thin frame. Merrick was the younger of the two that looked like what Hollywood would want if they wanted a catholic priest for a casting call in a movie, but slightly shorter than his Mentor.

"Is she going to be okay?" Sam asked, concerned.

"We hope so, Sam, but you never know how these cases can go," Saldonaldo answered as honestly as he could.

That was not the answer Sam was expecting as she pried further. "Does that mean it could come back?"

"They always come back," Merrick said glumly.

"But sometimes not in the same person," Saldonaldo added, which did bring Sam a more hopeful outlook to her question. Not that she wanted anyone else to fall victim to this demonic entity, but Maria, this sweet little girl, had suffered enough, she thought. Sam also knew she would have a hard time erasing the images of how the demon that had identified itself as "Charley" had distorted the little girl's face. A demonic entity that took on a physical appearance of its own as it spat out vile and vulgar obscenities at her and the priests and appeared to have intimate knowledge of their personal life and other languages that was not native or known to the child's tongue. Yes, she had indeed seen a lot of things in her years as a paranormal investigator and journalist that would blow most people's minds. But when children were a victim of these demonic forces, her heart always seems to ache harder, such as the case she had investigated in Louisiana involving Isabella Dupri.

Sam could tell it was something on Father Saldonaldo's mind as she watched him rub his thumbs together as he held his hands folded against his cassock.

"Sam, I don't mean to pry, but may I ask you a personal question if you don't mind?" he asked.

Merrick seemed to clear his voice nervously and swallow a lump in his throat, which Sam did not miss either.

Sam felt she already knew what the question would be because she had been asking herself the same damn thing ever since she exited the Dupree's home. "Sure, Father, go ahead," she answered, trying to sound as if she had not anticipated this inquiry.

"What did the demon mean when it looked at you and said, "She's coming?" he asked.

"Honestly, I have no idea, Father," she replied, much to Saldonaldo's and his assistant Father Merrick's disappointment.

"Did you notice the change in its face when it said that? It was almost beast-like," Merrick pointed out.

"Yes, I noticed that Father Merrick, it's something I don't think that I will forget anytime soon either," Sam confided.

Saldonaldo cleared his voice as if signaling to Merrick to cut this conversation short because he did not want this topic to take an uncomfortable turn for Sam, especially after all they had just been through earlier during the exorcism.

But Merrick blatantly ignored his signal and was not letting up. "If you can think of anything, please let us know."

"Will do, Father Merrick," Sam replied pleasantly, disregarding his pushiness.

"If you need anything else for your story, please let us know," Saldonaldo added.

"Thanks, Father Saldonaldo, I will do just that," Sam replied, as she shook both Priests hands in gratitude before she said her final farewell.

As Sam walked towards her car, she suddenly felt as if something or someone watched her every movement. She turned around and looked back at the duplex, only to find that both men had gone back inside. Sam's eyes went up to the second floor of the duplex. She briefly caught sight of the windows upstairs drapes being quickly drawn back. It looked like Maria was standing in that window, she thought. But no, impossible! She concluded, because the child had been incapacitated and confined to her bed after the hellish ordeal.

Sam's car made two beeps as she unlocked it with her remote. Once inside the vehicle and alone, everything that had happened with the Langelli case hit Sam like a whirlwind as she broke down and began to weep. She eventually got her composure back together as she wiped the tears away from her face with her hands. As Sam flipped down her visor to access her vanity mirror, she suddenly caught a reflection of an apparition staring back at her with glistening black pupils and rotten teeth grin on its face in her rearview mirror. Sam quickly turns around only to find out that no one was in the back seat at all. But the vision of what she thought she just saw still left her shaken as she regains her composure again.

"Get your shit together, Sam," she said to herself as she started up her car. As she pulled off from in front of the Langelli house and headed home, for some reason, she could not shake the nagging feeling that the most challenging battle lay ahead. Father Saldonaldo's earlier question suddenly nagged at her as well. What did the demon mean? When it stated, "She's coming." Sam was aware from experience that these demonic entities that occupied people could not be trusted. They always used fear, lies, and manipulation to control their subject and the surrounding people trying to help them.

What had it meant? An incoming call quickly sidelined her thoughts about it through her car's Bluetooth from her fiancé Brandon.

"Hey, babe, what's up?" he said. The sound of his voice automatically seemed to cheer her up.

"Hey Detective, I just finished up at the Langelli's place, and I am on my way home," she answered.

"Do you mind making a detour and joining me for a drink at Logan's?"

How did Brandon know that a stiff drink was something that she could use right now, she thought. "Sounds good babe, I could use a nightcap," Sam replied.

"That makes the two of us," Brandon said. Sam detected in his voice that his day had been maybe as rough as hers, which came as no surprise to her being that he was still a fresh Homicide detective on the gritty streets of Chicago.

"Okay, it's a few things I got to wrap up here at the precinct, and I will see you shortly, my love."

"I like the sound of that," Sam said.

"Me too," Brandon answered.

The call disconnected from her car's Bluetooth center as Sam hit the freeway headed towards her new destination Logan's, located in Chicago's downtown district. Sam glanced into the rearview mirror at the backseat. To her relief, no vestige of the hideous apparition appeared in her rearview mirror as a co-passenger, although she could not shake the one that comfortably nestled in the recesses of her mind.

CHAPTER SEVEN

Sheriff Alvarez had decided that he would now back trail their route because the bank robbers had not attempted to penetrate the roadblock of spikes and patrol personnel that he had set up ahead of the road he had been pursuing them down.

After assessing the situation at hand, he concluded that the suspects must have cut off into one of the numerous side roadways along the route during the pursuit and was now hiding out somewhere in the dense woodlands waiting for nightfall before they attempted to get out of his County undetected.

Alvarez knew that there were many privately owned cabins nearby scattered within five to ten-mile radiuses of each other, maybe a few miles more for some of them. He would have to put together a task force to search each one of them for any signs of evidence of the dangerous criminals he was after. To make it happen, though, he had to make a call first to the only other person he could think of that knew these surrounding woodlands better than himself or any other local around there. And that person was no other than Cody Smith, Harper Creek's game warden.

"Hey, Cap."

"Yeah, Sheriff, what's up?" Smith answered, sounding a little bit groggy to Alvarez like he had just woke up. He had after a night's romp with the naked, dirty blond that lay next to him that he had picked up at a local bar last night.

"You still sleep?" Alvarez asked.

"Was, even I deserve a day off," Smith answered.

"Sorry, Cap, did not know it was your day off," Alvarez apologized.

"Like I said, sorry to disturb you, but I got an urgent situation up here that I am going to need your immediate assistance with," Alvarez said.

"What gives?" Smith asked, concerned.

"This morning, a crew robbed one of our local banks, and I think that maybe holed up in one of the nearby cabins near Scouters Peak."

"What's up, daddy?" said the dirty blond as she turned over towards Smith yawning and wiping the sleep out of her eyes.

"I am not your daddy," he said as he brushed her hand off his arm.

For some reason, she had looked far different to him last night at the bar than what he now had sprawled across his bed. More pretty, not as old. "Damn," he said to himself, he is going to have to stop letting the JD (whiskey) make the decisions for his pecker from here on out. At least she, as far as appearances go, did not look that bad from the rear, he thought.

"What was that?" Alvarez asked.

"Never mind Al, let me get my shit together, and I'll meet you asap at your location," Smith answered.

"Thanks, Cap, I appreciate that," Alvarez replied.

"Who's asap?" the dirty blond asked.

"What?" Cap said.

"Who's asap?" she repeated.

Smith shook his head sideways, took a sip out of what's left in the bottle of Jack Daniels on his nightstand.

"My uncle from Kentucky," he answered, handing her the bottle.

The sound of welding emanating from the cabin's garage as Brick watches over John. "How long, old man, before our van is ready?" he shouted out.

John flipped the welding goggles up over his head. "Well, old man, I need to see if the weld has taken or else y'all asses are going to be calling for another tow down the road," he answered.

Brick put the barrel of his assault rifle to John's chin. "Very funny, now how long, shitkicker?"

John could see something in Brick's eyes that told him if he pushed too far, it might put him in a position where he could not help his family. If his brains were blown out of his head, that would be one of those positions, he concluded.

"Maybe another hour, maybe less," John answers in a defiant tone of voice.

"Hurry up, asshole, we ain't got all day," Brick barked.

"Everything's okay out here?" Needy asked as she approached the two men.

"Yeah, me and old John here were just having a friendly talk, that's all."

"How's it coming along?" Needy asked, looking over the van.

John looked over at Brick; he wanted to tear his head off but thought best of it and that it also might not be the brightest move right now. "I was telling Mr. Friendly that it shouldn't be much longer," he informed Needy.

Needy cracked a smile; she could see some of her Father in John, a sharp tongue, and a pair of steel balls to go with it. Again, her final decision on what to do with him and his family would not be an easy one.

"Hungry? I've got some sandwiches and sodas here," Needy said, handing each man a small brown paper bag.

"Like a wolf," Brick answered as he took the bag from Needy.

"Thanks for my own food," John said bluntly.

"You are welcome," Needy said with a grin on her face.

Needy watched as Brick devoured the sandwich she had given him in almost one bite. His soda went down just as quick in three swallows and a burp. John ate his sandwich much slower as if savoring and appreciating every taste.

Brick felt Needy eyes were on him. " Like I said, I was hungry," he stated, as he licked the crumbs off his fingers.

"I'll see about getting you another one," Needy said.

The sound of something rustling in the distance suddenly snapped Needy and her gunman to their attention as she withdrew the gun from her holster with a speed that gunslinger Wyatt Earp would have been proud to witness.

"What the fuck was that noise?" Needy said as she and Brick made their way slowly towards where they thought the sound came from while keeping an eye out on John.

Something appeared to be moving between the trees ahead of them; that was their focal point, but it was too dark for them to make out precisely what it was? As they continue to advance towards the unknown.

"Hey, boss, is everything cool?" Dez asks as he appeared out of nowhere with his assault weapon in hand.

Needy put her finger up against her lips in response to silence Dez and then pointed to the trees ahead.

Her eyes suddenly caught sight of a pair of eyes luminously glowing in the dark.

She and her crew raised their weapons.

A startled young deer bolted out of the trees and took off in a quick sprint off into the woods. "Don't shoot!" Needy yelled out in just enough time to spare the young deer an early demise.

John watched from afar as he contemplated whether or not he should arm himself with something from the garage and sneak back to the cabin and attempt to free his wife and son.

"Damn, Bambi, you almost bit the dust," Dez said, snickering.

Needy looked back at John; she did not realize how much distance she and Brick had created between her captives.

Needy felt she knew what John had been thinking because she would have been thinking the same thing herself if she was him. And although her crew appeared to be a band of misfits, she knew one thing about them that John did not know; they were a band of well-trained misfits by an ex-Special Forces Op. Staff Sgt. Needy Sellers.

As John's eyes locked on her, she pointed to the garage behind him that was only a short distance away. As John turned around, he saw Scooter emerge from the garage opening illuminated by the shop lights inside. He watched Scooter wave to him, cracking a smile in the halo of light. John also noticed the most important thing: the silhouette of an assault weapon in his hand now raised to his shoulder.

Fuck! Her men were like cockroaches, John thought. Everywhere.

Elwood, hidden in the shadows undeterred, watched them all closely, biding his time. Time to strike, time to kill.

CHAPTER EIGHT

A group of intimidating men with one woman that looks like an equal shit kicker made their way in the airport towards Luna as she claimed her luggage off the carousel. She grabbed her bag up off its conveyor belt before it passed her by while at the same time keeping her eyes on the motley crew of characters expeditiously headed her way. Not only did they catch her attention, but the eyes of other people in the airport luggage pick-up area that would glance but were too nervous about maintaining prolonged eye contact with these head crackers.

Luna was tired after the long flight from Romania and just wanted to get some rest, but if Marcellus sect had followed her and wanted to tango, she was always in the mood to dance, she thought.

"Well, I be damned," she said as the head crackers came into closer view. She recognized every one of them sonsofa-bitches now. It had been four years since she had last seen their ugly mugs, but it was no mistake who this rough and tumble crew of bounty hunters was? That she had run with and been in charge of up in Montana. Their reputation was so fierce that the mere mention of their name made even the hardest fugitives shiver with fear when they found out that this team was on their trail, on their asses. They were the last ones you wanted on your tail with their ruthless reputation and one-hundred-percent fugitive apprehension rate of suspects, dead or alive. *"Kick asses or doors down, or whichever one comes first,"* The Bone Squad.

"Well, I'll be a monkey's ass," Dean said as he went in with outstretched arms to embrace Luna.

"You might be," she said, triggering a chuckle from the others in the group, as they individually embrace her as well with a smile and a friendly hug.

"How was your flight in?" asked Mako, a bearded and large muscular man of Native American heritage.

Luna looked at him and smiled. Damn, he looked more ripped than she last remembered. "Good, but shit, I am hungry as a wolf," she answered.

"I bet," he said, as a wide grin broke out across his bearded face, revealing shiny gold caps on some of his back molars.

It was a consensus of quietness now amongst Luna and her old crew as she stood there sizing all of them up like the pack leader she was, absorbing the energy of their presence. Dean, Mako, Riley, Omar, and Wiz their Tech–guy. She could sense that they were doing the same to her, but as each of their eyes met hers, it was no doubt in her mind that they still knew that she was still the Alpha, that she was still Luna Dye, top of the fucking food chain.

"Let's get the fuck out of here boss, and get some grub in your belly," Omar said, breaking the silence, who was just as large and intimidating as Mako in presence.

Luna cracked that one-hundred-watt smile of hers and gave Omar a flirtatious wink. "Sounds good, cowboy," she said.

Riley felt the curious eyes on them all and shot one of the gazers a fierce look causing them to look away and keep stepping with luggage in tow quickly. Luna caught the exchange and chuckled. It was good to be back with her old crew; she thought as they made their way out of the airport. But most of all, she felt it was good to be free again to start setting plans in motion that she had dreamed about while in the nightwalkers captivity.

Plans to soon rain Hell down on all those who have crossed her and scores to settle with no mercy.

As Luna and the others entered the black tactical van in the airport parking garage, Wiz turned on the radio to Thin Lizzy's *The Boys Are Back In Town.*

The irony of the song at that moment brought a smile of satisfaction to Luna's face.

* * *

Relieved from his post outside by Scooter for a break, Freak stood there in the living room, finishing off the last of his sandwich. His eyes fixated on Deena as she put away the dishes in her kitchen cabinets. He still wondered what she looks like without that skirt on and that wool sweater she was wearing as his eyes locked in on what he thought was a nicely shaped ass for a woman of her age in that skirt.

In his mind, he could visualize her already mounting him and riding his manhood slowly with abandoned passion and lust with no regard for her husband. "What about your husband," he asked as he grabs her by that tight little ass of hers, thrusting himself deeper into her treasure box. "Fuck John," he heard her whisper in his ear as he came out of her, she slid down to his crotch, and gently begin to take him in her mouth.

"Yeah fuck John," he agreed, as he clutches her by the back of the head and pushes himself deep into that wet pouty mouth of hers that he sure had not seen this kind of action in an exceptionally long time. "But what are we going to do with John?" he murmured, grimacing between pleasure and pain as she devoured him in her mouth. She was hungrier than he had imagined. Her eyes did not directly meet him as she released him and licked the rest of him off her lips. "Kill him," she answered with an evil smile on her face.

Freak's wild eyes lit up. "Yes, I can do that."

"Do what?" Hallie asked, breaking Freak out of his hallucination.

"What? What? Are you talking about?" answered Freak.

Hallie looked at Freak oddly before she addressed him again. "You said, yes, I can do that."

"What in the hell were you talking about?"

Freak looked back at Hallie, dumbfounded before he answered. "Dude, I have the slightest goddamn clue about what in the hell you are talking about?"

Hallie shook her head sideways, dissatisfied with his answer. "No, dude, you need to lay off the drugs seriously," she said.

Freak grinned and gave Hallie the middle finger in response.

Hallie looked over at Dez. "You heard him didn't you?"

"Naw, I was too busy watching your boyfriend," Dez answered, nodding towards a sentinel, Jason on the sofa.

"I heard him; he is crazy," Jason said, looking over at Freak, who quickly took offense to Jason's direct allegation.

"Fuck you! You did not hear shit, piss boy!" Freak shouted out angrily as he began to make his way over to Jason with his weapon pointed at him.

Hallie just as quickly intervened, jumping in between Jason and Freak with her weapon drawn as well. "Freak, since you're finished with your sandwich, why don't you go have a smoke and get some cool air," she suggested non-negotiable as she handed Freak a cigarette and patted him on his chest.

Freak looked back at Dez with his assault weapon at the ready and who appeared to be backing Hallie. He took the cigarette from Hallie.

"You are not the boss," he said.

"Never said I was," she answered, face to face with freak and not backing down.

Freak gave Jason a dirty look before he reluctantly took Hallie's advice.

"Yeah, I guess I could use some cool air," he said, in a manner that implied it was a decision that was left up entirely to him. It was not.

Jason watched him closely as he left out the front door. "Freak how appropriate," he said.

"When we want your opinion, we will ask for it," Hallie replied sternly.

"Okay, you the boss," Jason said. And not to his surprise, unlike Freak, she did not correct him. Maybe she likes him stroking her ego, he concluded, and perhaps he could use this tactic to his advantage.

"Don't get what I did twisted. I did not want Freak to kill you before I take you for a test drive and test out your stick shift." Hallie said with a smirk on her face.

Dez laughed at her remark.

"What?" Jason replied.

"I see what you were working with when you were taking a piss, not bad for a tight little ass like you," Hallie said.

"And what if I am not interested in you taking me for any ride?" Jason countered.

Hallie pinched Jason's cheek. "Then maybe Freak can loosen you up for options," she said with a grin on her face.

Jason jerked away from Hallie, he was not amused at the thought of being anally raped, but he noticed that her crew member Dez appeared to get a kick out of her remark by his hearty laughter. What kind of degenerates had infiltrated their lives, he thought. Kidnapping, potential rapist, what next he thought, murder? Suddenly a cold feeling of awakening crept over Jason like a morning chill off the South Dakota mountains.

He would have to be more careful in his interactions with them, he thought. Because indeed, if they were capable of committing the first two offenses, he concluded. It was no doubt in his mind that they were ruthless enough to execute the latter, murder. Jason looked over at his Mother. Despite her disability, he knew that she was more vital than she looks, and one thing about her that he had admired about her all his life she never let anything hold her back from living her best life that included her disability. Jason was willing to give his life for her and his Father if necessary and did not doubt in his mind if it came down to it. They were both ready to do the same for him. Right now, he knew that he and his family were not only at risk but under close watch, but when the opportunity presented itself for him to make a move and attempt to disarm one of these assholes, Jason felt he would know.

"You can have a seat, grandma," Hallie said, pointing over to the space next to Deena's son, forgetting that Deena could not see.

"Mom on the sofa," Jason said.

Deena complied and made her way over to the sofa and sat right down next to her son.

"Good girl," Hallie said.

"How's that arm?" she asked Dez.

"I'll live," he said, frowning.

Dez looked around the cabin, taking it all in, the place was cozy and decorated nicely, but that did not negate the uneasy feeling he had about being there. In fact, he would have preferred to be anywhere else but this cabin in the woods.

Hallie picked up on his discomfort and concern.

"Hey, you okay?" she asked, rubbing his shoulder.

"I don't like this place, and the sooner we leave, the better," he answered.

It was something not right in the atmosphere that Dez sensed. He had picked it up as soon as they had got stuck in this part of the woods. He wondered if the others could feel it as well, or was he just being unnecessarily paranoid.

"I hear you, big guy, this is not my idea of how to party either stuck here with Norman Bates and his Mama and Papa," Hallie said.

Dez walked over to one of the windows in the cabin and pulled back its curtain. "Damn, is it ever going to stop raining?" he asked, as he noticed that the rain had started up again.

A code-like tapping on the front door erupted, which consisted of three taps, a pause, then tap, and another tap. Needy had created that distinct knock just in case someone else outside of her crew was trying to breach the cabin or perimeter before they leave. Hallie went over to the door and unlocked it as Needy entered, brushing the rainwater off her clothes. She automatically picked up on the tension in the room.

"How long before we blow this joint?" Dez asked, not attempting to hide the tone of impatience in his voice.

"Not long," Needy answered, not trying to hide the tone of annoyance in hers either.

"Daisy, I need you to gather up all the communication devices these folks own, cellphones, laptops, etc.," she ordered, still referring to Hallie by the alias she had given her prior to first making the family's acquaintance.

Hallie looked over and addressed their hostages on the sofa. "You heard her, right? I need all your cellphones and any other toys you got around here that all of you use to communicate with," she said firmly.

"My phone is on the charger on the kitchen counter," Deena answered.

"In my coat pocket," Jason informed Hallie.

"What about John's?" Needy asked.

"He usually leaves his cell in the truck," Jason answered.

"Is that right," Needy replied, looking for signs of deception from him.

"That's right in the glove compartment," Jason confirmed, standing his ground.

Needy looked over at Dez and nodded her head towards the front door. "Go take a look in the wrecker."

Dez menacingly glared at Jason. "Kid, you better not be bullshitting me!" he warned.

"The only way to find out is to go and look," Jason said, grinning, knowingly playing on Dez paranoia after listening in on the big guy's conversation with Hallie, who he thought of now as the **HBIC** (head bitch in charge).

Needy did not like the grin on Jason's face either and made it a point to let him know as much. "Don't play games with us, son, because I can guarantee you that you won't like the consequences, understand?"

The grin quickly disappeared from Jason's face as his eyes met Needy's deep emerald, green ones. He had watched her interaction amongst the others, and he had quickly picked up that she was someone not to tangle with unless you wanted to go all the way with her in the Octagon. He could tell she also had some type of specialized training by the way she carried herself. Military? Police? He did not know which one. But he was sure he was not too far off from his assessment of her background. And if this was so? He also had to come to another hard-cold fact that it might make whatever he had in mind to save his family a more difficult task than what his skill set was qualified to handle. Regardless, he could not see himself or his family going down without a fight. Fuck a skill set, he thought; I will improvise.

CHAPTER NINE

Dez made his way slowly towards the red wrecker parked next to John's workshop/garage to retrieve the cell phone that was supposed to be inside the truck's glove compartment. He could hear the noise coming from inside the workshop from John, whom he assumed was putting the finishing touches on their van.

A gray fog-like mist now hung thick in the air around the cabin, only penetrated by the eerily yellowish glow of light emitting from the garage. Dez observes as Brick steps out of the garage; upon hearing him approach, he nodded his head in acknowledgment of him, and then, just as quickly as he appeared, he disappeared back inside the garage. The old man needed to hurry up and fast as far as Dez was concerned because he did not want to spend another waking moment out there in the wilderness if he could avoid it. Besides that, his shoulder, where he had been wounded in the shootout, still hurt like shit! He felt lucky that the bullet had not taken a fatal detour and hit him in his chest or head. Good thing the pig was a lousy shot and could not see between those slitted pig eyes; he laughed at his thought. Dez slung the AR-15 around the shoulder that was not wounded as he made his way inside the wrecker to search for the cell phone.

He went straight to the glove compartment, and much to his surprise, "Bingo!" It was right there, just as John's pantywaist son said it would be. Dez reached in and retrieved the phone, stuffing it in his jacket's pocket.

"Let's see what other surprises Pops have in here," Dez murmured to himself as he rifled through the glove compartment. He soon discovered a clear plastic bag hidden under other miscellaneous items in the truck's glove compartment.

"My oh my, what do we have here?" Dez said to himself as he turned the vanity light on in the truck to get a better look at the neatly rolled joints in the plastic bag. He reached inside and took out one of the joints and slowly dragged it across and under his nostrils, inhaling its skunk-like scent.

"Pops, I think you got some good shit here," he said, with a grin on his face. Dez set his assault rifle up against the truck dash as he then proceeded to light up the joint in his hand. He took a long drag of it and then began coughing as he beat his chest to clear his throat. "Damn like I said, some good shit!" he exclaimed. As Dez grabbed his assault weapon and got ready to exit the truck, he heard what he detected as movement next to the wrecker that suddenly snapped him back to a defensive position and out of his momentary state of Cannabis bliss.

"Brick, is that you?" he called out as he stepped outside of the wrecker, looking nervously around in the darkness.

Dez's eyes widened as he felt the hot breath of something hovering behind him on his neck. Its musty outdoor stench hitting his nostrils full force. He spun around as quickly as he could to engage whatever had taken him by surprise, only to be met by something to him that looked like Bigfoot in the dark disguised as a man. Dez's eyes went straight to the blade in the beast's hand that went directly under his chin and through his skull, paralyzing him. The goliath lifted all six-feet-two of Dez off his feet and dangled him in the air like a rag doll before he retracted the bloody blade, and Dez's lifeless body dropped to the ground with a resounding thump.

El the man-beast picked him up like he was lifting a child and slung him over his shoulder. Grunted and then disappeared with his first kill undetected and quietly into the night as if he had never been there.

Needy looked at her watch on her wrist as she paced back and forth inside the cabin, trying to decide what their next move would be when they finally put this scene behind them.

She looked again at her watch and now realized that Dez had been gone over twenty minutes now and had not returned after she had sent him to retrieve John's cell phone.

"Dez should have been back by now," she said to no one in particular in the room.

"Maybe he stopped and decided to take a big shit after eating Grandma's homemade sandwiches," Hallie said, looking over at Deena on the couch.

"Home cooking will do that to you," Hallie added with a nervous laugh, hoping that was all it was to his long absence.

"Dez, what's your twenty?" Needy asked over the walkie-talkie she held in her hand.

"Dez, what's your twenty?" she repeated, worrying.

"Dez is not answering his radio; he better be taking a big one in the shit house," she said.

"I told you," Hallie answered, sitting on a wide lounge chair with one of her legs laid across one of the arms of the chair, just a little too cozily for Needy's taste.

Needy radioed into another one of her men she had posted outside watching the perimeter. "Scooter, what's your twenty?"

"Out here getting wet and watching the fucking trees," Scooter answers back sullenly.

"Do you have Dez in your visual?" Needy asked.

Scooter, standing not too far from the wrecker, looked around the perimeter in response to Needy's question, took a quick sweep with his flashlight around the area, illuminating the darkness in front of him.

"Nope, don't see him at all."

"Check the outhouse," Needy suggested.

Several minutes pass by quietly until Needy hears the squelch of the radio and Scooter's voice again. "No, not there either."

"What?" Needy said, now very concerned. Shit house or not, Dez should have been back by now, she thought.

"You keep an eye on these two; I am going to find Dez," she said to Hallie.

"My pleasure," Hallie said with a salute and a grin on her face.

Needy looked over at Deena and Jason, quietly sitting on the sofa, hands tied in front of them. She could sense the anxiety and fear coming off the both of them. As her eyes met Jason's, she silently tried to convey that this was not how she had expected things to turn out, but she was still in charge of how this situation would come to an end.

Nothing else to say, she exited the cabin in search of Dez, with the thought in her head that he better not be fucking around out there. Because they did not have time to be jerking around or playing games.

"Dez, where are you?" she shouted out as she made her way around the perimeter of the cabin, investigating the area for his whereabouts.

Scooter met up with her, and by the look on his face, she could tell he was just as baffled as she was about where in the hell Dez was? Where in the hell he could have gone.

Needy looked over at the garage.

Scooter followed her eyes. "I already checked," he said.

"Where in the hell is Freak?" Needy asked.

"Here, boss," Freak answered as he approached both of them slowly.

"What in the hell is going on?" he asked.

Needy shines her flashlight around them just in case something or someone decides to jump out at them and eat lead.

" Good question, that's what we are trying to find out," she answered.

Needy made her way over to the wrecker with Scooter and Freak beside her. As she shines her flashlight at the ground to verify Dez's fresh footprints in the mud and that he had indeed "made contact" with the wrecker as ordered by her to retrieve John's cellphone.

The beam of her flashlight suddenly lit up the half-smoked joint on the ground.

Needy bent down and picked it up, dragging it across her nose.

"What the hell is that a joint? Old Dez holding back on us, huh?" Freak said.

Needy only needed to take several more steps before her flashlight illuminated the blood and brain matter on the ground closer to the wrecker.

"What the fuck is that?" Scooter said nervously.

"What the fuck does it look like?" Needy answered as she bent down and touched the still wet blood mixed with bits of brain.

Scooter flashlight hit the palm of Needy's hand, illuminating the blood on her hand in the darkness.

"Look at that shit!" Freak said as his flashlight hit a set of large shoeless footprints that made their way to and from the wrecker.

"Who in the hell would walk around with no shoes on in this kind of weather?" Freak asked.

"I don't know, but we got a fucking problem!" Needy answered.

Needy could read the look on Freak's and Scooter's faces, and she knew just what these two assholes were thinking, and it was her responsibility to clear things up before their little brains start working overtime and fry themselves out with wild out conclusions.

"Well, I tell you two what. It's not goddamn Bigfoot!" she said.

"How can you be sure of that," Freak asked.

Needy looked at Freak and shook her head sideways in apparent disagreement. As she walked over to the wrecker looked inside the glove compartment. The cellphone was not there. She suspected Dez had already retrieved it and the weed, probably smoked a little bit of the weed before someone had taken him by surprise and ambushed him or at worst killed him.

She exited the wrecker and only then felt it was necessary to address Freak's question.

"You still need an answer to your question?" she asked.

"It might help," Freak replied.

"When did Bigfoot ever need an AR-15?" Needy asked.

Scooter looked at Freak.

"Dumbass," he said.

"Like you did not believe it too, you Fuck," Freak retorted.

"Ladies, cut the shit! I do not care if Bigfoot butt fuck the both of you in your dreams! We still got one of our own missing, and until we find out what the hell happened to him, all our asses or on high alert! Understand?" Needy said assertively.

Freak and Scooter both nodded their head in agreement after being scolded.

"Good! I need both of you to spread out and secure this area until we get the fuck out of this shit storm that we got ourselves into."

"I thought we were already on high alert," Freak muttered as Needy walked away.

The Bigfoot they were looking for watched them silently from a distance, hidden in the shadows, his blade still dripping with Dez's blood and brain matter. As he heard the sound of their footsteps approaching, he quickly disappeared again into the darkness of the woodlands, carrying the decapitated head of bank robber Dez Franklin in one hand.

CHAPTER TEN

The aroma of hot coffee and the transmissions from police radios filled the air inside the Sheriff's department as it bustled with activity. Alvarez had contacted the Federal Bureau Of Investigations regional office in Minneapolis. They had agreed to get some agents down asap to help him track down the team that had pulled the earlier bank robbery. It appeared to him while discussing the matter with Special Agent Childs. That this group of bandits that had hit *Harper Creek Bank & Trust* was so popular that had been on the radar of the FBI for some time now, had even earned a nickname for themselves, on the Bureau's most wanted list as "*The Go-Go Bandits.*" The FBI had noticed from the surveillance tapes of the numerous bank jobs that the bank robbers had pulled that the team of bank robbers not only and always appeared to be in a hurry. But one of them that they assumed was in charge always shouted out, "Let's go, go, go!" Hence, their nickname was born and now followed them.

The Go-go Bandits, huh? Alvarez thought with a smirk on his face. As far as he was concerned, the only place these degenerates were go, go, going, when he caught them was to prison!

"I heard you had a helluva run-in with this gang?"

"Huh?" Alvarez said, looking up from the file that the FBI had faxed him over on the bank robbers. He had almost forgotten Smith was sitting in his office right across from him.

"I said, I heard you had a helluva encounter with this gang?" Smith repeated himself.

"That's an understatement. I wish you had been there to lend a hand," Alvarez answered.

Smith took a sip of the warm coffee in his Styrofoam cup. "Me too," he agreed.

" Let me tell you something, Cap, those assholes were armed to the Tee and going for broke," Alvarez said.

"Heavy artillery?" Cap asked.

"AR-15's, Heckler & Koch's and a badass attitude to go along with It," Alvarez answered.

"Sound like people I'd like to get to know," Smith said as he took the last sip of the warm coffee out the cup, crunched it up, and threw it in the wastebasket.

"Al, you know we don't have time to be waiting on a bunch of stiff suits to get down here; we need to get a search party up there to those cabins and start to flush those assholes out before they are long gone; before sunrise."

"Yeah, Cap, I was thinking the same thing too," Alvarez replied, stroking his mustache, which was a habit as he leaned back in his office chair.

Alvarez slapped his hand on the desk. " You right, Cap, I'll have those Fed boys meet us on-site; by then, and hopefully, we have those bank-robbing assholes flushed out and in custody."

"Alive or dead?" Cap asked.

"After taking headshots at me and mines, do you think it goddamn matters to me one way or the other?"

"Good answer," Cap said.

"Nah, easy question," Alvarez replied.

Alvarez walked over to two doors that looked like closet doors in his office and unlocked them.

"Well, I be damn," Smith said, as his eyes went to the high-powered assault rifles loaded on the wall racks hidden behind the faux-closet doors.

He walked over to the rifles to get a closer look. "New Inventory?" he asked, inspecting the rifles.

"Yeah, I figured a long time ago, we might get someone or something that one day will come to pay our town a visit again, that likes to play ruff," Alvarez answered.

Alvarez lifted one of the AR-15's off its rack and handed it to Smith.

Smith knew damn well what Alvarez was referring to also. Years ago when a murderous shape-shifter had visited their town and wreaked havoc. All while one of their own turned out to be just as deadly and brutal as the beast that they were chasing resided undetected in Harper Creek right under their noses.

"If that happens, we need to be able to play just as hard," Alvarez said regarding an earlier statement that he had made to the game warden.

Smith nodded his head in agreement as he flipped the AR-15 over in his hands. His eyes went back up to the gun rack. "Is that an M203 Grenade Launcher?" he asked.

Alvarez smiled. "Is that what it looks like?" he answered.

Smith shook his head sideways as a smile crept across his face. "You weren't shitting about being prepared, was you."

"No, I never shit about being prepared, Cap."

Alvarez pointed at his clock on his office wall before he spoke again. "We got six, maybe seven hours, before daylight again to get a task force up there in the woodlands and start flushing out those cabins."

"Can I get a couple of those AR-15's," Cap said, smiling.

"Of course and anything else that you might need," Alvarez responded.

Smith's eyes went towards the grenade launcher mounted on the wall rack as Alvarez's eyes followed.

"Just not that," Alvarez said with a smirk on his face.

* * *

"I did the best I could with those airbags, but I guarantee you can drive all the way to Mexico on that rod now, and it won't break," John said.

"Who said we were going to Mexico?" Needy asked, sternly, with a menacing look on her face.

John looked confused back at Needy because he only meant what he said figuratively and not disrespectfully. "No one, I was only…"

Brick cut him off with a slap on his shoulder. "Relax, shit kicker, she was only screwing with you."

"Freak, take Pops back to the cabin. We will meet you back there shortly," Needy said, the sour look on her face never changing.

"Let's go, Johnny boy," Freak said, pointing his weapon at John and then motioning it towards the direction of the cabin.

John put his hands in the air and did as instructed, but in his mind, he would have liked to grab the weapon out of Freak's hands and shove the barrel up his ass.

When Needy felt that Freak and John had created enough distance between her and the two remaining members outside, she addressed Brick.

Brick could see that she was visibly upset. "What's up?" he asked.

"Dez is missing!"

"What?" Brick asked again, not sure if he heard her correctly the first time.

"Dez is fucking missing, I sent him out to retrieve a cell phone out of that wrecker over there, and he has not shown back up."

"Maybe he bailed," Brick replied.

Needy shook her head sideways in disagreement with Brick's assessment. "Nah, that's not his style, plus I found what I believe is his blood and flesh nearby the truck."

"Fuck me!" Brick said.

"I suspect someone or something attacked him and then took him off to God knows where?" Needy said.

"Fuck me!" Brick replied.

"This does not make sense; Dez is a big guy and tough as nails and can handle himself," Scooter said.

"Maybe he ran across something tougher," Needy said contemplatively.

"I knew this place was bad fucking news!" Brick blurted out.

"You think the pigs are playing games with us?" Scooter interjected.

"No, I do not think that's their style either. This shit is something else we are up against." Needy answered.

"Well, the van is fixed. Why don't we get the hell out of here!" Scooter proposed, not trying to hide a heightened sense of dread that he was starting to feel around them.

Needy cut him a look of disgust. "If it were your ass out there, would you want us to do that? We do not leave a man behind, understand?"

"What I know is Dez may be hurt, but we do not know if he's dead," she said.

"She's right; Dez is like a brother to us. We can't just say fuck him without making a concerted effort to look for him," Brick said.

"Shit! I do not have a good feeling about this," Scooter said grimly.

"I still think we should go," he added, sticking to his guns.

Needy had heard enough, she thought. The more time they took debating what the next move was, the bigger of a peril Dez's life might be in wherever he was at and whomever he was with after being ambushed, she determines.

"Then you are free to go Scooter with your portion of the money, but you are not taking the fucking van with you," she said firmly.

She had never taken Scooter for a coward, but she knew he was not the bravest of the soul out of her bunch either. Maybe he was right, she thought. But the ex-soldier in Needy would not allow her to believe so, and it stood against everything she represented as a person as a leader.

"Times up. What's your decision?" she asked him.

"Let's go find Dez," Scooter replied.

"That's what I thought," Needy said.

"As I stated earlier, we are now on high alert until we get the fuck out of this area, if it breaths, move, and farts, and we cannot identify it. We shoot first and answer questions later, understand boys," she said.

Brick and Scooter both nodded their heads in agreement.

"Good, I need you two to stand guard out here while I go fill in the rest of the crew on what the hell is going on out here! Stay awake and be safe," she ordered.

Brick looked at Scooter with a grin on his face.

"What?" Scooter asked.

"It's good to see you have a pair of balls, Scooter," Brick said sarcastically.

"I always had a pair, steroid freak; that's why I am trying to save them," Scooter countered.

"Me too if my balls were the size of marbles," Brick said with a chuckle.

"Funny guy," Scooter said right before he gave Brick the middle finger and walked off to his post.

El watched his targets closely from a vantage point in the darkness, the long blade in his hand, mentally begging for another taste of blood.

And although his mind was not as clear as it was years ago, before he had made the wilderness his home due to the head injuries he had sustained during an event, he could not recall. That primal lust to kill was something that he had tried to bury in the deep recesses of his mind, only for it to come back repetitively and visit him in his dreams. After being befriended by Deena years ago, he had decided to set aside his killing instinct after she had discovered him foraging around her cabin. She had kindly offered himself something for his belly and given him some of John's old clothes, although she suspected that some of them might be a tad bit too small for a man of size. She did have a pair of coveralls that was way too large for her husband John but seemed to fit El perfectly. Their maternal relationship was a secret that they had kept between themselves for years, and El only came around when John and Jason were not present. He was sure that his appearance would probably not only come as a shock to them but also be very intimidating. But he had discovered afterward when he first met Deena, and she showed no reaction to his appearance; it was because she was blind.

Therefore, he had determined Deena was not seeing him with her eyes; she saw him with her heart. He could care less about her husband or son; the only value they had to him is that they meant something to her. If it were not for that, they would have been long ago, expendable as well to him without a second thought.

Strange though, he could feel changes in his body as well as his mind over the years. He felt as if he was growing stronger, and his six senses had heightened beyond what they had typically been. Bits and pieces of his past had slowly come back into his memory after the severe concussion he had sustained after his fall off a cliff into the deep dark waters of a South Dakota River.

The only thing that was murkier to him in his memory than the waters he had fallen into was the circumstances leading up to him falling off the drop-off. El remembered being attacked by some large animal that night, but he did not remember what that animal was? And how he had made it alive out of those cold waters the next day. But one thing that he did not forget, or was it instinctual? He could never return to the life he once had again until El was able to remember who the hell and what the hell he was? And what was the chain of events that had transpired prior? That put him in the circumstances that had led to almost his death or, in hindsight, his rebirth.

Flashes of who he might have been or done occasionally came back into his memory, of some guy driving a large semi-truck and picking up hitchhikers on the way to his delivery point. He could see the truck driver grinning and picking up the Lot lizards that sold their bodies and souls cheaply at the truck stops in his flashbacks and dreams. He could also see how that truck driver would abduct, torture, and kill some of those lot lizards he picked up along the way. But El could also see that the killer in his dream found this kind of abduction, child's play at best.

It was as easy as spinning a web like a spider and just waiting for the foolish fly to land in its sticky trap. No, El found out that the killer within him got the most satisfaction when hunting and stalking his prey before the catch. EL had no doubts that the killer and he was one of the same. He just no longer retained the memory of what had driven him to this point. The only thing that drove him now was primal rage and his hatred for intruders in his territory. He was almost more animal than human now, and his senses were so acute he could smell the sap cultivating inside the surrounding trees, in the wilderness which had become his home.

The only human connection he had established was with Deena, out here in this remote area. An odd relationship based on his past. That still gave him a slight sense of humanness to his innate sense of misanthropy.

El the man-beast ripped the meat apart in his hand quickly, devouring it hungrily and filling his belly as the raindrops fell on his bearded face.

He had built himself a well-camouflaged temporary makeshift shelter hidden away from the normal pathways and prying eyes of the woodlands' beaten paths. But he would not remain here for long, he knew, not as long as the intruders were still present.

El looked over at Dez's body that he had hidden in some brush. He cleaned the rest of the meat off the bone, grunted, and threw it at Dez, face locked in a deathly stare. A bloody stump at the shoulders was now where Dez's arms used to be. El bit down on something hard in his mouth and grimace, then spitted it out in his hand. It was a ring that had been on one of Dez's fingers.

CHAPTER ELEVEN

Needy watched over her niece as she laid in her hospital bed, stroking her arm gently as she slept. The nurse had come in and given Hannah some pain medication in her IV and something to help her rest.

Tears began to form in Needy's eyes as she went to all the injection marks in Hannah's thin arms. Why her? She thought. Had Hannah not been through enough with the dysfunctional family that she was born into in this cold world. Was her childhood now going to be taken away as well? She wondered.

Needy's faith had never been as strong as she wanted it to be, despite being raised in a Catholic church. As she got older, her views and position were more Agnostic at best. Nevertheless, she found herself praying silently, often, as she had been taught for the Cancer to leave Hannah's small body for good. If there was a higher deity she had determined, she only hoped her prayers were not in vain and heard.

Hannah had gone through another round of chemotherapy treatment for her leukemia that her doctor had recommended. This time with the hopes, this round of treatment would eradicate the cancerous cells in her body. Needy could only hope at best that he was right this time.

"My little angel," she said softly to herself as she watched Hannah's breathing as she slept for any signs of distress.

Hannah's mother, Alice, entered the room with two cups of coffee in her hands, handing one off to Needy.

"How's my baby, " she asked as she walked over and stroked Hannah's face gently.

"She's finally asleep," Needy said as she blew into the cup of coffee to cool it off some before taking a sip.

"She looks like an angel when she is asleep," Alice said.

"Yes, she does," Needy agrees.

Alice sat down in the second chair next to Needy. "I just want you to know, Sis, I appreciate everything that you have done for us, especially Hannah."

"I know Alice, no need to keep thanking me," Needy said humbly before a knock on Hannah's door interrupted their conversation, causing both of their attention to go towards who was now entering the room.

"Come in," Alice said.

Needy watched as all the blood seemed to drain from her sister Alice's face, causing her to go as white as a sheet as Gary entered the room, holding a vase of flowers in his hands. It had been over two years now since the last time they had both laid eyes on him, and by the looks of him, Needy determined not much had changed.

"Gary?" Alice said, bewildered by his visit.

"Hi Alice, Needy," he said, barely looking towards Needy's way and making eye contact, but it was no doubt he could feel the eye contact she had on him, and if he could read her mind, he was sure it would say what in the fuck are you doing here now Gary?

"Hi, Gary, long time," Needy said dryly.

"Yeah, long time," he responded, self-conscious of his absence in his daughter's life as he walked over and placed the flowers on the nightstand next to Hannah's bed. He stroked Hannah's brow as he stood over her watching her sleep.

"Why are you here?" Alice asked, frowning.

Gary cleared his throat. "I know that I have not been the best father, but she is still my daughter," he replied defensively.

Alice folded her arms before laughing at Gary's remark. "Now that's an understatement," she said.

Needy nodded towards Hannah that was still asleep despite the brewing confrontation between her parents. "Look, maybe you two should have this conversation outside of this room," she suggested.

"Look, I did not come here to fight. I just came to see how my daughter is doing," Gary said.

"She's doing fine," Alice replied, who was now toe to toe and in the face of her ex-husband.

Gary stood silently in front of her shaking his head in objection, as a smile crept on his face.

Needy did not like that reptilian smile on his face. She did not like him at all.

"I guess some things never change," he said.

"And I guess some people never do," Alice responded defiantly.

"Needy, can we talk?" Gary said, catching Needy off guard.

"Whatever you got to say to me, you can say in front of my sister," Needy answered.

Gary stroked the scruffy goatee on his tired face. "I don't think so," he replied in a tone that told Needy that this snake in her eyes had something up his sleeve but what she did not know.

"It's okay," her sister said as they made eye contact.

"Nice seeing you again, Alice," he said with a grin on his face.

"Likewise," she answered.

Gary walked back over to Hannah's bed, kissed the inside of the tips of his fingers, and placed it softly on her forehead.

Needy, just like Alice, could not believe what she was witnessing right before her eyes. Because up until now, the only thing that Gary ever displayed for his daughter was an attitude of gross indifference and abstinence.

"Good luck," Alice said to Needy as she and Gary left the room.

Whatever Gary had on his mind? Needy instinctively felt it was best not only do they leave Hannah's room but also step outside the clinic.

"What's up, asshole?" Needy said, letting Gary know right off the bat that she had little time or patience for any bullshit he had intentions on bringing her way.

Gary still had that cheap grin on his face, and Needy noticed that it appears that he had not changed clothes in a few days. She wondered if he was back on that shit again.

"Look, I know we have never seen eye to eye on jack shit! But you need to know first and foremost that I am not as dumb as I look," he said.

Needy smiled. "I do not think you want to drive down that road, Gary," she replied.

"Really," Gary said, as Needy observed his eyes light up in a weird way to match his bizarre smile.

"You know I got to thinking how my ex-wife is paying for all these expensive treatments for Hannah on her mediocre salary?" he said, as he watched to see if the stoic expression on Needy's face would change; it did not.

"Really? And what brilliant conclusion did you come to Einstein," Needy asked?

Gary pointed his finger at Needy before he answered. "You! That's the conclusion I come to, boss lady."

He took out a pack of cigarettes and offered Needy one, which she graciously declined. She observed the pack of cigarettes shaking in his hand like a Maraca.

Gary lit up the cigarette nervously and took a long drag before continuing with what he thought of as a proposal to his ex-sister in law.

"As I stated, I am not as dumb as I look. I think you have been putting those Special Ops skills to use and getting bank loans that you do not have to pay back if you get my drift."

"Go on; I am listening," Needy said, never denying or admitting to Gary's allegations.

Was this fool wired, she thought.

Gary passed her a ruffled-up FBI wanted flier with the typical grainy image of a team of bank robbers pulling a heist.

"Nice picture," Needy said as she handed the picture back to him.

"If you believe all of this is true, why don't you just turn me in for the reward money to the FBI.," she asked.

"Look, I am not a total heartless bastard. I appreciate what you are doing for my baby girl, Auntie Needy," Gary answered.

How someone like him had put two in two together did not matter to Needy as she assessed the situation before her. But she was concerned that the smoke he was now blowing up her ass could cause a fire. She was now mentally ready for his pitch, which she knew would be nothing short of blackmail to keep a secret that she had not admitted guilt or innocence to.

"What are we talking about?" Needy asked.

"I need ten-thousand dollars by the end of this week and ten more in two -weeks," Gary answered.

"That's a lot of money," Needy said.

Gary smiled. "Freedom isn't cheap," he replied.

"How do I know you won't come back for more once I pay you this money?" Needy asked, presenting Gary with the proverbial question that always arises during blackmail. A question that she knew he would be anticipating, but she already knew the answer to before he even answered out of his lying reptilian mouth.

"You don't. I guess you are just going to have to trust me on this one," Gary said, smirking.

Needy smiled, breaking the stoic look that she had maintained during their entire conversation. And when she did, it made Gary nervous.

"I will get you your money, and we will never have this conversation again," she said with a tone of voice that gave no room for further compromise or discussion about the matter.

"Do you understand?" Needy reiterated.

Gary took another drag off the cigarette; he did not want to give Needy the impression that he was intimidated in the least. He flicked the butt of the cigarette to the ground and smothered it out with the heel of his foot.

"Twenty thousand dollars, no games," he answered.

Needy observed Gary as he walked off and got into an old pick-up truck. She took out her cellphone, zoomed in on the license plate, and snapped a picture of it as he pulled out of the Clinic's visitor lot. He would get the Twenty thousand dollars that she promised him, but she would make sure that he would also receive the consequences of the money she would give him.

She would also make sure he complied with the essential term of the deal between them. That was nothing short of blackmail and extortion in her eyes, really, and that was he would never mention this again to her or anyone else - permanently.

CHAPTER TWELVE

Scooter thought he had heard the sound of something moving in the nearby brush as he stood guard nearby the cabin. He shined his assault rifle-mounted flashlight in the direction of where he thought the sound had come from, illuminating the darkness in front of him.

He hit the talk button on the side of his radio but spoke softly inside of the walkie-talkie so that he would not give away his position. "Boss, I think I just heard something moving about twenty-five feet in front of me, maybe less."

"What's your twenty?" Needy asked.

"About fifty meters out from the cabin nearby the main roadway," he answered.

"Brick, can you make that twenty?" Needy radioed in, into her other outside guard.

"Affirmative," Brick responded quickly.

"I am on my way," Needy said as she broke the radio transmission silence.

* * *

Scooter almost jumped right out of his skin as he saw something out the side of his eye, moving so quickly it was almost like a blur in his vision. He spun around to engage it, but it was gone by then, so he never got off a shot.

"What the fuck was that?" Scooter said nervously as he slowly made his way over further to where he thought he had seen movement, his finger on the trigger and at the ready to pop off a bullet more quickly, this time if needed.

Scooter jumped back, startled as the silhouette suddenly emerged from the darkness in front of him, holding something in its hand.

"Asshole, step out where I can see you!" he yelled out.

The silhouette stood there silently, not moving, not complying with his orders.

"Last chance, asshole!" Scooter yelled out as he raised his weapon, ready to put some lead behind his warning.

"No, last chance for you," he swore he heard the thing say in front of him in a deep guttural voice that sent chills down his spine and straight to his trigger finger.

"Fuck you then!" Scooter said as he sighted in on the threat and began to press the trigger to his assault rifle; at the same time, he was unaware that he had stepped inside a trap. As he pressed the trigger to fire off a round, the noose that he had unknowingly stepped into tighten around his legs and quickly closed in like a snare snatching him off his feet as the enormous figure yanked the rope towards himself. Scooter got a few shots off aimlessly in the air before the weapon flew out of his hand.

Scooter fought hard to free his ankles as the thing that stood before him pulled him towards it with what he could feel was an unbelievable amount of strength! He suddenly remembered the push blade knife he kept in his pocket. He took it out and ejected the blade and began feverishly cutting at the rope.

"Come on, you sonofabitch!" he screamed out, as he cut deeper into the rope until it finally snapped!

The sound of gunfire suddenly erupted from behind him, startling him! As he went to gain his composure and get back on his feet.

He watched as the rope quickly disappeared into the darkness, retrieved by whatever tried to reel him in like a flopping fish on a hook.

"You forgot something, Scoot?" Needy said, tossing him the assault weapon he had dropped as she helped him back onto his feet.

"What the fuck was that about?" Brick said, also on the scene.

"Did you see it?" Scooter blurted out, eyes bulging.

"Yeah, I saw something? But whoever it was on the end of the rope definitely meant you no good!" Needy answered.

"Whoever it was? That sonofabitch is strong as an Ox!" Scooter said, still rattled.

"Needy, we need to get the hell out of these backwoods and leave this shit to the inbreds and rednecks!" Scooter shouted out.

"He's right, we got a Hills Have Eyes muthafucker running around out there in the darkness trying to off us, and we don't even know why?" replied Brick.

"And it's only a matter of time before the pigs show up for dinner," Scooter injected.

"Goddammit, Dez is still out there; need I remind you both!" Needy shouted out angrily.

"Yes, out there and most likely dead!" Scooter retorted.

Needy stood silently debating their options, which she had to admit was quite limited at this moment.

"Okay, we leave now," she finally said.

"What about the blind woman, her husband, and her asshole son?" Brick asked.

Deena turned and looked Brick squarely in his eyes. "We are not going to touch them, do you understand?"

"But they have seen our faces," Brick pointed out.

"It must be a better way, and I will figure it out," Needy assured the both of them.

"That van better be fucking ready,' she said.

"I don't care if we have to Fred Flintstone our way out of here in that fucking van. It's time to go!" Scooter said nervously.

* * *

Deena felt strange that she had to ask for permission in her own house to get a glass of water but much as she hated to admit it. These were the circumstances until this ordeal was over and these intruders had left.

Freak stood behind her watching her intensely as she filled the glass in her hand with water at the sink. Freak's eyes went to her ass in the summer dress she wore. He noted again that she did not have a lousy bottom for a woman of her age, and it still appeared to be firm. He eased up slowly behind her and squeezed her ass, startling her!

Causing her to spill some of the water she was about to drink. She brushed his hand away from and off of her body.

"What are you doing?" Deena said, making sure that she kept her voice low as she addressed what Freak had just done because she did not want to put her husband or son's life in unnecessary danger.

"What does it look like?" Freak whispered in her ear as he placed his hand back on her ass, squeezing her butt cheeks.

"I bet you having had a good hard fuck in ages," he said.

Deena could now feel Freak's erection on her buttocks as he pressed up harder against her.

"I know old man John over there is not sticking it to you like you deserve. Why don't you let me take this granny pussy for a ride," Freak cooed in her ear.

Deena spun around and tossed the rest of the water in Freak's face. "You got a dirty filthy mind, young man!"

Freak wiped the water off his face and ran his now wet fingers across Deena's lips. "You got me, all wet baby, now I am going to have to return the favor,' he said, chuckling.

"Get the fuck out of my way!" Deena retorted as she moved Freak aside.

"I was never stopping you from leaving," Freak said with a wicked grin on his face as he extended his hand for her to pass.

Deena made sure that she got her composure together before she walked back over to the sofa with her husband and son. She was sure they had not witnessed Freak accosting her because of the blind spot she and Freak were in when it occurred.

She could still smell the musty cigarette scent off his clothes, feel the heat of his breath and the pressure of the bulge in his pants against her ass. He was a young bad boy she knew. But she was ashamed because, at the same time, she was declining his advances. Deena also felt herself getting wet with desire over things she had not heard a man say to her in more than twenty years now. Freak looked over at her with that Manson-like grin on his face, like he knew what she was thinking. And although Deena could not see, she could feel his eyes still on her, feel his rough hands still caressing her ass.

"You are a lucky man John," Freak said, still grinning.

John said nothing as he looked Freak straight in those crazy eyes of his. He did not have to because Freak immediately picked up on the non-verbal cut-throat stare John gave him. The message was clear, "If you touch my wife, I will fucking kill you!"

Lucky for him, he thought that John had not seen that little grab-ass action that he had with his old lady; he would not want to give the geezer a stroke at his attempt to make good on his non-verbal promise, he thought.

Freak's twisted thoughts were suddenly broken by a loud tapping in code on the cabin's door.

Hallie quickly responded, opened the door as Needy and Scooter rushed in with a look of urgency on both of their faces. Hallie immediately picked up on something wrong in the room.

"What's going on?" she asked.

Needy did not waste any time getting straight to the point. "Dez is missing, and we need to go!" she said.

"Dez is missing?" Hallie repeated.

"Yes, something or someone grabbed him out there, and I found blood over by the wrecker," Needy stated.

Hallie turned towards Deena and her family sitting on the sofa and pointed her gun directly at them. "What the fuck is going on?" she shouted out at them.

"She's right. What the fuck is going on?" Needy asked. Backing Hallie's inquiry.

"We don't know what you are talking about?" John shot back defiantly.

Needy always thought she was good at sizing up people, and right now, John was either a good liar, or she was not as good as she thought she was, Needy concluded.

Needy looked over at Jason. "What about you?"

"My dad is right; we have no idea what you folks are talking about," he answered.

"What about you, Mommy Dearest? Do you know what the hell is going on?" Needy asked.

"Figure it out for yourself," Deena answered sharply with a smug look on her face.

"That's not an answer, dear," Needy said.

"Deena looked over towards Needy, following her voice. "That's all the answer you bitches gonna get outta me," she said gruffly.

Freak chuckled at her remark. " Damn, now we know who got the balls in this family," he said.

"Put that gun down runt, and you might find out different," John said, tired of Freak giving him shit.

"Are you calling me out, old man?" Freak shouted out wide-eyed.

"Enough! Did you fucking clowns hear any goddamn thing I just said!" Needy shouted out. Cutting Freak off and at the same time de-escalating the situation brewing between the two-men.

"We need to go!" she reiterated.

"What do we do with these three stooges?" Scooter said, stroking his goatee.

"Well, I found something that might be of concern to the Anderson's in their bedroom," Needy said, taking a white envelope out of her pocket.

"How did you know our last name?" asked Deena.

"What's that?" Jason said.

"Well, it seems like your Mom and Dad's cozy little cabin here is in foreclosure because of a Lien put out on it by Good ole Uncle Sam," Needy said as she handed Jason over the paperwork.

Jason took the IRS notice and looked it over. " Mom, Pops, why did you not tell me this?"

"Tell you what? Your ass is broker than us," John answered, which got a chuckle out of Needy's crew.

Jason cringed in shame. "But... But... "But nothing," interrupted John as he snatched the paper out of his Son's hand.

"This is me and your Mom's business, not yours!"

Needy motioned for Freak to bring over one of the black backpacks that they were carrying.

Freak handed Needy the backpack; she unzipped it and reached in and got three stacks of one-hundred-dollar bills. Five thousand dollars was in each pile. Needy sat the money on the table in front of the three of them. Fifteen-thousand dollars in cash. More money than they had seen or had in a very long time.

"What's going on?" Deena asked.

John picked up one of the stacks and passed it to his wife.

"Oh my God," Deena said as she flipped through the stack wrapped in a $100 money band.

Deena reached out and patted on the two other stacks on the table.

"How much is this?" she asked.

"Fifteen thousand in cash, that should be enough to pay off your IRS bills of $10,000 and still leave you with leftovers to celebrate," Needy answered, and pointed out.

"This is dirty money; we can't take this!" Jason objected.

"Shut up! Jason, she ain't giving you shit!" his father interjected.

"Well, we are letting him live. I hope that's not too much of a burden on you both," Needy said sarcastically.

Hallie cracked a wide smile at Needy's comment.

"We've always been honest, hard-working people never asked anyone for anything," John said pridefully.

"You did not ask for this; we brought this to your doorstep," Needy said.

Needy then pointed to the money on the table. "Furthermore, do not consider this a handout. You earned this," she said.

"Thank you," Deena said.

"Mom?" Jason said, still contentious about his parents accepting the stolen bank money.

"Awww, shut up, Jason!" Deena said as she gathered up the three stacks of money off the table.

"Is the van ready, John?" Needy asked.

"Yeah, it should get you where you need to go."

Needy looked around at her crew. " Okay, let's rock n roll and blow this shit stack," she said.

Freak was giving Jason his Charles Manson-like stare-down, again. "Are you sure you want to let this one live?" he asked, gritting his teeth.

"Only if he can keep his mouth shut, and we do not have to come back."

"He will keep his mouth shut, and you won't have to come back," Deena assured Needy. John nodded in agreement.

Needy slung the backpack on her back. "Good, thanks for your hospitality, folks, but I think we've overstayed our welcome."

"You can say that again," Jason mumbled underneath his breath.

Hallie walked over and kissed Jason on his forehead. "What a waste of Ding-dong," she said.

Freak tongue stroked his upper lip back and forth as he looked over at Deena. He imagined if they had stayed a little longer, he would have got to sample those good-ies and probably would have had to kill her husband if he objected. Hell, what did he know? He thought the old man might want a piece of him too, especially after he had seen how he was knee-deep balls in and putting it down on that sexually pent-up wife of his and making her fantasies come true. As far as Freak was concerned, John should be patting him on the back while he was hitting them butt cheeks and cheering him on.

"Freak, stop daydreaming! It's time to go," Needy said, breaking his train of thought on what could have been.

"He waved over at Deena and blew her kiss with that grin still on his face as they made their way out of the door.

"Man, you need some serious help," Hallie said as she watched Freak's actions.

Needy turned back around as if she had forgotten something. " By the way, I suggest that no one attempts to leave this cabin until at least two hours has passed by, is that understood?"

"Understood," John answered, for all of them.

"Good," Needy said.

"Be careful," Deena said, with what looks like a smile on her face. Needy could not be for sure, but the warning itself was enough to catch her off guard and a cause for concern.

"Yeah, thanks," Needy said, feeling awkward in her response.

"Goddamitt, those gunshots earlier were loud enough to wake up the dead and give up our location," Needy said, once on the outside of the cabin as she briefed her crew.

"From here on out, noise and light discipline folks until we are far away from this area, understood?"

Her crew nodded their heads in agreement.

"Good. Let's get the hell out here," she said.

"About time," Scooter said.

CHAPTER THIRTEEN

The cold martini was just what the doctor ordered as far as Sam was concerned as she took a sip out of the chilled cocktail glass. She looked around Logan's as she and Brandon sat at the bar, soaking up the place's moderately busy atmosphere for a weekday.

"So what's new in your world detective," she said before she plucked one of the olives off the stick into her mouth.

Brandon smiled. "Off or on the record," he answered as he swirled the Jamerson whiskey on the rocks in his glass.

Sam looked at Brandon seductively, leaned in, and gave him a peck on the lips. "Whichever one you prefer," she answered.

"The latter," Brandon said.

"At least for now," he added.

Sam wrapped her pinkie finger around his playfully. "Off the record," she agreed.

Brandon spoke softly just in case an extra pair of nearby ears was listening.

"I think we might have a potential serial killer on the loose," he said.

"Again? Are you talking about the recent murders and missing women on the news?"

"Yeah' we are trying to figure out how they are all connected, but we are pretty sure it's the work of the same PERP."

"Do you have any suspects?"

Brandon looked quietly at Sam before answering; he could probably unconsciously see she was in reporter mode and did not even know it. But it was too late now for him to bail out of this topic of conversation.

"We think it might be the work of this joker that calls himself "Hands-On" and has been taunting us," Brandon answered.

"Wow, I heard about him, a real nut job!" said Sam.

"Yeah, but a smart nut job, the worst kind," Brandon replied.

"Now that I recall, I thought his stomping grounds was California?" Sam asked.

"Yeah' it was, but unfortunate for us, it seems he has got a taste for the Midwest now," Brandon answered.

"Mums the word," Sam assured Brandon.

"Babe, are you okay?" Brandon asked about the earlier conversation that they had before meeting up at Logan's.

Sam stirred her Martini slowly with the cocktail pick. "I am doing the best I can, with what I gotta work with," she answered contemplatively.

"What the hell does that mean?" Brandon said.

Sam looked at Brandon and burst out in laughter.

"Not a goddamn thing!" they both said in unison, laughing.

Sam pointed at her drink on the bar. "Boy, I can sure use another one of these."

Brandon leaned over and kissed Sam on her forehead. "And have you end up in the drunk tank tonight? I'll make you one at home," he said, winking.

"I am going to hold you to that," Sam said.

Brandon got up off his barstool. " I am going to hit the restroom before we leave."

Sam pointed Brandon in the direction of the bar's restrooms.

When she noticed two men across the bar, she did not know, staring in her direction with a smile on their faces.

Sam managed a friendly smile at them and went back to minding her own business as she got the bartender's attention so that she could pay her and Brandon's bar tab before they left.

The bartender came over, smiled, and took her credit card, and went to the nearby cash register to ring up and close out her tab. To Sam's surprise, one of the men who had been eyeballing her from across the bar proceeded over and approached her from behind.

"Hi there beautiful," the stranger said, smiling.

"Hello," Sam said, not wanting to be rude but thinking at the same time she was affording this man the courtesy that he was not extending to Brandon.

"My name is Tim and Me, and my bud was wondering would you like to come over and join us for some drinks." He asked.

"No thanks, I am here with my Fiancé, and we are about to leave,' she said as nicely as she could under the circumstances.

Tim attempted to put his hand around Sam's waist, but she quickly brushed his hand aside.

"Oh, that L-seven you was sitting with, we ain't worried about him," Tim said rudely.

Sam ignored the man's insult. "I said no thanks, but you and your friend enjoy the rest of your evening."

Sam watched as Tim's face suddenly changed from a pleasant expression to one of anger. "Look, you uppity bitch, all I am asking is you join us for one drink!"

Sam backed away from Tim, creating a safe distance between them. "Excuse me?" she said.

Tim smiled. "Look, I am sorry, one drink baby." He reached in again to pull Sam towards him aggressively; she quickly responded defensively by catching hold of his wrist and twisting it, bringing his arm behind his back as Tim let out a scream of pain. With the other hand, Sam grabbed a tuft of his hair and slammed his face straight into the bar.

"I am not your baby!" she said.

Tim, stunned by Sam's quickness and strength, threw his free hand in the air to surrender. "Okay' okay' I am sorry!"

Sam let the man up, releasing him.

All the patrons in the bar begin clapping regarding how Sam had handled herself, embarrassing her assailant even further.

Tim could feel the eyes of his friend on him, mocking him, calling him a sissy. Now he felt he had to see this through. He quickly grabbed an empty bottle off the bar, smashed it, and lunged towards Sam to cut her with its jagged edges.

Sam saw him coming back towards her out the side of her eye and swiftly reacted, kicking the bottle out of his hand; she then quickly executed a roundhouse kick into Tim's chest, knocking the wind out of him, sending him sprawled out on the bar's floor.

Tim's friend looked on with his mouth dropped in fear and surprise. Sam looked over at him, ready for him to make his move, he did. Straight out the front door of the bar in a mad dash.

Brandon ran out of the restroom with his hand on his still holstered service weapon. "Is everything okay?" he said, as his attention went to the man sprawled out on the floor.

The bartender was the first to respond to Brandon's question. "Yeah, he ordered a drink called "Whup ass," she said.

"And let me assume who he ordered it from," Brandon asked.

The bartender smiled and pointed at Sam as she handed her back her credit card. "No charge, Ms. Jackson, the drinks are on us," she said.

Brandon lifted Sam's assailant off the floor and smacked him upside the head. "I ought to arrest your dumbass, but since you got your ass kicked, I am going to cut you a break."

"Thanks, Mister," Tim said, his cocky demeanor now gone.

"And?" Brandon said, as he still had a firm hold on him.

"My apology Ma'am, for ruining your night," Tim said.

"You did not ruin my night. I needed the practice," Sam said as she brushed off her clothes.

Brandon released the man and shoved him towards the door. " Get a cab and take your sorry ass home."

"I cannot leave you alone for a second babe, without you getting into trouble," Brandon chuckled.

"What do you expect me to do? He called you a square," Sam said.

"I am a square," Brandon replied.

Sam smiles and kisses Brandon on the lips. "I know, but I am the only one that can call you that."

CHAPTER FOURTEEN

With the assistance of the County's Game warden, Sheriff Alvarez was now en route to Harper Creek's more remote areas. Places where people built homes up because they desired less human company. Residents with independent solid survivalist attitudes to make it on their own and survive off the land. He did not have a problem with that and admired anyone who could survive the South Dakota winters out here in such remote locations.

The only problem he knew was with this particular lifestyle was that it was not only the wildlife and the environment that one had to worry about when living off the grid. It was people and strangers like the ones he was chasing who could use these locations to hide out and for other nefarious purposes. Not to say that he thought all the residents that lived up in these woodlands were good people. Alvarez had busted too many meth lab operations up in these parts to entertain that kind of delusional perspective.

Alvarez leaned forward, stretching his seat belt as he watched the rain start up again and begin to beat against the front windshield of the SUV driven by his deputy while he shotgun. "Goddamn rain is going to make the off roads muddier and this manhunt harder," he said.

"I know sheriff; hopefully, we can get up to the first cabin in the area without giving away our position," Shannon said.

Both of their bodies shook as they hit a bump in the road.

"I do not know how the Feds is planning on getting their asses up here in this kind of weather unless they plan on coming by boat," Alvarez ruminated.

Shannon glanced up at the rearview mirror, looking at the illuminating headlights from one of the three other law enforcement vehicles following behind them in a convoy formation. "Yeah, I can't see them sending up a bird in this type of weather."

They hit another jarring bump in the road, causing them both to shift in their seats. "Jesus, Shannon, are you trying to hit every bump in the goddamn road!" Alvarez yelled out as he took hold of the grab handle above him.

Shannon looked over at her boss with a sly grin on her face. "Sorry, chief, we should be reaching the first cabin soon," she said.

"I hope so for the sake of my damn hemorrhoids," Alvarez said, as he shifted in his seat again, trying to get comfortable.

A familiar voice then came in over the patrol vehicle's radio, taking Alvarez's mind off the rocky terrain that was presently causing him so much discomfort.

"It's getting bad out here, Al."

Alvarez picked up the radio's mic and pushed the talk button. "I know, Cap; hopefully, we can get this done before the weather gets worse," he answered.

"Roger that Al, but if this rain does not let up, we have to worry about the danger of potential mudslides in this area and trust me, we do not want to be out here if that happens."

"Duly noted Cap," Alvarez answered as if not overly concerned. Despite being aware that Smith was right, the last thing he wanted to do is call the search off when the ink was not even dry on the warrants he had gotten from Judge Albright.

"I tell you what, Cap, you keep your eye out on the weather, and I will keep my eye out for the suspects," Alvarez said.

"Is that a fucking joke?" Smith said, not amused.

"No, but if a big ass rock hit the bank robbers van in that mudslide, I am sure you will be the first to know," Alvarez answered.

"Asshole," Cap snapped back.

"I know, over and out," Alvarez said, with a grin on his face.

Deputy Shannon tapped Alvarez on his shoulder and pointed at the yellow warning sign on the road.

Alvarez glanced over at the mudslide sign and sighed. "Not you too?" he said.

CHAPTER FIFTEEN

Needy and her crew had loaded up and were back in the van minus one and headed back towards the hardball and out of the woodlands. But she had decided that they would use the back roads as much as possible when available to stay out of detection of law enforcement, whom she was sure was still hot on their tails.

Contrary to that dilemma, she was glad so far that the van appeared to be holding up pretty well on the rocky and muddy terrain after its repair. But she still did not feel comfortable riding this terrain too long with the recently welded tire rod. One good bump, she concluded, might be all it took, and then they would be fucked and back to the square root of one.

Scooter strained to see through the darkness as he drove down the muddy road even with his high beam lights illuminated. "It's darker than Satan's asshole out here," he said, squinting his eyes.

"It's okay, just try not to hit anything like a big fucking tree on the way out," Needy said.

Something significant suddenly hit the side of their van, causing Scooter to almost swerve off the muddy road over into an embankment, tossing the van's passengers around upon impact.

"What the fuck?" Scooter shouted out as he struggled to gain control of the wheel to keep from going off the road into an embankment.

"Stop! Stop!" A shaken Needy barked out to Scooter as he finally gained control of the skidding van.

Scooter complied and brought the van to a screeching halt.

The van had no side windows, only rear ones, so they could not see what had struck their vehicle from the driver's side.

"Are you guys okay back there?" Needy shouted out to the rest of her crew in the rear of the van.

"Yeah, all good back here, but we won't be if we get any more hits like that," Brick answered.

Hallie brushes herself off. "You damn Skippy. I am starting to feel like a fucking milkshake back here."

Needy made the quiet sign with her finger against her mouth and then pointed in the direction of the van rear doors. "If it moves, breaths, walk or crawl, light it up," she said softly.

Her crew open the back doors and begin to exit the van slowly, one at a time with their assault weapons locked and loaded and ready to engage whatever threat presents itself on the outside in whatever shape or form.

Needy exited the vehicle from the side passenger door and instructed Scooter, their driver, to remain seated and alert. Just in case they had to get the hell out of dodge quickly.

He reluctantly complied and sat with his pistol in his hand, ready to blast anything and anyone he did not recognize that attempted to breach the van doors. Beads of sweat began to form on his forehead as his eyes nervously darted back and forth across the landscape in front of him as he attempted to see clearly in the void of darkness ahead.

Needy shone the flashlight to the significant dent on the driver's side of the van, then on the large boulder laid on the ground that she believed was the missile or object thrown at their van.

"Jesus, that thing must weigh one hundred and fifty pounds or more," Freak said as he nudged it with his foot.

"Yeah, that's one big ass rock," Needy said as she scanned the darkness for any movement nearby them in the tree line or area.

"No, that's one strong motherfucker to throw a boulder that size at a moving object. I could not do that type of shit on my best days when I played college football," Brick said.

"Yeah, some Bigfoot shit," Freak nervously replied.

"No, it's just some motherfucker playing games with us that's too chicken shit to show his ugly face!" Hallie shouted out.

"We here fool what you wanna do?" she taunted.

"Cut the shit, Hallie!" Needy growled.

"Why?" Hallie asked defiantly.

"Because I have a feeling we are fucking being watched, that's why," Needy answered above a whisper of her voice.

"I think I see movement over there," Brick said, pointing to a dense tree line area about twenty-five yards out as he held the night vision monocular to his eyes.

"I have an idea Hallie; you go with Brick. Freak and I are going around this asshole and going to come up from the rear and flank him in," Needy said.

"Sounds good," Hallie answered.

Brick turned to Needy with a bewildered look on his face. "What?" Needy asked.

"How do you know it's a man?" he asked.

"Do it fucking matter?" Needy answered curtly.

"Nah, I guess not," Brick conceded.

"Man, how many times were you hit in the head with a football?" Freak said with a grin on his face.

"Look, you walking anomaly, I am not too busy to make mud pies with your ass out here," Brick warned, cutting Freak a mean glare.

"Hey, you two can fuck, kiss, or makeup later. I do not give a royal shit! I will shoot you both if you two don't get your head and asses in the game," Needy asserted.

"I am in coach," Brick answered.

Needy's attention went towards Freak and off of Brick. Her stare down was much more intimidating than Brick's, to Freak. Maybe, because he knew she could back her threat up in a millisecond before you knew what hit you and realize that you had fucked up and no apologies or regrets in this world could save you once Needy went full Lobo wolf.

"My head and ass are your's boss," he said.

Hallie smiled. "Be glad she is not a nine-inch thorny dildo then," she chimed in.

"I am a nine-inch thorny dildo, now move y'all asses," Needy said.

"I kind of like that analogy," Freak said as they all begin to make their way towards the tree line.

Needy rolled her eyes. "I kind of figured you would."

Freak smiled. "Boss, can I ask you a question?"

"Yeah, what?" she answered.

"Were you always a bad bitch, or were you born that way?"

"Both," Needy answered, focused on the road ahead of them.

"Remind me not to get on your bad side," Freak said.

"Too late you already have," Needy answered.

"I think I will shut up now," Freak said.

"Yeah, that might be best," Needy agreed.

* * *

"It's like walking in fucking quicksand out here," Brick said as he and Hallie tracked through the thick mud that seems heavier on their boots with every step they each took.

"You got that right, Brick, and when we find that trick bitch I am going to gut him from the root'em to the toot em," Hallie said.

Brick wiped the rain out of his eyes. "Do you know that you are one crazy white bitch?"

Hallie smiled. "Yep, but really would you want a sane white bitch out here with you right now?"

"Good point," Brick said, his finger on the trigger, weapon at the ready.

The noise of something moving up ahead brought both of them to a dead silence as Brick brought the night vision monocular back to his eye to see what had made the sound in the darkness in front of them.

"I think the sound came from that direction," Brick whispered and pointed as he and Hallie slowly made their way towards the dense area of trees.

Snap! "Fuck!" Brick screamed out in excruciating pain from the spikes of the bear trap clamping down on his foot as he unexpectedly stepped inside of its metal jaws. Hallie heard the trap's snapping sound and watched Brick go down to the ground in anguish.

"Help get this fucking thing off me!" Brick shouted out in pain, as he attempted to pry the jaws of the bear trap off his now profusely bleeding and injured foot.

Hallie kneeled and attempted to open the bear trap with her hands, but the spring-loaded trap would barely give. The sharpness of the spikes-like teeth bit into her fingers. "Shit! I need something to stick in it to pull it apart," she said as she looked around on the ground for something to use as a prying tool.

"Be careful. This area is probably booby rigged with more of these fucking things!" Brick warned.

"Find a fucking stick or something and get this shit off me," Brick yelled out! As he watched Hallie wander off in the dark.

He sat his weapon down beside him and attempted again to pull the bear trap apart and off his foot. He could now feel his foot in his boot beginning to swell, which he knew would make getting the bear trap off even more challenging if that happens.

"Fuck this," Brick said to himself as he begins unlacing his boot. Then an idea came to him as he took a knife out of his pocket that maybe he could cut away some of his boot and slip his foot out of the trap.

As he started cutting, he suddenly heard the sound of someone approaching him. "Hallie," he called out in the darkness.

No answer, as the night went quiet again around Brick. What in the fuck was taking her so long? He thought as he put the knife away and grabbed up his weapon as he nervously shined his flashlight in front of him.

"Hallie?" he called out again.

"Hallie," A deep guttural voice repeated behind him.

"What in the fuck... was Brick's last words as he looks up at the large man-beast standing behind him. Before the man-beast took Brick's head swiftly in its gigantic hands and twisted it into a gruesome unnatural position that caused the bone in Brick's neck to snap to accommodate his head's new location, almost facing backward on Its shoulders. The man-beast released Brick's head and watched as his body collapsed lifelessly to the ground of mud.

The sound of someone approaching once again put the man-beast into evasive mode as it disappeared back into the darkness of the night just as quickly as it had appeared after taking out another member of Needy's crew effectively.

Hallie returned to the site less than a minute later to where she had left Brick with a solid piece of broken tree branch, in her hand that she had found and thought would aid in getting the bear claw off his foot.

"Okay big baby, I got you," she said as she approached Brick.

Her flashlight illuminated Brick. The ghastly vision of his body propped up in a sitting position, his head twisted backward on his body with a glazed-over look in his eyes like he had just seen the devil as he stared directly into her eyes blankly. Hallie dropped her flashlight as a scream of terror left her mouth.

"What the fuck was that?" Freak said as he and Needy heard Hallie's scream, break the silence of the surrounding darkness that engulfed them.

"Let's go; I think that was Hallie," Needy said as she broke out in a fast trot towards where the scream had come from in the night.

"Watch your step," Freak said, not knowing that was the best advice he could give his leader as they navigated through the mud and darkness of the terrain.

"Fuck me!" Freak said as his face became a ghastly pallor as he laid eyes on Brick's body.

"Is this how you found him?" Needy said as she walked over to inspect Brick's body, shining her flashlight into his abnormally positioned head on his body.

Tears were rolling down Hallie's face. Needy could see that she was visibly upset by this horrific vision of one of their crew killed in this manner. What kind of asshole could have done something like this? She thought. But she knew she already had the answer to that question, and that was the same kind of asshole that probably killed Dez, the same type of asshole that was strong enough to lift a one hundred and twenty-five-pound boulder and throw it at their van like it was a freaking volleyball. The same kind of asshole that was now picking them off one-by-one and probably was having a jolly lolly fucking good time while doing it. A raving fucking lunatic or lunatics with an insatiable blood-lust that she knew was out for them for God only knows what reason or maybe no reason at all.

Regardless, when all was said and done, one thing Needy knew for sure that he, she, them, or whoever was responsible would have to be dealt with and dealt with soon. Before she has no crew left, she concluded.

"Is this how you found him?" she asked again.

Hallie shook her head yes between sobs and pointed to the bear trap on Brick's foot.

"I was looking for something to get that damn thing off his foot, and that sonofabitch must have sneaked up on Brick and killed him!"

"I should have had his back," Hallie said guiltily.

"Well, look like he can watch it now," Freak said sarcastically.

"Shut the fuck up, Freak," Needy said, not amused by his humor.

"Man, I was just saying he looks like some *Exorcist* shit like green soup is about to hurl out of his mouth or something."

"I said cut the shit, Freak! Get this contraption off his foot and get his body back to the van," Needy ordered.

"And do what with it?" Freak asked.

"What do you mean?" asked Needy.

"I mean, why take his body back to the van if he is already dead?" Freak answered and wanted to know.

Needy knew it was time for patience, and it was a time that she could kill someone over blatant stupidity. Lucky for Freak, she chose the first option.

"All I have to say is, if I answer that question, I am going to be taking two fucking bodies back to the van," she threatens.

Freak felt that lump of fear in his throat again. "I digress then," he said.

"Scooter, is everything okay in your area?" Needy said in her walkie-talkie.

"Living the dream," Scooter shot back.

"Brick's been killed. We are on our way back," Needy said.

" What? Fucking shit!" Scooter said, upset.

"Did you get the asshole that did it?" he asked.

"Like, I said, we are on our way back. Be careful," Needy said, too ashamed to answer Scooter's question. Brick's blood was on her hands, and she knew it because she felt personally responsible for every swinging dick on her crew anatomically relative to that metaphor or not.

"Damn, he's one heavy fucker," Freak said as they lifted Brick off the ground.

"Stop your whining," Hallie said.

"One on point, and we will switch off on carrying him until we reach the van," Needy said.

"Got it," Hallie replied.

"Good, now let's get the fuck out of here," Needy said.

CHAPTER SIXTEEN

The Bone Squad headquarters was a nondescript building in Billings, Montana, nestled in a manufacturing business district. A perfect location that Luna had chosen for her bounty hunting team operations a long time ago. As she walked around the inside of the spacious building that used to be an old warehouse, Luna was quite impressed with how her old crew had kept things up around the old place.

Luna looked inside an office decorated with a painted skull and crossbones on the wall. "Shit! Is that my old office," she said.

Mako grinned. "Yeah, just like you left it, boss."

Luna walked inside the office. "I do not remember it being quite this posh."

"Well, we made a few upgrades," Mako answered.

Luna sat down in the opulent leather chair behind the office's desk. "I'll say a shit load of upgrades," she replied.

"Only the best for the best," Dean said.

"It looks good on you, boss," Riley added.

Luna massaged the arms of the big leather chair. "It feels good, but enough ass-kissing, let's get down to business," she proposed, never one to mince words.

"That's the old Luna we know and love," Omar said.

"Here, here," Wiz said, raising a bottle of beer in the air.

"Who's been running this team since I've been gone?" Luna asked.

Omar raised his hand. "Guilty as charged," he answered.

Luna looks sternly at Omar for what to him seemed like an uncomfortable amount of time even though it was seconds before she took a sip out of the glass of whiskey on her desk.

She raised the hardball of whiskey and slammed back the remnants of what was left in the glass, wiping her lips off with the back of her hand.

"I only have one problem with that," she said in an aggressive tone of voice.

"What's that?" Omar asked defiantly, knowing that it was never wise to show fear around Luna no matter what the consequences were, good or bad.

She threw Omar the empty glass, which he caught quickly with one hand.

"You need to stop watering down the fucking whiskey!" she answered to riotous laughter by her crew, including Omar.

"Like I said, it's good to have you back, boss," Omar said, smiling with relief.

"It's good to be back," Luna replied, followed with that one hundred-watt smile of hers that could light up any room.

"By the way, blame Wiz for the whiskey; he is a genius with computers and techno stuff but does not know jack shit about buying good booze," Omar said.

"My bag, it was on sale at Walmart," Wiz said, throwing his hands up in admittance with a grin on his face.

"No worries, it's better than the piss water I've been drinking for the past four years," Luna replied.

Omar walked over to a liquor cabinet in the office, opened it, and pulled out a twenty-five-year-old bottle of Bunnahabhain scotch whiskey. "I have been saving this bottle for a special occasion," he said.

Omar walked over to Luna with the bottle of whiskey. "And I am sure we can all agree that this occasion is special."

Luna took the bottle from Omar and examined it and its ingredients. She reflected on her short stint as a bartender as she rolled the bottle in her hands.

"Now, this is what I am talking about," she said.

Omar looked over at Wiz. " It appears that I threw you under the bus, but remember I just pulled your ass out from underneath it as well," he said.

"My hero," Wiz replied sarcastically with a grin still on his face.

Omar tapped Wiz on his shoulder in camaraderie. "No harm, no foul, my friend, now help grab us some glasses so that we can enjoy some real whiskey.

"Here, here," repeated Wiz to laughter from his crew.

After the last glass was filled amongst the crew, Omar proceeded to make a toast as he raised his glass in the air. "Here is to Luna who will always be and remain at the top of the food chain and her game," he said.

Fuck he remembers Luna thought, flattered that Omar was able to recite her affirmation.

They all downed the whiskey and began barking loudly in riotous unison. It was good to be back with the wolf-pack, Luna thought, with her old crew, The Bone Squad.

She slammed the hardball down on the desk as the whiskey went down to do its magic; she caught Omar staring at her out of the side of her eye. It had been a long time since she had desired the company and feel of a real man inside of her loins. The bloodsucker that Luna had carnally given herself too, definitely did not count as one in her mind. She smiled as she pictured her oppressor's decapitated head on her vanity desk with his dick stuffed in his nasty mouth like a fat cigar.

Marcellus must have got a kick out of that trophy she left, Luna thought.

She rose from the desk, walked over to Omar, and grabbed him by the crotch, not to anyone's surprise either in the room. She softly placed her tongue in his mouth, pressing herself up against the ever-growing erection in his pants.

Luna whispered in his ear as she grabbed him by his hands to take him into another room. "Let's fuck." Omar smiled as he looked into Luna's eyes that now had that "eyeshine," something that only animals possessed when you looked at them in the dark. It's going to be a wild night, he thought. He only hoped he was up to the task and Luna's energy.

Riley caught the eye of Luna as well as she proceeded to exit with Omar. She was an attractive young woman with a hot body that would do whatever Luna asked of her - whatever.

Luna stretched her hand out for her to embrace it. "Are you coming?"

Riley smiled. "I thought you'd never ask," she answered as she took Luna's hand.

Luna turned back around to address the rest of her crew in the office. "Boy's I advise you not to wait up. It's going to be a very long night."

Her crew begins barking again, which turns into a constant howling, as their faces appeared to shift and change during their revelry.

Luna Dye top of the food chain was back.

CHAPTER SEVENTEEN

The van's windshield wipers squeaked back and forth on full blast as Scooter attempted in vain to keep it cleared, so he could have some kind of visibility just in case the killer that was out there had decided to sneak up on him and make him the next victim. Quite frankly, he had reached the point where he was ready to go with or without the rest of his crew as he looked nervously at his watch and then at the van's digital clock on its radio's face. How long had they been gone now, he thought ten, maybe twenty minutes? More? He had lost track of time.

Why in the hell had Needy made him stop, he thought. They should have kept going, regardless of what was thrown at or hit the fucking van, he concluded, until they hit the hardball again. Or have gotten to a safer destination to sort this crazy shit out.

Scooter knew something was not right about this location. Now he regretted that he had not been more outspoken in stressing his position and opposition to Needy about the *bad karma* that he picked up from this location, from back at the house. He had a feeling that those motherfuckers back at the cabin probably knew more about what the hell was going on than they were letting on. Why he wonder, had Needy paid them all that money? When she could have saved them the expense. By just putting a bullet in the back of each of their heads. Hell, he felt like doubling back and doing it himself and confiscating the fifteen thousand dollars that Needy had paid them for their silence. What did they have to show for her decisions so far, he thought, but two dead members of their crew, he finally deduced.

He now contemplated if he could still trust Needy to make the right decisions? Had she gone soft, he wondered.

"Fuck this shit," Scooter murmured as he took another drag on the cigarette in his hand and then proceeded to roll the van's window down and flicked out the bud. But as he began raising the window back up, a loud crunching sound not too far away caught his attention. "What the fuck is that noise?" Scooter said as he stopped the window midway.

Suddenly it hit him precisely what the noise was? It was the sound of a tree being chopped down nearby him, nearby the van. Scooter unlocked the door to exit the van, but it would not budge. It was as if something was jammed against it from the outside and stopping it from opening. He then tried the passenger door, but it would not open either. Scooter could still hear the hacking away of the tree.

"Fuck!" he shouted out in anguish as he then begins raising down the window of the passenger van again. He threw his assault rifle out first and then proceeded to exit out headfirst through the driver's side open window, falling the rest of the way to the ground below. The sound grew louder, closer.

"Fuck!" he said again, as he looked up in shock and seen a large pine tree falling towards the van. Scooter grabbed his weapon up off the ground and scrambled to his feet. A loud explosion erupted behind him as the tree came down on the rooftop of the van, concaving it in, followed by a plume of tree dust and a metallic odor that now filled the night air.

Scooter looked on in horror and anguish at the destruction that the tree had done to the van as the cold reality set in on him, also that he had only been seconds away from losing his life.

The sound of approaching footsteps jarred his attention away from the van as he swung around, ready to fire upon the intruders.

"Scooter, stop!" yelled out Needy with her weapon raised and ready to engage just in case he had a hearing problem.

Scooter lowered his weapon at the recognition of Needy's voice.

"No need to carry you any further," Freak said as he and Hallie dropped Brick to the ground.

"What in the fuck happen here?" Needy asked as she looked on in awe at the tree sitting on top of their van's roof.

"Call me simple, but it looks like a big ass tree fell on top of the fucking van," Scooter answered sarcastically.

"I know that dumb ass, but how?" Needy replied angrily and in no mood for Scooter's flippant rhetoric.

"I… I heard what sound like a chopping sound, and then I was locked inside the van, and if I had not gone through the fucking window, I would have been tree sap!"

"That would have been a sight to see," Freak said, grinning.

"Fuck you, asshole," replied Scooter.

Needy shook her head in disbelief. "That does not make any sense. You know what kind of strength it would have taken to cut down a tree that size?" she said.

"The same kind of strength to throw an almost two-hundred-pound rock at our van," Hallie answered this time.

"What do we do now?" Freak asked nervously.

"Get our fucking money out of the van and double back to the cabin," Needy answers.

"So, in other words, we are back to where we started," Scooter said.

Needy walked up to Scooter. "No, we have two of our men dead, and the van is not fit for fucking scrap metal, so no, Einstein, we are not "back" where we started."

"But going back to the cabin, do you think that's a good idea?" Scooter asked.

"Do you have a better one, Scooter? Get your ass in gear and go get those fucking backpacks out of that van before a tree falls on our asses." Needy orders.

Freak looked down at Brick's dead body lying in the mud. "What about him?" he asked.

"What about him? Unless he can get up and start walking, he is not coming," she answers coldly.

Needy looked down at Brick and made the sign of the cross. "Rest in peace, big dog," she said.

"Can you be straight with me boss," Hallie asked.

"Like an Arrow," Needy replied.

"We are in deep shit, aren't we?"

"Up to our fucking elbows," Needy answers.

El watched them silently in the darkness. He could not allow that to happen, he thought. For any of them to make it back to the cabin alive! For anyone of them to make it out these woods alive.

He felt himself growing stronger every day. More powerful, more deadly, more primal. As the days passed by, was he becoming more animal than human? El did not know, nor did he care.

El looked up at the full moon glowing in the night between the tree line. The beastly hairs raised upon his neck as he savored the thought and taste of their blood in his mouth.

Soon he thought…

CHAPTER EIGHTEEN

lvarez and the task force he had assembled were searching through the first cabin out near Cotter lake. "All clear!" Deputy Shannon yelled out as she went through one of the empty rooms in the dwelling.

"Shit, they must be further out than I thought," Alvarez said as he looked around the empty cabin that appeared not to have been disturbed or occupied for over a month or more.

"It would be nice if we could get a Copter up to aid in the search, but the weather is shit right now," Smith said.

"Damn, how far is the next cabin from here?" Alvarez asked.

Smith took a map out of his jacket and spread it out on a nearby table. "No more than twenty miles from here," he answered.

Alvarez took off his Stetson and ran his hand through a head full of salt and pepper hair. "Damn, that's a lot of territories to cover Cap in these weather conditions."

"It's your call, Al. I am just along for the ride."

"You know who that cabin belongs to up there, Smith?" Alvarez asked.

"Yup, the Andersons, John and Deena, an older couple, have been vacationing up there for years."

"Is there any way we can contact them up there to make sure they are okay?" Al asked.

"I am afraid not. No landlines out in these parts, and the cell phone tower signal would be a hit or miss in this type of weather unless you got a booster," Smith answers.

Alvarez turned to address Shannon, who had now joined him and Smith. "Well, if they have a CB radio or Ham, I am sure they are monitoring it right now due to the adverse weather conditions, so let's put out another BOLO (be on the lookout) on the suspects in the area," he suggested.

"I'll get right on it, Chief," Shannon said.

"Smart deputy," Smith stated to Alvarez as Shannon walked away from the two of them to fulfill her boss's directive.

"The finest," Alvarez agreed.

"Yes, she is," Smith said, as his eyes followed Shannon wantonly.

Alvarez rolled the toothpick in his mouth. "I do not believe we are on the same page, Cap," he said.

Smith grinned and looked at Alvarez wide-eyed. "No, disrespect, but yes, we are," he answers.

Alvarez knew like everybody around town that Cody Smith was a notorious man whore. But he just wanted to let him know in his own way that Shannon was off-limits because she was like a daughter to him, and the last thing he needed was Smith corrupting her with his penis and meanderings.

"Twenty miles, huh?" Alvarez asked, intentionally changing the conversation.

"Yup, that would be about right," Smith answered as he looked down at the map again on the table to pinpoint their destination.

"Then we need to get going now," Alvarez said urgently.

Smith smiled. "Somehow, I knew you would come to that ... "Hey Chief, you are not going to believe this one!" Shannon shouted out, interrupting their conversation.

"Yeah, what you got, Shannon?" Alvarez replied.

"I got a witness on the phone that says he has seen the suspects," she answered excitedly.

"What in the hell, give me that phone," Alvarez said.

Shannon handed Alvarez her cellphone.

"Sheriff Alvarez, who is this?"

"My name is Jason Anderson..." "John, and Deena's boy?" Alvarez asked, cutting Jason off.

"Yes, sir, that be me," he confirmed.

"Well, I will be damn Jason; it just so happens we are on our way up there to your location. What you got their son?" Alvarez asks.

"I believe I saw the suspects that robbed that bank this morning that you are looking for," he answers.

"Is that so, and how long ago might that be?"

"About twenty minutes ago, maybe less," Jason lied.

"Well, goddamn, what took you so long to call in? They are probably in goddamn France by now," Alvarez said, frustrated.

"I was not so sure it was them?" Jason responded with enough self-doubt in his voice to make his answer somewhat believable.

"How many of them was it?" Alvarez asks.

"I think I saw three of them creeping around these parts," Jason lied again.

"Did you see what they were driving?"

"A white Ford Econoline van," Jason replied.

"Well, you got the model right, but the color is all wrong, Son are you sure it was white?" Alvarez asked, confused about how all of his information was right up to that point.

"Well, I am not color blind, sheriff," Jason answered defensively.

"I never said you were," Alvarez countered, not in the mood for sensitivity at this moment.

"You and your family stay put. Lock all your doors and arm yourselves. We are on our way up, their son." Alvarez instructed.

"Sheriff, we will patiently await your arrival," Jason said condescendingly.

"You do that," Alvarez instructed as he ended the call and handed his deputy back over her cell phone.

"What's up, Chief?" Shannon asked.

Alvarez stroked his razor-lined mustache on his face. "The Anderson's kid said he spotted the suspects creeping near his parent's cabin about twenty minutes ago."

"That would be by Bent Lake," Smith interjected.

The other deputies and game warden officers, four total, had joined them after searching the perimeter and inside the cabin.

"Okay, we just got a tip that someone spotted the suspects by Bent Lake; let's get our asses over there but be careful and smart while we are doing it," said Alvarez.

"Hey Chief, I know that look. What's going on?" Shannon asked as she and Alvarez made their way hastily in the pouring rain and thunder to their patrol vehicle.

Alvarez wiped the rain off his face with a handkerchief from his pocket. "I think that snarky-ass Anderson kid knows more than what he is telling," he replied.

"How so?" Shannon asked as she started up the SUV.

Alvarez stuffed the hanky back in his pocket. "I just got a feeling, and after being in this business as long as I have. One thing you learn not to ignore is your feelings about these kinds of things."

"Duly noted," Shannon said.

"Yup, that kid's is more "full of shit" than a dairy cow," Alvarez quipped.

Shannon smiled. "I'll remember to use that metaphor Chief."

Alvarez turned towards Shannon and chuckled. "Really? Well, you might find yourself using it more than you like in this line of work, " Alvarez said.

"I can only imagine," Shannon answered.

"Can you?" Alvarez asked as he contemplatively stared ahead at the road. Shannon did not answer. She didn't need to. Shannon had been around her boss long enough to know that sometimes all his questions did not require an immediate answer. She also knew that his mind was probably a million miles away and focused on apprehending the suspects at large.

"This weather is a bitch," she said, changing the subject of the conversation.

"That might give us an edge," Alvarez replied, with a smirk on his face.

"What do you mean, Chief?" Shannon asked.

"I mean, if it is slowing us down, It is slowing the suspects down as well. Maybe even more," he answered confidently.

"Does that mean you still think we got a chance of apprehending them, Chief?" Shannon asked.

"About as much of a chance that they have of getting away, deputy," Alvarez answered, stroking his mustache again.

Shannon nodded her head in agreement. She had to admit to herself, her boss had a good point. Shannon had never apprehended a group of bank robbers before. Hell, she had never made a felony arrest in her life in Harper Creek. Only misdemeanor bullshit arrests like trespassing and disorderly conduct in the small town that her department oversaw. This type of arrest would be a good stripe on her sleeve, she thought, and an even better one on her resume.

"Fuck, I need a cigarette," Alvarez grumbled.

"Chief, I thought Mrs. Alvarez made you quit those cancer sticks?"

"I did. That's why I could use one right now," he retorted.

Shannon smiled as she reached in her jacket pocket, pulled out a pack of cigarettes, and handed them over to Alvarez.

"Fucking lifesaver you are," Alvarez said as he took one out of the pack, lit it up, and took a long drag on it. He then rolled down the window and blew the smoke out.

"Just don't tell Mrs. Alvarez I don't want her kicking my ass," Shannon said.

"Yours and mine both," Alvarez replied, as the sound of thunder erupted so loudly it seemed to shake the SUV he and Shannon were sitting inside. He flicked the rest of the remaining cigarette out of the window.

"Thanks, Chief. I do not want us electrocuted before we get there," Shannon said sarcastically.

Alvarez handed Shannon back her pack of cigarettes. "No worries, I think that thunder came from my wife because of these," he said with a grin on his face.

CHAPTER NINETEEN

Sam awoke to what she thought she heard was the sound of something moving about in her and Brandon's Condominium. "Babe, did you hear that?" Sam said as she nudged him in his sleep. "Hear what?" he mumbled, still half asleep.

"I think I heard a noise come from the front living area inside our home."

Brandon wiped the sleep out of his eye as he came too. "What?"

Sam put her finger against her mouth. "Shhh... listen."

A loud, clanging noise brought Brandon to a sitting position in the bed. He reached over and quietly opened the nightstand drawer beside him, retrieving his duty weapon, a Sig Sauer 9mm.

Brandon slowly made his way to the kitchen with his weapon pointed in front of him with Sam behind him. "Anyone in here?" he shouted out in the darkness.

Hi-Cee, their orange tabby, suddenly lunged out of the darkness and leaped upon their breakfast nook, startling the both of them. "Shit! Hi-Cee," you scared the bejesus out of us," Brandon said as Sam flipped on the light switch.

Brandon lowered his weapon and stroked the fat cat's fur as It purred. Sam pointed to the swing metal pots on the rack above the nook in the kitchen.

"Was you chasing a mousy boy?" Brandon said as he cupped the cat's face in one hand. Hi-Cee meowed and began licking Brandon's hand.

Brandon looked up at the worried look on Sam's face.

"Look, babe, it was probably just a mouse. I will get an exterminator out here later on today to take a look," he said.

After they both had searched the rest of their condo and found nothing amiss, Sam and Brandon retired back to bed. Something again moving about woke Sam out of her sleep. She looked over at Brandon, who was snoring. Sam decided not to wake him up this time because she had decided that she did not want to come across that she was overwhelmed and hypervigilant due to her post-traumatic stress disorder.

But she was sure that she had heard something moving and felt a presence in their home. Sam looked over at their cat, an orange Tabby that had entered their bedroom and was now staring wide-eyed and catatonically up at the ceiling.

Sam's eyes slowly went up to the ceiling, and that is when she saw Isabella Dupri's corpse hanging on the top above her with a wide rotten tooth grin on its face, as it defied all natural laws of gravity. The corpse's white, cold dead eyes were penetrating her soul as It pointed down at her in an accusatory manner.

The aberration then begins fiendishly laughing as black drool slithered down its rancid mouth and dripped onto the bed below. Sam looked on in horror, frozen, unable to move as she tightly gripped the bedsheets at the leering entity.

A black snake-like slimy tongue now flickered out of the aberration's mouth before it begins to grow longer and extends itself like an Anaconda until it touches Sam's forehead, giving it a wet sloppy lick. It then receded into the thing's mouth. Sam struggled to move her body and feel Brandon in an attempt to wake him up. No matter how hard she tried, her muscles would not comply with her request. Sam closed her eyes to see if that would make the little girl monster with the slimy black snake tongue that was hanging upside down on her ceiling go away. Maybe she was hallucinating, she thought. When she opened her eyes, the little girl had now transformed into a ferocious werewolf hanging from the ceiling as it snarled at her with the same cold white dead eyes.

Sam now watched helplessly as the ceiling began to crack under the weight of the enormous beast. She tried to speak and scream out for Brandon to wake up, but the words came out of her mouth too softly.

The ceiling finally gave way as the creature plummeted towards her bed after righting itself in a position to attack to rip them both apart. Sam threw her hands up in front of her face to protect herself. Before, a scream finally erupted from her throat.

"Brandon woke up abruptly to the sound of her screams. " Jesus Sam, are you okay?" he asked, startled.

Sam looked up at the ceiling, which was still intact. But it had all seemed so natural. Well supernatural. It had all seemed so genuine. Brandon took hold of Sam's hand in his. "Sam, those nightmares again?" he asked, concerned.

"I'll be okay. It was just a bad dream," Sam said, playing it down.

"By the way, you were screaming. I would say that's an understatement," Brandon replied, not convinced that Sam was forthright with him. But he understood why as well. She was tough as nails and stubborn as hell, but he did not want her to think that the traumatic event that happened to her when she was younger and had now followed her into adulthood was a battle that she ever had to fight alone. Because for him, it was not about his ego or manhood. It was about the love he felt for Samantha and the fact he did not want her to think that there was ever anything that she could not come to him about and discuss that would push him away.

"Babe, maybe you need to go see a doctor?" he suggested.

"And tell him or her what? I was kidnapped by a serial killer, saved by a werewolf, and attacked by one after?" she answers sharply.

"Sam, I see your point. But I didn't mean it like that," Brandon said, trying to avoid their discussion turning into an argument.

"I know baby, I just had a rough day, and I really need to get back to sleep," Sam replied, not wanting to discuss the matter any further. She leaned in and kissed Brandon on the lips. "Go back to sleep. I'll be fine, I promise," she assured him.

"You are stubborn as hell Ms. Jackson," Brandon said, reluctantly conceding.

Sam smiled. "I know that's why you love me," she replied as she kissed her fiancé again. He embraced her in his arms. She felt comfortable and safe in his embrace. And despite her independent nature, that is where she thought she needed to be right now. Sam felt terrible though that she had not been as straight with Brandon as she would have liked to be about her dream, or was it a hallucination? She did not know. Maybe he was right, she thought, and she needed to see a doctor again about the nightmares and stress that she had been experiencing lately.

As Brandon finally fell back to sleep, she slipped out of his arms, still looking up at the ceiling into the darkness. And when she stared hard enough, Sam would have sworn that she could even see that specter of Isabella staring back at her in the dark. Maybe, Sam thought. She would see a doctor, as Brandon had suggested. But tonight, Sam felt she had no other choice but to combat whatever demons came her way, on her own. The sound of Brandon's snoring broke her thoughts and also brought a smile to her face. It reminded Sam that she was still attached to reality no matter how abstract it may have seemed at the moment.

As Sam eventually falls back to sleep herself, the pans and pots on the kitchen rack begin to sway if moved by an unseen force. A cold draft of air followed through the condo into Sam and Brandon's bedroom, causing her to pull the sheets tighter to her body for warmth. Hi-Cee sat up at the edge of the bed. His eyes illuminated in the darkness as he watched their doorway protectively as if he were expecting someone or something to walk through that doorway any moment now. "Meow," any moment now.

CHAPTER TWENTY

"How do you know we are going the right way?" Freak said as they made their way back to the cabin. "If we are not, I guess we are fucked," Needy answered bluntly to his remark as they made their way through the mud that appeared to be getting deeper and thicker by the minute due to the downpour.

"Don't worry, dick head. She knows where we are going?" Hallie said, backing up Needy.

"Any more concerns?" Needy asked, who was frankly tired of the bitching and complaining from her subordinates.

"Yeah, what if when we get there, the whole goddamn backwater assed police department for the town of that little shitty bank we robbed is lying in wait for us?" Freak stated.

Needy stopped walking and turned to address Freak she finally had, had enough of his fucking quibbling, between the fucking night mosquitoes that was having them for a late night dinner. "Look motherfucker if you think you have a better option, please take it. If not, shut the fuck up! And I better not hear another word out of your dick trap until we get back to the cabin," she said, annoyed.

"Do I make myself clear?" she asked.

"Crystal," Freak answered nervously.

"Man, what in the fuck did you just step in?" Hallie asked Freak as her flashlight hit Freak's pants leg covered in blood and guts.

"Fuck if I know, maybe a dead animal," he said.

"Needy shines her flashlight on the back trail that their footsteps had just made in the mud.

"Fuck me!" she said, as her flashlight lit up the dead body of Brick. As the light hit his face, they could now see his face was just an open cavity, no eyes, nose, or mouth. Brick's face was now a hollow mushy cavity that had the impression of the sole of a boot that had just stepped inside of it, flattening it out even more.

Freak raised his boot's sole and looked back at what's left of Brick, some of him still clinging to his boot. A sour taste formed in his mouth right before a projectile of vomit erupted from his mouth onto the muddy ground.

"What kind of fucking animal could have done this?" Scooter asked between clenched teeth as he stared at Brick's body that was only recognizable by the clothes he wore.

"Pick your choice Grizzly, Wolf, Cougar, Human? All I know is we need to get our asses in gear and back to the cabin," Needy shouted out.

Hallie held her hand up against her nose as the stench of Brick's corpse finally hit them. "It looks as if it ate his face-off," she said.

"Freak, are you okay?" Needy asked.

"No!" he shot back, between coughs and spittle, still bent over holding his stomach.

"Well, get your shit together. It's time to go," Needy ordered.

As Freak wiped the vomit from his mouth and raised to gather his composure, an ax thrown from out of the darkness at lighting speed met him squarely in the forehead penetrating his skull, sending him toppling to the ground.

"What the fuck!" Needy said, as she and the rest of her crew immediately turned around and began firing a hail of bullets in the direction that they had presumed the ax had come from. A loud growl of pain erupted from something in the dense tree line. Needy threw a signal up to cease-fire as she listens to any further movement in the area of engagement. She looked over at Freak, who convulsed for a few seconds and then died.

"You think we hit that son of a bitch?" Scooter asked, tense and nervously.

"I don't know," Needy answered as her eyes darted back and forth between the trees. All she knew for sure was she had never faced an en emy or adversary that was so quick and proficient at killing in her life.

"This ain't right," Hallie said as she swung her weapon back and forth at a tactical one-hundred-eighty-degrees.

Needy walked over to Freak and pulled the ax out of his skull, which made a crunching sound as it came out. She then angrily hurled the ax down a muddy embankment. "Get the money and his weapon," she ordered. After, Hallie and Scooter had retrieved the backpack of money and an assault weapon. Needy instructed them to roll Freak's body over the same muddy embankment that she had thrown the ax over.

The three of them stood over the embankment as Freak's body rolled aimlessly down the muddy slope into the dark of the night, into oblivion.

Needy's mind went back to her niece Hannah. She was one of the strongest people she knew, her words the last time she saw her ringed in her head. "I love you, Auntie Needy." "I love you to pumpkin," she recalls herself saying.

"When will I see you again," Hannah asked as Needy pictured her lying in her hospital bed.

"Soon, pumpkin, soon."

"You promise," Hannah asked.

"I promise."

The image of Hannah faded out of her mind. Her thoughts and awareness of her present reality kicked back in with her survival instincts. Needy muttered softly under her breath. "I will get out of this hell-hole, Hannah, I promise."

* * *

The smell of bacon and steak permeated the air in the Bone Squad's headquarters, mixed in with the aroma of pancakes and eggs. "Good Morning, boss. How you like your steak," Mako asked as Luna entered the dining area in a flowing sheer white gown that did little to hide her curvy figure, nor did the Victoria Secret's undergarments she wore underneath.

Luna winked at Mako and smiled. "Very rare, of course, and make sure I see some blood," she replied. "You got it, boss," he said, grinning, as he flipped a fresh steak on the grill.

As Luna sat down at the head of the spacious dining table, Dean walked over and sat her down a cup of coffee. "Black, no cream and sugar," he said. "Thanks," she said as she took the cup of coffee sipped out of it and smiled. "And a pinch of salt," Dean added.

"The only way I like it," Luna replied.

Luna had to admit it felt damn good to be back home and in her Alpha mode as the Bone Squad's leader. While breakfast was being served up amongst the pack, and every swinging dick on the team was present, she decided it was time to now get down to the business at hand.

"Listen up, everyone, four years ago, as you all are aware, I was kidnapped by Marcellus and held captive against my will."

Omar slammed his fist down on the table. "Fucking night walkers, we ought to kill them all!" he shouted out angrily.

"We will get there," Luna answered with a sly smile on her face.

"But what you do not know about is the events that led up to it and who is responsible," Luna pointed out to her crew, that was hanging onto her every word.

"Who was it?" Riley asked.

"Solo Chase, one of our own," Luna answers, studying the impact and emotional reaction to her response on the faces of her crew, *disappointment, anger, betrayal, revenge.* She expected no less and was satiated with the latter.

"Fucking wolf scat!" Riley shouted out.

"I did not know you were still interested in that traitor," Dean said, with a hint of jealousy that Luna detected in his voice.

Luna cut Dean a sharp glance and stood up to address his remark. "What dog, I am fucking is never your business, what dog, I kill is," she answered bluntly.

Dean threw his hands up apologetically. "My bag, no disrespect, meant boss."

"None taken," Luna countered.

"Now may I continue," she said.

Dean said nothing as no one did at the table; they knew better than giving their boss permission and permission to an Alpha.

Luna looked across everyone's faces at the table, silence. "Good, I traced Solo hiding out in a small town in South Dakota playing little house on the fucking prairie with the locals, whom I believe facilitated in my capture."

"Fucking civilians," Riley interjected.

That perfect smile came across Luna's face. "Eat up, my babies, we are taking a fucking road trip, maybe with a few pit stops along the way," she announced.

"Where too?" Omar asked as he stuffed three slices of bacon in his mouth.

Luna had been waiting for this moment after four years of imprisonment. It was just as she had envisioned locked up in that cell in the Carpathian Mountains of Sinaia

Romania. It was time for her to bring hell to those who thought they could so quickly dispose of her like trash to her unnatural-born adversaries, the bloodsuckers.

The smile never left Luna's face as she repeated the name of a place that she had not uttered in years. The name of a place she had planned long ago to exact vengeance on and kill as many of its inhabitants as she could that she thought was instrumental to her imprisonment. And yes, collateral damage was readily accepted if necessary to achieve her end goal in the process.

"Where too?"

"Final Destination: Harper Creek, South Dakota," she answers with a smile on her face and a more than a mischievous glint in her eye.

"Yeah, what's our business there?" Omar asked.

"Chaos!" Luna replied grimly.

CHAPTER TWENTY-ONE

What in the hell had happened, he wondered? And how in the hell had Luna escaped such a fortified compound so far away he did not have a resolute answer to that question either. The only positive thing he could think of about the whole goddamn situation is that Marcellus had contacted him right away to let him know she had indeed escaped. And he was lucky for his other resources that had tracked her down to Billings, Montana, where he discovered that she had linked back up with her old bounty hunting team of like-minded killers that she had created. Fortunately for him, though, he had been able to penetrate their compound and plant listening devices and discover that Luna was now heading back to Harper Creek. And he suspected it was for no other reason but to seek revenge. Maybe Sam had been right, he thought; perhaps he should have killed Luna when they had the chance four years ago when she went on a rampage and killing spree in Harper Creek.

How could he be so naïve, he thought? That Luna would stay in bondage forever, that she would not find a way to escape eventually. He had to make the call. He had no other choice.

"Hello," said the recognizable voice on the other end that he had not spoken to in years.

"Gin," he said softly.

"Yes, this is Dr. Gina Jackson," she answered, not recognizing his voice immediately. But wait, who in the hell was this, she thought? Only one person she knew called her Gin. No, it cannot be, she thought.

"Excuse me, who is this?" she asked.

"This is Solo. How are you?" he said.

Gina covers her mouth in shock! She had not heard from Solo in years and thought that she would never hear from him again, and therefore it was just better to get on with her life and career, which Gina did. But despite the years that had passed. One thing was sure. She could not deny the love that she felt in her heart for him that had never ultimately died. Emotions that she had buried deep within herself (about him) were coming back up to the surface as he reached back out to her.

"Solo," she repeated, still shaken by this unexpected reunion. Her emotions inside were mixed. She did not know if she should be happy or pissed at him for taking so long to reach back out to her until now.

"I am fine, and you?" she asked.

"I miss you; what else can I say," he answered back with a tone of despair that Gina detected in his voice, that let her know this was more than just a simple check up on a past "ex-girlfriend" phone call.

"What's going on, Solo?" Gina asked, now worried.

"It's Luna, she has escaped and is now back here in the United States, and I think she's headed your way. That means putting it bluntly, you and everyone in Harper Creek is in imminent danger, Gin," Solo answered, not wanting to pull any punches on the message that he was trying to convey to his ex-lover.

This news hit Gina like a whirlwind, almost taking her off her feet as she felt her heartbeat speed up as she let the information sink in. "Luna has escaped?" she replied, confused.

"But how?" she asked.

"Years of meticulous planning, no doubt, and I suspect she was probably waiting for that one breach in security to make her escape. We are talking about a very ruthless and cunning woman Gina."

"I remember quite vividly, thank you," Gina answered, and indeed she did. After all, Luna had been the one over four years ago that had decided that she would stop at nothing to get Solo back in her clutches, including killing her daughter Sam and her, which she almost came close to doing.

"Good, then you need to get out of there asap," Solo stressed.

"Have you contacted Sam yet?" Gina needed to know.

"No, not yet. Sam is still in Chicago, correct?"

"Yes, how did you know that?" Gina replied.

"Gin, You have to know, my relationship and responsibility to the both of you did not end on the day I said goodbye."

"Solo, I never thought of "you" having a hero complex," Gina stated.

"Me neither," countered Solo.

A sense of urgency now overcame Gina. "I need to contact Sam and warn her that, that maniac has escaped."

"Please do," Solo agreed.

"By the way, Solo, this is my home, and I love this town and the people that live in it."

"What in the hell does that mean, Gin?"

"You know damn well what it means. I am not running," Gina said firmly.

"I see you still got that fire in you," Solo replied.

"Yes, and I would be damn if I let some bitch that can turn into a werewolf put it out," Gina answered defensively.

"I have no other option then but to get my ass down there as soon as I can," Solo asserted.

"I am not asking for your help, Hero," Gina said.

"You don't have to, you know damn well; this is my fight too," Solo pointed out.

"Be safe, Mr. Chase."

"You as well, Dr. Jackson," Solo replied.

* * *

"Sam, you have an incoming call on line one," said the switchboard operator at the Night Turner Tribune. "Okay, thanks," Sam responded.

"Samantha Jackson, Night Turner Tribune."

"Hello, Sam."

Sam did not realize how long it had been since the last time she had spoken with her mother due to both their busy work schedules until she heard her voice on the other end of the phone.

"Hey Mom, what's going on?" Sam asked, trying to sound cheerful.

"Sam, I am afraid we got a serious problem."

"What's that?" Sam asked, detecting a tone of dread in her mom's voice.

Gina spoke in code, but Sam knew precisely what matter she was referring to in her phone call. "I just got a call from Solo. That nasty weather is coming in soon." Did Sam hear her mother correctly, she thought? Had she just spoken the *code words* that they had agreed on over four years ago, they would use if they ever got wind that the shapeshifter that had terrorized their town years ago was free again?

"Sam, are you still here?" Gina asked, after giving what she had just told her daughter, time to sink in.

"Yes, mom, please be careful. I will be on the first flight I can catch back home."

"Sam, don't worry, I will be okay; just take care of yourself and Brandon, and I will see you soon."

"Thanks, mom. I love you."

"Show me and just get your ass here safely and in one piece," Gina said.

Her mom's remark made Sam smile, although the last thing she felt like doing was smiling at this time. "I will. I promise."

"I love you guys too, be safe," Gina said.

Sam turned around swiftly in defensive mode as her Editor in Chief - Avery Dent, tapped her on her shoulder from behind, startling her as she quickly knocked his hand away off her shoulder. Avery took a step backward, surprised.

"Sam is everything okay?" he asked, noticing that she appeared visibly upset about something and was certainly not herself.

Sam rubbed her forehead. "Oh, sorry for being so skittish. I feel like I might be coming down with something," she said apologetically.

"I'll say, you almost knock my head off Sam, why don't you take the rest of the day off, go home and get some rest," her boss suggested.

"Thanks, Chief, but I got too much work to do," Sam protested.

"That work can wait. I insist," Avery asserted.

"By the way, great job on the Dupri case," he said, referring to the demonic possession case she had just investigated and completed. "Now go home and get some rest."

"Thanks, Chief," Sam conceded; as she watched Avery stroll away back to his office, she knew damn well that she would need more than a day off to address the kind of virus that was coming her way. A virus named Luna Dye, that had plans to wipe out her hometown, including her existence.

Sam gathered up some personals and paperwork off her desk. As she proceeded out of the newspaper's building, the dream she had recently about Isabella transforming into a Lycan came flooding back into her memory. She now wondered had it been a premonition or sign of the things to come.

"Fuck," Sam murmured to herself as she thought of how she was going to tell Brandon that she had to take an emergency flight back to Harper Creek because her home town was about to be seized on by a psychotic werewolf that she thought was locked away for good in a dungeon abroad.

Sam's thoughts then went to her mother's ex-lover and nucleus of this evolution, Solo Chase. Not that she was blaming him for the trail of carnage that Luna left in her wake. But the fact that had he only listened to her the first time and destroyed Luna when they had an opportunity to do so, she was sure that they would be in a different situation right now. Or would they? She thought. As Solo's words and the event associated with it also came back flooding her memory, why that was not such a great idea.

"We need to end her, to make sure this never happens again," said Sam wielding a lethal dagger in one hand, as she stood over a tranquilized Luna spread out on her living room floor after attempting to kill her and her mother.

Solo put his hand out to block her from plunging the silver dagger into Luna's chest, into her heart.

"Not this way Sam, if you kill her here, it will be like opening the gates of hell in this town because everyone close to her, that she has turned, will be at Harper Creek's doorsteps, seeking revenge. "What the Hell? It looks like those gates were open regardless," Sam said to herself as she got inside her car.

* * *

"We should not be that much further from the cabin now," Needy said as she and the two other surviving members of her team made their way even more cautiously than before, back to the Anderson cabin. Needy, hand signaled to the last two of her crew to stop walking and spread out as she heard what sounded like footsteps approaching.

The stranger in hunting gear came out of the darkness with his high-powered hunting rifle pointed at Needy as she quickly drew her submachine gun on him in a face-to-face stand-off. "What in the Sam Hill is your ass doing out here, young lady?" he asked.

"I was going to ask you the same thing, old man?" Needy answered, never taking her weapon or eye off the stranger.

"Well, I know that firepower you got there ain't the standard for hunting," he said.

"What in the hell is the standard out here?" Needy counter, which causes the old hunter to chuckle. "Well, you got a good point there, stranger," he agreed.

The barrel of a weapon nudged the back of his head. " Put your weapon down, Pops, before I blow the back of your skull out," Hallie ordered.

"Well, I guess y'all got me with my pecker hanging out," the stranger said as he submitted to Hallie's request and sat his weapon slowly down on the ground, then raising his hands in the air voluntarily as an act of submission.

Scooter appeared seconds later out of the darkness with his weapon drawn on the stranger. "Who in the fuck are you?" he asked.

The stranger looked at Scooter and then back at Needy.

"You heard him Pops, who in the fuck are you? And why in the hell are you out here?" Needy stated assertively.

"Well, I can tell you one thing I am not out here wiping my ass with acorns and singing Christmas songs, that's for damn sure," he answered sarcastically.

Needy shook her head in dissatisfaction with his answer. The last thing she wanted to do, she thought, was waste time fucking around with this old Cooter. Maybe she needed to make herself clearer to him, she thought.

"I am going to give you one more time to answer, funny man. And if I do not like your answer, your brains right along with your witty demeanor is going to be in that mud," Needy said, in a tone of voice that immediately conveyed to the stranger that there was no bullshit in what she had just told him. He looked over all three of them, and he immediately picked up a sense of desperation, that they were running from something other than the police out here in the woods.

"The name's Joe. I live around here," he said.

Needy lowered her weapon. Joe had saved his own life, at least for now, she thought. "And what in the hell are you doing out here, in this kind of weather, Joe?" she asked.

"I am not looking for y'all if that's what you mean?" he answered flatly.

"Do you know who we are?"

"I reckon, y'all must be the yahoos that robbed that bank earlier," he answered, non-invasively.

"We need to smoke the old shit kicker now and get going," Scooter yelled out.

"Smoke me if you want, but I don't give a flying one nut squirrel's ass about you all robbing no banks. All they do is steal people's money any goddamn way," Joe said defiantly.

"Anyway, looks like to me, y'all got bigger problems," he added.

"What the fuck is that supposed to mean?" Luna asked.

Joe begins chuckling as he speaks to Needy specifically. "First, you look like you are a few men short, and I don't think you know what in the hell you are up against out here in these parts."

"Is that a fact?" Needy shot back.

" Yes, like bear shit stinks, and the cops are the least of your worries out here, little lady," he said.

"Get to it, old fart," Needy said, with no more patience for Joe's animal metaphors.

Joe looked at them all wide-eyed now as he answered Needy enthusiastically. "You don't know, do you?" he asked.

"Know what?" Needy asked.

"Elwood Cyphus Holmes haunts these woods, that's what!" he said.

"Elwood fucking who?" Hallie asked.

Joe looked at Hallie and shook his head in disgust. "Elwood Holmes, dingbat!"

"You motherfucker!" Hallie said as she lunged at Joe, only to be cut off and held back by Needy's outstretched arm.

"Cool it!" Needy said. After she had calmed Hallie down, she then turned and addressed Joe. "From here on out, I suggest you watch your fucking mouth, you old shit stain."

"May I continue?" Joe asked unperturbed.

"Very carefully," Needy advised him.

"I guess you all were too busy robbing banks to hear that there were some killings around here years ago. The locals thought first it was animal attacks because the kill-ings were so vicious. But it turns out we had our own homegrown prolific serial killer right here in Harper Creek that was responsible for countless murders," Joe said.

"Yes, I think I heard something about that, but didn't he die from an animal attack himself?" Needy asked.

Joe started laughing again. "That's what the local sheriff department said, but they never recovered his body, and he was not attacked or killed by no normal animal."

"Old coot, you've been out here sniffing pine trees and eating shrooms too long," Scooter said, mocking him.

"What do you mean by no normal animal?" Needy inquired.

"From what I heard, Elwood and a werewolf went down in the black rivers not too far from here. They never found him or the beast that attacked him and took him over that cliff down into that watery abyss," Joe replied.

Scooter threw his hands up and began pacing. " I told you this old fart was bat shit crazy!" he exclaimed.

"Let's just kill him and go," he said.

"Shut the fuck up!" Needy shot back to Scooter.

"Where do you keep your money, Joe?" she asked.

"I am old school, definitely not in a fucking bank," he answers gruffly.

Needy sized up Joe, the old cooter, may have been a smart ass, but she did not get the impression that he was a liar. It was conviction in his voice that told her he sincerely believed every word he had just spoken. "You're out here looking for him, aren't you?" she asked.

"Yes, I believe that fucker ain't dead and until I am. I won't rest until I find out so," Joe answered, not giving a damn at this point if they believed him or not. He was in his truth, and that is all that mattered to him.

"Give him back his weapon," Needy ordered.

"What?" Scooter answered.

"You heard me, give him back his rifle," Needy asserted.

Scooter picked the rifle up off the ground, pulled back its bolt, and began discharging its rounds as they plopped to the ground. He then reluctantly handed the weapon back over to its owner Joe. "Here, asshole," he said.

"The feelings are mutual," Joe replied as he took possession of his rifle.

Needy picked up one of the bullets and examined it closely. "Well, I be damn, what is this silver?" she said, scrutinizing the slugs.

"Yep, the only thing that will kill werewolves, besides separating their goddamn heads from their bodies," Joe assured them.

Needy turned her attention back to Hallie and Scooter. "Listen up, you two, there are two ways to look at what he just told us, either he is coo-coo for cocoa puffs are maybe there is some actual truth in what he is telling us, regarding what we may be dealing with, out here."

"It's all true," Joe interjected, insulted that they were branding him crazy.

"Fucking werewolf?" Hallie repeated, still unconvinced.

"Let me know when you got a better explanation for all the weird shit that has been happening to us out here," Needy replied.

"How did you get into these woods, Joe?" Needy asked.

"I got an ATV parked three miles down the road hidden in some brush," he answered, right before a bestial howl erupted in the night air jarring all four of them to silence.

"What the fuck was that?" Scooter asked, shaken.

Joe looked at Scooter with a smirk on his face. "My imagination," he answers.

CHAPTER TWENTY-TWO

Needy took the backpack off her back, went inside, and pulled out five thousand dollars in cash. "Here is something for your trouble," she said as she offered Joe the money. "For my trouble or my silence?" he asked as he looked at the thick band of money.

"Both," Needy answered as she held the cash out, still waiting for him to accept it.

Joe rubbed his beard as he stared at the cash with the five thousand dollar band wrapped around the one hundred dollar bills. It was more money than he had seen in a long time because he lived on his meager pension hand-to-mouth.

"Don't worry, it's insured they won't miss it," Hallie said, grinning.

"Naw, I don't need your blood money. Keep it! You've earned it," Joe said to Needy as he declined her offer.

"And as far as my silence goes, what does it matter if all of you are dead by sunrise anyway," he said.

Needy smiled and put the money back inside the backpack and strapped it back on behind her back. "Have it your way, Pops, and good luck with your search," she said.

Joe eyeballed all three of them before he spoke again. "Thanks, by the way, as far as I am concerned, if you three get out of these woods with your life and that stolen cash, you deserve to keep it."

Maybe the old man was crazy as a loon, Needy thought. She turned back and looked at him. "Like I said, good luck," she repeated.

Joe said nothing this time as he watched Needy and her crew make off into the woods. At least to them anyway, because he felt that all three of them might as well have been a dead man walking out here in these parts of the woods. The problem was, he thought. They did not appear to know their fate. "Good luck, you are going to need it way more than me, assholes," he said, as he begins gathering up his ammunition off the ground.

As Joe picked the ammo off the ground, he caught the sound of something growling nearby that appeared to be approaching him in the darkness. He quickly reloads his rifle nervously as he looks around to see what direction the growling was coming from in the dark. As he pulled his rifle bolt back, chambering his last round, his rifle made a resounding snap.

"Come on, you sonofabitch, I got some hot lead for your sorry ass!" Joe shouted out.

"Growllll," Joe spun around and let loose several rounds into the darkness from where he had detected movement. The sound of something squawking in pain emanated out of the nighttime air and direction that he had fired shots, where he thought he heard movement.

Needy and the last of her team stopped in their tracks as they heard the gunshots. "What in the hell is that crazy old buzzard shooting at?" Hallie asked.

"Who knows," Needy said.

"You think we need to go back."

Needy debated Hallie's question for a moment and quickly determine that her niece Hannah needed her much more than the old fart that should have been home watching *Jeopardy* instead of hunting for werewolves as far as she was concerned. "No, we don't have time for any more bullshit! Move out," she said.

"I got you now, you sonofabitch," Joe yelled out as he advanced on the area near a slope where he thought he had injured a different kind of animal, a werewolf. As Joe shined his flashlight down on the ground, he could now see a spotty trail of blood loss by whatever had been approaching him before he opened fire and wounded it. He just hoped that one of the bullets had landed in the right spot and that the creature was now bleeding out. The blood trail now went dead as Joe shined his flashlight in a wide axis in front of him for any sign of movement.

"Growlll...." it seemed to come out of nowhere as Joe spun around to engage it. A creature that was part man and beast knocked the rifle clean out of his hands with one mighty swipe, sending the weapon flying aimlessly in the air and to the ground out of his reach. Joe fumbled for his sidearm a 44. Magnum as the creature advanced on him quickly.

Joe's brain exploded in pain as the creature landed a decisive blow to the side of his head that sent him straight to the ground in the wet mud. He felt as if he had just been hit in the head by a brick! Joe knew that he could not survive another blow like that as the woods seemed to be spinning around to him now. The creature to him now looked like a blur as it continued to advance upon him to finish him off. Joe begins to back crawl in the mud in a sitting position to escape its next assault upon him.

The man-creature in primal rage went in for the kill as it lunged at Joe, who was now at the edge of the muddy slope. Joe, not thinking, just reacting, made one last effort to get out of its way as he scampered backward only to go over the edge and roll down its embankment, landing in a deep bed of mud below. He could now hear growling, and the sound of the man-beast footsteps approaching as he laid half-conscious, camouflaged in the bed of muddy soil.

Joe laid as still and quiet as he could in the mud as he watched the creature sniff the night air for his scent. As the man-beast turned towards him, its eyes that glowed eerily in the dark locked directly on him. Joe swallowed a lump of fear down his throat as he watched the thing that looked half wolf and half man to him continue to stare in his direction. The creature sniffs the air one last time before it finally bolts off into the darkness of the woods.

Joe begins to breathe again, unaware all this time that he had been holding his breath. The fear in his eyes illuminated from the mud that now camouflaged his face.

* * *

Marcellus had now been summoned to an emergency board meeting by the Blood Order and as head of his sect. He knew that he would be held responsible for the breach in his security team that allowed, as they described, that mad dog Luna to successfully escape his compound while also successfully killing some of his foot soldiers in the process. If his head guard Dragos had survived, he would have killed him viciously himself, he concluded.

Fucking idiot, Marcellus thought. How fitting that Dragos died with his dick stuffed in his mouth due to his blatant incompetence. Because of his head guard's unchained libido, Marcellus knew all he could do now is pick up the pieces to salvage Project: Cerberus, which he had created and started with his own two hands, that was now at risk of being terminated by the Blood Order.

Marcellus now sat at a long executive table with other high-ranking members and leaders of different sects throughout Europe and the world that made up the order. But the one vampire present that deserved and commanded the most respect was an ancient and overlord by the name of Constantine Vladimir, a force to be reckoned with that sat at the head of the executive table. He was also an eccentric that fancied Victorian day clothing with a modern-day twist.

The meeting was coming to an end, and Constantine had made up his mind after hearing Marcellus's testimony what his decision would be. He did not doubt that the other leaders and elders would support that decision.

"Although we are all quite pleased that you have accepted full responsibility for this travesty under your command, I feel we have no other choice but to halt Project Cerberus," he said bluntly.

Constantine looked around the table at the faces of the other nine leaders before he addressed them all. "If there are any objections to this action amongst the order, please state your position," he said.

None of the others raised his or her hand in objection. It was just as he had anticipated unanimous support across the board. All the better, he thought. He felt famished and needed a good meal of the healthy blood plasma supplied by his United States contact and fellow associate Jonathan Piper to satiate his thirst and hunger.

"I understand and respect the Order's decision, but please give me the opportunity, Honorable Constantine, as you stated, to rectify the situation," Marcellus said.

"And how do you plan on doing that?" Constantine responded.

"Allow me to assemble a team of my best soldiers, and I can assure you I will bring Luna Dye back to this compound before the Order to answer for her crimes," Marcellus proposed.

"Dead or Alive?" a sect leader named Artemis shouted out across the table.

"Trust me; she will wish she was dead when my team and I capture her," Marcellus assured Artemis with bravado and confidence in his voice.

"The same team that allowed her to escape," Artemis countered, not impressed by what he perceived as Marcellus's false sense of self-importance to The Order. Never a fan of Marcellus. Artemis's position was The Order was around long before Marcellus came into existence and would still be around if his immortality got revoked. Relative to Artemis's perception of Marcellus, he did not fare any better in his rival's eyes. Marcellus found him to be a vampiric weasel that repeatedly kissed Constantine's pale ass to curry favor with him, in addition to being a greedy opportunist also, that would betray anyone foolish enough to trust him.

Marcellus scowled, revealing his canines. "I will put my soldiers up against your band of misfits anytime, Artemis!" he challenged.

"Enough!" Constantine shouted out in anger as he pounded his fist on the table, a blow that was so powerful it was felt by all that was seated as the table shook from one end to another.

"We are all on the same side unless you two have forgotten," he said, reprimanding both men before the Order.

"Yes, we are," Artemis agreed, as he felt the heat of Marcellus's eyes and scorn upon him.

"The Order accepts your proposal, Marcellus. You and your team may leave immediately for the United States to extradite Luna back here to Romania to answer for her crimes," Constantine said, much to Artemis dismay, who had enough wisdom, not to challenge Constantine and the rest of the Order's final decision.

"Thank you, great one, Alexandra will take over my command during my absence," Marcellus said, as he extended his hand in the direction of a beautiful and regal-looking vampire with an alabaster complexion and long dark hair tied into an exquisite bun. Her ice-blue eyes almost seemed to glow in the dimly lit conference room known as "The Chamber" by the Blood Order members.

"This meeting's concluded," Constantine said to the relief and satisfaction of Marcellus. The latter thought that it could have gone much worse for him as he observed the other members of the Order, including Artemis, leave the Chamber. But before Artemis exited, he caught him side-eyeing him with a look that he could only interpret as envy and jealousy as Artemis quickly looked away when he made eye contact with him. "Coward," Marcellus thought.

Constantine approached him and placed his longhand with overgrown fingernails that were more like talons on his shoulder. "Do not disappoint me," he said firmly, which came off more like a warning to Marcellus.

"I assure you I won't, Sir," Marcellus said, knowing damn well the consequences if he did.

As he watched Constantine leave the chamber, he turned to Alexandra, who was still in the room with him and now standing beside him. "Be careful while I am gone that Artemis is a rattlesnake," he said quietly.

"Do not worry, Marcellus. I can handle that dickless snake," Alexandra replied with confidence.

Marcellus looked over Alexandra. She was one of the best and brightest soldiers that he had in his sect and more than any man's equal or, in most cases, better. "Yes, I am sure you can, Alex, I am sure you can," he repeated.

"There is only one problem though with snakes," he said contemplatively.

"What's that?" she asked.

"You never know what rock they are going to crawl from underneath and strike you when you least expect it," he answered.

"Well, that is the nature of a snake. Is it not?" said Alexandra.

"That is the nature of Artemis," Marcellus said as he embraced Alexandra in his arms and kissed her softly on her cold lips.

CHAPTER
TWENTY-THREE

Needy, Hallie and Scooter had now made it back to The Anderson's property without any further incident. But as they all stood in the shadows in the woods a reasonable distance from the cabin. Needy knew that it would be foolish to try to strong-arm their way in and that they probably would be met with gunfire if any sign of their presence is detected again near the home. And since she was not there for that type of family reunion. Especially at the end of a 12 gauge shotgun. The only thing she wanted from the Anderson's is their transportation and to get herself and her remaining crew as far away as she could from this area before they were discovered and apprehended by law enforcement which she suspected was still hot on their trail like bloodhounds on an escaped convict's ass.

She wondered that despite paying Anderson's hush money if they had already taken the other road and sold her out? Contrary to the deal she had made with them earlier.

After all, she was aware of the fact that she and her crew did have a nice FBI bounty on their heads to be collected by any snitch that gave information that was important or pertinent enough to lead to their arrest. And she was sure that if the Anderson's found that out, they no doubt in her mind, could see that as a nice little bonus to the cash that they had already received to alleviate their money woes. And significantly, Needy ascertain if they thought that she and her crew's chances of making it out the woods alive were slim to none, she reasoned.

Needy stood silently by watching the cabin for any signs of unusual activity through her night vision binoculars. She spotted Anderson's SUV unmoved, still in their driveway.

"How are your hotwiring skills?" she turned to Scooter and asked him.

"Still up to par," he replied with a grin.

"Good, we here for the car, and that's it," she said, wanting to make herself clear in case he or Hallie had any ideas in their minds or heads of going off-script. At this stage of the game, Needy knew she could not afford anymore fuck ups. She could not afford any more needless loss of life on her watch.

"All clear," Hallie said as she returned to the two of them after circling the cabin on foot.

Needy wiped the rain out of her eyes. "Good, are you ready, Scoot?"

Scooter nodded his head yes. "Okay, we got your ass covered. Make it quick and stay low," Needy said. "I got this, boss," Scooter answered before he made a beeline towards the sport utility vehicle in the driveway, sloshing through foot-deep mud on his way over to the car to their salvation.

"Fuck!" Needy blurted out! As she observes, a light popping on in the cabin. She and Hallie immediately concealed themselves deeper in the darkness's recesses amongst the tree line to avoid detection. They both now watched the light on inside the cabin that cast an eerie yellowish glow from the outside with bated breath, and their weapons pointed towards the cabin's front door. As far as Needy was concerned now, if one of the Anderson's came out, they were as good as dead. Needy started counting the seconds the light remained on her head.

One, Two, Three, Four, Five, Six… the light inside the cabin finally went off, much to Needy's relief as she let out a long deep sigh from pent-up anxiety. She focused her night-vision goggles over on the Anderson's SUV and locked in on Scooter crouched down beside the driver's door, giving her the thumbs up before entering the vehicle. Needy cracked a slight smile; about time, something was going goddamn right, she thought much to her chagrin of how things so far had played out.

Scooter quietly entered the Toyota 4Runner Pro, and before he went to hot-wire the SUV, he carefully flipped down the sun visor, causing a pair of keys to drop down in his lap. "Things are looking up," he said, smiling.

He planned to put the car in neutral and coast it quietly and far enough away from the cabin so that the owners would not hear him stealing it. When he felt the SUV was a comfortable distance away. Scooter, would start it up and drive off with it. Scooter got out of the vehicle to push and steer it once he put the gear in neutral. Needy from afar could see he was having difficulty moving the car on the muddy surface, so she ordered Hallie to stand her ground and cover her as she ran over to assist him.

"Look like you can use some help," she said as she got behind the vehicle and began pushing. As the sport-utility vehicle started picking up traction and distance, Scooter and Hallie jumped in as Scooter put his foot on the brake to stop the car from freewheeling. He turned the ignition key quickly, starting the vehicle up, and threw the car into drive as he and Needy now made their way down the dark muddy road. "Hot damn," shouted out Scooter gleefully.

"Over there," Needy said, as she caught a glimpse of the light from Hallie's flashlight as she signaled them. "Let's get the fuck out of here," Hallie said as they pulled up on her, and she jumped inside of the back of the Toyota with her weapon and backpack full of stolen cash.

As they navigated their way through the woods and rugged terrain in the darkness, a feeling suddenly crept over Needy. "Turn here," she shouted out.

Scooter quickly followed her orders without hesitation and whipped the car in the direction that Needy had requested. After a quarter-mile down, the road turned into a paved intersection. "What the hell?" Hallie said, smiling as the Toyota hit the hardball.

"How did you know," Scooter asked Needy as his sweaty hands gripped the steering wheel tightly.

Needy looked at Scooter apprehensively. " I did not know," she answers.

Hallie turned around in her seat and looked out the back window of the SUV at the green road sign that illuminated in the darkness that said, now leaving Harper Creek. "Fuck Harper Creek!" she shouted out defiantly.

Scooter laughed nervously. "Hot damn, I second that emotion," he said.

"Watch out!" Needy shouted out. As a large buck, deer suddenly darted in front of the Toyota, caught in the glare of its headlights. Scooter attempted to swerve out of the animal's path, but his reaction was too slow as he collided head-on with the giant animal. The deer crashed through the windshield, causing the SUV to veer off the road down a muddy ravine into a tree as it finally came to a crumpling and smoking rest.

As Needy slowly begins to regain consciousness from being temporarily knocked out by the collision. She turned to check on Scooter and immediately recoiled back in horror at the sight of him being impaled through the neck by one of the bucks large antlers. He emitted a death rattle and struggled to breathe as blood ran down his mouth. Needy eyes went to the sizable bloody animal resting over the hood of the Toyota 4 runner. She could not help notice that its life had expired from its cold dead stare. When she turned and looked back at Scooter, the rattling had now stopped, and he had the same frosty look of death on his face.

"Fuck!" Needy shouted out in anger as she attempted to assess how badly she was injured as she unbuckled her seat belt. She then turned to the back seat to check on Hallie, unconscious and bleeding from the head.

"Do not do this to me, Hallie; please wake up!" Needy shouted to her as she began shaking her to bring her back awake.

Needy heard a slight moan come from Hallie and slapped her face to revive her further. "Come on, don't fucking die on me now bitch!"

Hallie finally opened her eyes to Needy's relief and began to respond to her. "What the fuck happen?" she said, as she touched the blood running down her face. "Bad luck," Needy answers as she proceeds to unbuckle Hallie's seatbelt.

Hallie noticed Scooter's head slumped back on the seat and part of the large animal through the windshield. It was not until her eyes came on the sight of the buck antler sticking out the back of Scooter's neck did she completely lose her composure and recoil back in horror as well at the gruesome sight in front of her. "Jesus Needy! What the fuck happen to Scooter?" she said in anguish.

"What the fuck almost happen to me? Now we need to go," Needy said as she proceeded to open the door and exit the car. The sound of something growling and large moving towards their vehicle stopped her in her tracks from escaping. She looked at Hallie wide-eyed and said nothing before she punched her in the chin knocking Hallie out cold and unconscious. Needy then proceeded to play dead as she smelled the stench of the creature as it approached them in the wrecked SUV.

She could hear it sniffing in the air as she remained as still as she could, even mentally slowing down her heartbeat. As she squinted her eyes to fake death, she could make out something that was like nothing that she had ever seen in her life before, something that stood almost seven feet tall, that appeared to be part human and part animal with a wolf-like face. Needy sat frozen as she listened to the sound of it walking around the sport utility vehicle. She then watched in awe as it savagely began to pull on the dead buck and drag all close to two-hundred pounds of its carcass off the hood of the SUV. With one powerful tug by the creature, she watches in horror as it quickly snatched Scooter's body through the broken windshield, causing the rest of it to implode.

Needy had known fear before as a war veteran who served in a Special Forces unit and did two Iraq tours. But this shit was on a completely different level; she had to admit even for her level of experience and expertise as a soldier as a human being.

"Get your shit together, Needy," she said to herself between deep breaths. She knew that whatever that creature was? It would be back for more after it was finished with Scooter and the deer carcass. But she would not be sticking her narrow ass around to find out, she concluded.

Needy turned around and shook Hallie in the backseat. "Wake the hell up," she said. Hallie began to come to again as Hallie touched the side of her sore jaw and chin.

"What the fuck just happen?" she said, with no memory that Needy had just knocked her out.

"I just saved your ass," Needy answered.

"Now we need to get the fuck out of here because I don't know if I can do it again," she said.

CHAPTER TWENTY-FOUR

With their team of officers, Alvarez and Smith had come up empty so far with their search for the crew that had hit their local bank earlier in the day. Alvarez still suspected that the bank robbers could not have gotten too far in the treacherous and hazardous weather they were having in the area. If mother nature had not been an ally in assisting them in catching the brazen bank robbers, she sure was not doing those assholes that had hit his bank any favors either, he determines, as he and Smith's team pulled into the Anderson's place. The place appeared quiet and was also in the dark as they made their way up the long unpaved driveway in the downpour of rain.

"Chief looks like they are not expecting any visitors," Shannon said.

"Yes, it does appear that way," Alvarez said; as he knocked on the front door, the sound of a dog barking erupted from behind it.

After a few seconds had passed, Jason finally came to the door looking disheveled, like he just woke up. "I thought you had canceled on me, Sheriff," he said, rubbing the sleep out of eyes.

"Not a chance," Alvarez answered as he attempted to look behind and around Jason for any signs of suspicious activity.

"Well, I told you all I know," Jason said.

"Good, may we come inside to discuss that further," Alvarez said, not swayed by Jason's admission of transparency.

"Discuss what?" Jason said.

"All you know," Alvarez answer, either this kid was dumb as he looked or was playing dumb or both, he thought. Regardless of which one he would get to the bottom of his bullshit, he concluded.

"Sorry about that, sheriff, sure step right on in," Jason said as if he had forgotten a monsoon of rain was pouring down on Alvarez and Shannon's heads.

"My parents are asleep," Jason said. Alvarez nodded his head in acknowledgment, although he was sure that he had not asked him any questions yet.

"Sorry, I did not think you were going to make it out here in this bad weather, so I guess I just fell to sleep," Jason said.

Playing dumb and over apologetic, never good signs, Alvarez mentally noted, as he took his Stetson off and shook the rain off of it while still looking around the cabin for anything out of order, anything out of place.

"Yeah, it is a shit storm out there, but I still gotta do my job, and that job is keeping the good citizens of Harper Creek safe, including you," Alvarez said.

He had responded like that intentionally to see if Jason would question what he had just said.

"Yep. I guess you're right," Jason replied with a fake smile. And just like he had expected, Jason did not prove him wrong.

"You mind if we take a look around here," Alvarez asked, as his suspicions about Jason's demeanor and the fact that he may be hiding something grew stronger by the minute.

"No, but as I said, my parents are asleep upstairs, and I appreciate it if you and your Swat Team don't disturb them," Jason answered condescendingly.

"Those parents," Alvarez said, pointed up at the staircase where John and Deena appeared in their pajamas and lounge robes at the top landing of the stairs.

"Good heavens Sheriff Alvarez, what brings you out here to our house so late in this atrocious weather," John shouted down from above them.

Alvarez studied Jason's face, and to him, he appeared more than relieved that his father and mother had just shown up and saved his ass from potential self – incrimination. Like he thought earlier, playing dumb and over apologetic was never good signs from a potential witness or suspect.

Alvarez waved up to Jason's parents. "Good evening John, Deena. I apologize for the late-night house call, but I had to come out and check on the tip Jason here gave us regarding the suspects we are looking for that pulled that bank job earlier in town."

John looked over at Jason. "Is that right," he said, as he and Deena now stood beside them on the lower floor.

Jason did not answer out of embarrassment because he knew the deal that his father and mother had made with Needy and her crew. He was sure right now that his parents felt as if he had betrayed them by going behind their backs and ratting Needy out when they had given her their word that they would say nothing. What the hell, and in a sense, Jason had to admit to himself, they were right if they felt that way. But that was never a primary concern of his. After all, what in the hell was he getting out of it, he thought. And if they caught the bastards, he was sure it was some excellent reward money in it for him. Yes, Jason had it all figured out, that even if the bank robbers declared that they had paid his parents hush-money to keep quiet. If and when they were apprehended, his disposition was, who in the hell was going to believe thieves' statement over two seniors and law-abiding citizens, he thought. He wondered if he appeared too nervous or gave off the impression he was shitting bricks right now to Sheriff Alvarez and his sexist observation, Alvarez's cute little blond deputy with the tight ass that was with him.

"Well, since you good folks are awake, I am going to ask you two the same question that I asked your fine son Jason here. You folks don't mind if we take a look around here, do you?" Alvarez asks.

"No, not at all, sheriff," Deena answers.

"Do you suspect that the people you are looking for may have been around here?" John asked.

Alvarez smiled. He wondered if John was playing him too like a cheap Stradivarius violin. "According to your son, he stated that he saw them passing through, is that right, Jason?"

"Yes, that be about right, sheriff," Jason said, as he gave Shannon a smile, which was never reciprocated by the deputy, who remained poker-faced throughout the conversation.

"Sheriff, I would not put all my stock in what my boy said if I was you. People like Hikers and Campers do occasionally pass through. It might be nothing," John said, attempting to cast doubt on his son's tip.

"You might be right, John. But just to be on the safe side, we are still going to check it out," Alvarez said.

"Can I get you guy's some hot coffee?" Deena interrupted.

"Yes, thanks, Deena, that's mighty kind of you," Alvarez said. He was aware that John's wife had lost her vision a few years ago due to glaucoma. Alvarez admired her tenacity and courage in dealing with the disease. And he also knew overall that this family was good, hard-working people, and respected in the community. Their son Jason not so much. The only thing that he knew about him is that he had returned home to South Dakota and had been living with his parents for six months now after a failed startup he had in Iowa. After agreeing to the search, the Anderson's allowed entry to Alvarez's deputies and Smith's team, who now had the luxury of sipping on hot coffee out of the cold rain in the warmth of their living room.

"All clear, Chief," Shannon said after she and the other officers could find nothing suspicious or out of place.

"Thanks, Shannon," Alvarez said before he took his last sip of the hot coffee that did a decent job, if he must admit of not only putting some caffeine but warmth back into his body.

"Oh, by the way, John, when we pulled up, I noticed the Toyota 4runner was not in the driveway," he said.

"It was there earlier before we went to bed," said John, who did appear to be genuinely surprised to Alvarez at that revelation.

"I did hear some noise outside earlier, and I turned on the lights, but I did not see anything," Jason said.

"Well, why did you not mention that earlier," Alvarez asked.

"I don't know. I guess because I did not think it was that important."

"How long ago was this?"

"About twenty minutes ago, maybe more," Jason answered.

"Give Deputy Shannon the make, model, and year on that vehicle. We need to put a B.O.L. out on it now," Alvarez said, visibly upset that Jason had held this information from him earlier.

"You think the guys that robbed the bank stole our car?" Jason said.

"It's missing, isn't it?" Shannon said.

" Fucking assholes, must have double back," Jason pointed out. Alvarez noticed that the blood seemed to leave John and Deena's face when Jason made this statement.

"What do you mean double back? Are you saying that the bank robbers were here before?" Alvarez asked.

"No, No, that's not what I meant. I am just saying that I saw some of them creeping around this area earlier, so they must have cased our place and stole my truck after we all went to bed, that's all," Jason said nervously.

"To all units, B.O.L. for a 1998 Toyota 4runner, Yellow, License plate 9SC 423," said Shannon into her walkie-talkie.

"10-4," responded a voice back to her on her radio. "Roger that," said another spokesperson.

"We need to get going. I appreciate the cooperation, folks," Alvarez said.

"Anytime, sheriff," John said with a look of satisfaction on his face. No more than his son Alvarez noted.

"Thanks again for the coffee Deena," Alvarez said.

"Anytime, sheriff," Deena said, repeating her husband's graciousness.

Alvarez stopped at the door and turned around as if he had forgotten something, as he addressed Jason directly. "Oh, by the way, if there is anything else that you may not have remembered when you called in the tip. Please give us a call and let us know."

Jason gave Alvarez the best fake smile he could put on before he responded. "No problem will do, sheriff," he said.

Alvarez looked at him and said nothing and smiled at him back in return. The difference was his was real because something in his heart told him that Jason knew more than what he was telling, but his parents might be in on it as well. And if they thought that bullshit that they just fed him was going to digest well with him like a good meatloaf and mashed potatoes dinner, his wife, Mrs. Alvarez, was known to whip up with a side dish of jalapeno cornbread. Then they just underestimated his intelligence and his taste buds, he concluded.

CHAPTER TWENTY-FIVE

*P*iper Industries, Chicago, Illinois. The crowbar that was sticking out of Jonathan Piper's chest that went through his heart hurt like shit. And by all accounts, if he had been merely mortal and of flesh and blood, he would have been deceased by now as he laid on the floor of his warehouse tugging and pulling at the crowbar that had just been plunged into his chest by a date he attempted to murder name Laura Pennington. She had gotten the best of him. He had to admit, as he tried to make her his midnight snack and add her to his lucrative blood plasma business. Luckily for her, he had underestimated her will to live and survive, and she had fought him bravely for the right as far as he was concerned to live another day. He had given her the impression that the crowbar through his chest was the endgame to his existence, but it was just a minor inconvenience to him as he tugged and pulled on it as it ripped through his flesh and cartilage.

Jonathan dwells on how Laura would undoubtedly bring back the authorities to his building after telling her wild tales of how a winged bat monster vampire was trying to kill her. And he had comatose bodies hooked up to blood bank machines that were siphoning their precious blood - all of the latter and present, which was true in one aspect or another. But one thing Jonathan knew, he could not get caught lying there on his back on a cold warehouse floor, looking like a dying vampire when she did so, and the authorities arrived. That he contemplated would not be a good look on Jonathan Piper and his company. No, not a good look at all.

One more good tug, he thought through clenched teeth, and then the damn wretched piece of metal should dislodge out of his heart and chest. Jonathan let out a scream which reverberated throughout the entire warehouse as the crowbar came out of him more quickly than he anticipated. His pupils and eyes turned alabaster white as he coughed up residual blood from the trauma of the metal stake coming out of his body as it continued to tear through flesh and bone.

"What took you so long, dear friend?" he said, with a broad vampiric smile on his face as he looked at the tall and muscular imposing figure of Iman, his driver standing above him with the bloody crowbar in his hand that he had pulled out of Jonathan's chest and heart.

Iman just smiled and nodded his head. "Yes, yes, morning traffic is a bitch indeed, but so are blind dates," Jonathan said.

Iman extended his hand to help his boss up off the ground. "No, no, no, just let me lie here for a moment and collect my bearings and my pride," Jonathan said, as he felt the rapid healing process of his injuries begin, such as the gaping cavity in his chest and his torn internal organs and ruptured heart.

Jonathan sprung to his feet as Iman then handed him a fresh shirt to put on. "Thank you, Iman," he said as he took the shirt from his chauffeur/personal assistant.

Jonathan beat his chest with one hand. "Like I said, back like new. But what a harrowing experience that was," he said, as he took the crowbar out of Iman's hand and bent it into a horseshoe shape and tossed it aside.

"Let's get this place cleaned up, Iman before we get the surprise arrival of other guests."

"I agree with you," Jonathan added. His telepathic link with his driver allowed him to read Iman's thoughts without Iman ever having to utter a single word to him and transfer his thoughts and will to Iman.

"I will get this clean up immediately, Sir," he heard Iman's voice say to him in his head. "Thank you," Jonathan replied telepathically to him as he made his way to his bar to fix himself a stiff drink to take the edge off of what had gone down last night between him and the blind date he had attempted to sadistically murder. Jonathan walked over to his full bar in the warehouse's penthouse suite and poured himself two shots of Remy Martin Louis XIII in a cognac glass and quickly downed the liquor in the hardball before pouring himself another two shots. The sound of his cell phone vibrating relentlessly on his bar counter caught his attention and took his mind away from the fiasco and Remy in his glass as he picked up the cellphone and answered the call.

"Hello, is this Jonathan Piper?" the voice asked on the other end of the phone.

"Yes, this is him. How may I help you," he said.

" Mr. Piper, this is Solo. I have been trying to reach you all day."

"Yes, Solo Chase. How is your antiquities business going? I take it you have something new you want to show me."

"The business is fine, and no, that's not why I called Mr. Piper," Solo said.

"Then why did you call?" Jonathan asked as he took another sip of his cognac.

"Luna Dye has escaped," Solo answered glumly, again getting straight to the point of his phone call."

"Oh' your werewolf problem," Jonathan said, unphased.

"Yes, my werewolf problem. I appreciate what you did, Mr. Piper, and I just felt you were entitled to know just in case you hear anything about her or she attempts to contact you."

"If she attempts to contact me, I assure you that will be the last time that you will hear about that rabid feral dog, Mr. Chase," Jonathan assured him.

"Although I admire your level of self-confidence, if I were you, I would not underestimate someone so blatantly dangerous," Solo said.

"Thanks for the warning Mr. Chase, but I doubt if I will lose any good sleep worrying about Ms. Dye showing up on my doorstep. But in case she does, you will be the first to know after I am finished with her," Jonathan said in an ominous tone of voice.

"Thanks, Mr. Piper, I respect your position," Solo said.

"Good, if you get a new artifact that comes in that you think might be of interest to me, please do not hesitate to give me a call," Jonathan added.

"Will do," Solo said as he ended the phone call. He knew Jonathan Piper was a rich, arrogant asshole with an elite security team at his disposal and contacts to the underworld. But he still felt that, and all the money in the world would probably not save Piper's Fortune 500 ass, if Luna wanted to get to him. Evident to him, though, after this conversation, Mr. Piper did not share his same convictions. Solo had done his job as far as he was concerned and warned him as a display of gratitude for his assistance in imprisoning Luna Dye. The rest was left up to Mr. Piper. Solo looked down at his watch on his wrist and realized that it was time to get going. He had a plane to catch to Harper Creek, South Dakota. To protect people that he knew did not have Jonathan Pipers' assets in this world but indeed to him was no less important.

" Thanks for the warning Mr. Chase, but I doubt if I will lose any good sleep worrying about Ms. Dye showing up on my doorstep. But in case she does, you will be the first to know after I am finished with her." Solo smiled as he grabbed his suitcase off his bed. If it was only that easy, he thought. Something told Solo not to wait for that phone call as he rushed out of his motel room to get to the airport.

CHAPTER TWENTY-SIX

Sheriff Alvarez had determined that the weather was now too dangerous to continue searching for the bank robber suspects up in the more rural area of Harper Creek because of the torrential rainfall and possible mudslides in the area. He believed that the suspects had not yet made their way entirely out of his town or County. He also thought that his twenty-four-hour checkpoint and roadblocks at the borderline out of his county line might be able to do one or two things dig them deeper in his territory wherever they were hiding or fish them out when they were trying to leave.

Special Agent Childs had already contacted him from the FBI Minneapolis office and notified him that he and his task force, due to the inclement weather, would not make it into Harper Creek until in the morning, which he expected would happen. That revelation left him and the game warden and their officers on their own, which he did not have a problem with working out the logistics of that disposition. But Alvarez was smart enough to know when it was time to pack it in and get back into the game with a fresh set of eyes and a clear head, especially when you were getting your ass kicked by unseen forces like the weather beating down on your head.

"You sure you want to wrap this up, Al?" Cody said.

"Yes, Cap. This weather is a wretched bitch right now, and it's not worth putting our personnel at risk," he answered.

Smith wiped the rain out of his eyes. "Yeah, I guess you're right. We gave it a good shot, huh?" he asked.

"Yep, and we will give it a better shot in the morning because I do not believe we are that far behind those assholes."

"You still believe that the suspects that hit our bank are lingering around in this area?" Smith said.

"Like stink glands on a skunk," Alvarez answered, sure of himself.

Smith smiled, and wiped the rain off his face. "I hope you are on the money with this one."

" I hope so too. I got a twenty-four-hour checkpoint and roadblocks set up at our borderline into the next County and a *BOLO* on that stolen 4runner," Alvarez said.

"Sounds good," Smith said.

Alvarez patted Smith on his shoulder and shook his hand. "Thanks again for your help Cap, I'll see you in the morning."

"Maybe," Smith yelled back, throwing his hands up as he headed back to his patrol vehicle.

Alvarez laughed at his response as he made his way over to his patrol vehicle to get out of the pouring rain where Shannon was patiently waiting for him inside.

"What are you thinking, Shannon?" he asked once inside the vehicle.

"How it would be nice to be out of this cold ass rain curled up on my sofa with a warm blanket over me with a glass of white wine watching reruns of *F.r.e.i.n.d.s,*" she said.

"Yeah, that would be nice," Alvarez said, which brought a smile and a chuckle from Shannon.

"Now, if you are asking about the suspects, I think they are somewhere nearby holding out until the coast is clear and this weather lets up," she said.

"I think you are correct, deputy, and if we are both right. I hope they catch the fucking Flu out here in the process."

Shannon started up the patrol vehicle, which rumbled to life as she revved the engine. "Something tells me Chief that may be the least of their worries out here," she said.

Alvarez smiled. "You know one day, Shannon, you are going to make a good sheriff," he said.

"Screw that I would rather be the Mayor and sit on my fat ass like Mallowater," she quipped.

"Nah, I think you are overqualified for that job," Alvarez said.

"Thanks, I'll remember not to use you as a job reference," Shannon said, laughing.

"Excuse me, Shannon. I have an incoming call," Alvarez said.

"Hello, Sheriff Alvarez."

"Hi Sheriff, I am afraid I got some horrible news to share with you," she said.

"Hello Doc, this whole day has been bad news. I doubt if your news can make it any worse," he reassured.

"You do, well try this one on for size, Sheriff.

"Do you remember Luna Dye?" she asked.

"Are you kidding me? How could I forget that monster," Alvarez responded.

"Well, that monster has escaped Romania and is reportedly headed this way for payback," Gina paused, waiting for what she had just told Al to sink in.

"Al, are you still here?" she said.

"Yes," he answered.

"I guess that old saying is true," he said.

"And what's that?" Gina asked.

Alvarez looked at the passenger window at the rain beating down on it before he responded. "When it rains, it fucking pours," he answered.

CHAPTER TWENTY-SEVEN

(THE DEADLY SIX)

J onathan Piper strolled through his warehouse, inspecting it for any signs of disorder after he had ordered Iman to get it cleaned up. He noted that Iman had done an excellent job as usual in the allotted time he had given him to complete the task. Because if a stranger had entered the warehouse now, they would have never been able to detect the mayhem that had transpired throughout the warehouse earlier. Whereas the human Sarah Pennington had been fighting for survival, fighting for her life.

He was surprised that he had not heard from the authorities yet, and he wondered if perhaps his last blind date Ms. Pennington, had maybe decided that it was not in her best interest to go to law enforcement about what had transpired there. After all, it had been two days now since the incident, and none of his stooges that he had on his payroll at Chicago P.D. had contacted him about any complaints filed against him. Maybe he should visit her; he thought to assure her silence.

Hell, maybe he was wrong, he thought as the sound of his doorbell buzzing echoed throughout the warehouse. Jonathan walked into his security room to see who was outside ringing his doorbell on his (CCTV) monitors. What in the hell, Jonathan thought? As he looked at the screens that did not show the presence of anyone. The warehouse doorbell buzzed again as he looked at the screens one more time closely, puzzled.

"Iman, check the outside perimeter, he ordered." Jonathan heard one of the roll-up doors rising in the warehouse. Seconds afterward, he watched on one of the security monitors as Iman walked out of the warehouse and opened one of the numerous roll-up doors to execute the directive he had sent him telepathically.

Jonathan scanned the camera around the outside perimeter but pulled up nothing but Iman inspecting the exterior grounds. "Nothing Sir, maybe it was just a malfunction," Jonathan heard Iman's voice in his head say as he went to meet him as Iman re-entered the warehouse.

Iman pushed a button on the wall's side next to the stainless steel roll-up door. As the door began lowering suddenly, a hand came underneath it and stopped it and began raising the over two hundred pound door back up with ease. Jonathan stepped back from the door in surprise as Iman withdrew the .44 magnum that he carried concealed. Jonathan quickly motions for him to stand down.

"Jonathan Piper," Luna said as she lifted the roll-up door the rest of the way up, which was now above her head and made her way with her crew slowly inside the warehouse.

"In the flesh," Jonathan said with a grin as he sized her and the rest of her team-up.

"Not to be inhospitable, but I do not recall extending you or your strays an invitation," he said.

"I dare you to say that again, punk!" Omar said.

Jonathan smiled. "I said, I do not recall extending…

"Enough!" Luna shouted out angrily.

"Look, nightwalker, we did not come here to play games, I just want to know before I kill you and your boy toy here," she said as she looked over at the hulking Iman. "How did you hook up with Solo Chase and play a role in my long vacation in Romania."

"Well, I never reveal any of my associates' information but now that you mention it, Luna, how was your vacation in Romania?"

Luna smiled. This Piper character was a real piece of work, she thought. " Thanks for asking, but If you must know, I overstayed my welcome," she said.

"Shit happens, I guess," Jonathan said condescendly.

"It sure does," Luna agreed as she watched Jonathan closely. She was aware that he was not someone to underestimate and that he could be just as deadly as he was charming. But little did she know he had heard the same thing about her through his sources.

"No, Iman, I think you are wrong," Jonathan said as he addressed his assistant.

"Who in the hell are you talking to, nightwalker?" Mako asked.

"My assistance here, of course," Jonathan said as he pointed at Iman.

"I did not hear him say one fucking word," Dean said.

"That's because he's the big handsome silent type," Jonathan shot back.

"But perhaps Luna, you may be able to settle me and Iman's disagreement."

"Regarding what?" Luna asked.

"Well, I told him that your team was known as the Bone Squad, but he seems to think it's the Blow Me Squad. Which one is it?" he asked.

Luna and her team started laughing as Jonathan looked on at them, amused.

"Rip them apart!" Luna shouted out angrily as her entire crew began shapeshifting into Lycans quickly.

Iman stepped back and drew his .44 magnum and let loose with the cannon against Luna and her team as they charged at him and his Boss. The bullets ripped through the fully formed muscular beasts tough skin but seemed to barely phase them as they came at the both of them with maniacal fierceness.

Jonathan's eyes turned bloodshot red as a surge of his abnormal strength as a vampire shot through his body. Omar lunged at him and was the first one upon him, but Jonathan quickly grabbed him by the throat and kept Omar snapping and growling jaws from ripping his throat out. He threw Omar off of him, and the Lycan went crashing into the Rolls Royce Phantom parked inside the warehouse. "Not my fucking car!" Jonathan yelled out! As he now felt one of the Lycans teeth sink into his hand, he quickly pulled away before it crushed his hand in its deadly jaws and struck the Lycan in its face with a powerful counter blow knocking the creature back off of him.

In Lycan form, Riley went in for the attack on Iman as he expended the last of his rounds from his .44 magnum at her. She grabbed him and threw all of his muscular six-foot-two frame (sliding) across the warehouse floor.

"Iman, do it!" Jonathan said telepathically to Iman.

"Are you sure, sir," he responded in the same? "Yes, now!" Jonathan shouted back as he assessed they were out-numbered, and it would be only a matter of time before the two of them would no longer be able to fight off Luna's ravenous pack of wolves.

Iman reached inside his jacket as he got back on his feet after being thrown to the floor and pulled out a black remote. Luna had not transformed herself and was still in human form. "What are you going to do with that thing? Change the channel," she said, laughing.

"Exactly," Iman answered back to her surprise as he pushed a button on the remote in his hand, immediately shutting off all the lights in the warehouse, sending Luna and her pack into pitch-black darkness. As the lights came back on amongst the growling and mayhem, Jonathan and Iman were gone, and the only thing visible as evidence of their presence was a blood trail that they both had left behind in their escape.

"Fucking cowards!" Luna growled, upset that despite her pack's natural night vision, the two men had somehow given them the slip.

"Not at all. We just wanted to even the playing field, my rabid friends," a voice echoed over the warehouse loudspeaker system.

Luna immediately recognized who the voice belongs to; it was Jonathan Piper's. As she felt a cold chill come over the warehouse as she stood in the middle of the floor flanked by her team of Lycans. A mechanical buzzing noise suddenly erupted and reverberated throughout the entire warehouse. As her Lycans grabbed their ears in pain from the shrilling ear-piercing sound, the temperature in the warehouse dropped so quickly and unnaturally that Luna could now see her breath.

She and her team now watched in awe as six black caskets ascended above them at a three hundred and sixty-degree angle, putting them in the center. "What in the fuck is this?" she shouted out.

Jonathan's voice came back again over the loudspeaker. "Sorry, Luna, that me and my assistant Iman had to leave so abruptly."

"No worries, I will see you again," she said as she looked at the loudspeakers.

"Maybe? Meanwhile, I have some of my wives that will keep you and your associates' company," Jonathan said.

"How lovely, " Luna said, as her keen senses were telling her it was time to go into fight mode, time to change. The ascended caskets begin opening slowly one by one as a cold mist first slithered out of each one. When the coffins were open, Luna and her pack could see a beautiful woman resting in each casket dressed in the same white gown. Despite their beauty and life-like appearances, she could smell the scent of death on each one of them. Luna watched as their eyes opened, and they all seemed to come to life at the same time in synchronicity.

They all glided effortlessly out of their caskets as if they were all ghosts or specters as they levitated above their vessels of death, staring below at Luna and her team through piercing illuminating pupils of crimson red.

"My, my, what do you call these creatures?" Luna said as her facial features began to change as she begins to shapeshift into a Lycan.

The sound of laughter erupted over the loudspeaker in response to Luna's question. "Your demise," Jonathan said.

"Kill them all and let the devil sort them out," Jonathan commanded his team of levitating assassins hovering over the Lycans.

All hell and mayhem now broke out as "The Deadly Six," whom they were referred to within his organization, began attacking the Lycans with brazen fearlessness that Luna and her crew "The Bone Squad" had never dealt with before. The vampires flew in like apparitions and began biting and slashing them with claws almost as deadly as the Lycans possessed.

Luna and her crew now fought an all-out battle with supernatural creatures that she soon learned were not your average vampires. These demons may not have been in beast form like them, but that had nothing to do with their lack of savagery and the abnormal strength that they displayed as they fought against seven-foot Lycans. They became like fucking oversized mosquitoes to her as soon as she swatted one off; another one was on her hairy seven-foot frame. In addition to that, as soon as they got a hold of one of them in their big, clawed hands, the deadly six vaporized into thin air and then manifested themselves out of the Lycan's grasp, which tactically made them a more lethal and formidable opponent.

Luna looked over at Mako, who had knocked one down to the ground in its physical state. She proudly watched as Mako tore into the vampire with his claws, spraying its dark blood all over its white gown. Mako went for the throat, but before he could administer the final death blow, the creature dissipated quickly into thin air. It was then it became clear to Luna it was like they were fighting fucking ghosts. Luna looked over at the six opened caskets and growled. Was it possible those coffins were their Achilles heel? She reasoned. If that is where these hell demons came from, she thought they would not be going back in them. She looked at her packmates, postured, snarled, and lunged at a casket, and began ripping it apart. The other Lycans followed suit and began tearing the other coffins apart despite being constantly attacked by the deadly six, slashing and biting at them ferociously.

"Nooooooo!" screamed one of the deadly six as it floated above the Lycans. Seeing there was only one casket left. It immediately flew inside the opened coffin, quickly followed by the others as the coffin closed shut when the last one was in and began descending underneath the floor before Luna or her pack could stop them from escaping. Luna begins punching the floor as the concrete starts to crack. The other Lycans joined in.

The lights to the Rolls Royce Phantom and the noise it emitted starting up stopped the Lycans in their tracks. Luna turned towards the massive automobile to see all of it 5644 lbs, now barreling down on her at more than one hundred miles an hour.

The car struck her head on as she toppled over the hood and landed on the floor. Her pack gave chase as the Rolls Royce sped out of the warehouse's opened roll-up door, but they soon gave up the pursuit due to their visibility and exposure to civilians.

Luna and her crew now begin to shapeshift back into human form. When they had finished, they all stood naked inside the warehouse.

"What in the hell are you looking at?" Riley said to Dean, who had a smile on his face as he gawked at her body.

"Let's get the hell out of here. This place smells like vampire shit," Luna said.

CHAPTER TWENTY-EIGHT

S am felt terrible that she had to tell Brandon on such short notice that she had to fly out back home, but really what other choice did she have? She thought as she packed her bags to make that trip back home to South Dakota. Their cat Hi-Cee sat on the bed watching her curiously as she stuffed some personals in a carry-on bag that she was bringing with her on the plane.

"Sam, are you sure you don't want me to come with you?" Brandon asked as he watched her prepare to leave.

"No, I'll be fine, it's just a few things that I need to take care of, babe, and I'll be back before you know it," she answered, downplaying the seriousness and urgency of her trip. Because the last thing that she wanted to do, she thought, was put Brandon's life unfairly at risk in South Dakota when he was already putting his life at risk on Chicago's dangerous streets as a detective. The less he knew as far as she was concerned about the pending danger she might be facing, the better. Also, there was a flip side to this matter concerning Luna, Sam determine. What if the information that Solo had provided about Luna coming back to Harper Creek panned out to be nothing more than a false alarm. She would not want Brandon worrying about her over nothing.

"Wow, I sure was not expecting you to be flying out like this. I had our whole night planned out," Brandon said disappointingly.

"I know, babe. I will make up to you when I get back. I promise."

"I look forward to that," said Brandon as he planted a kiss on Sam's cheek.

Sam bent over and stroked Hi-Cee on the bed, causing him to start purring. "Boy, you take care of daddy while I am gone, okay," she said.

Brandon lifted one of Sam's travel bags off the bed while she picked up the other one.

"I guess it's just you and me, boy," Brandon said to Hi-Cee.

"Try not to feed him too much sushi," Sam said, smiling.

"Are you kidding? Who can resist a sushi-eating cat," Brandon joked, causing Sam to bust out in laughter.

"My ride's here," Sam said as she looked at the rideshare application on her phone.

"Can I at least help carry your bags down babe," Brandon asked?

"Yes, that's the least you can do," Sam joked as she kissed Brandon on the lips.

* * *

As Luna and her crew walked back to their van and Harley's, they passed a homeless man in a nearby alley that happened to be enjoying his morning elixir as he observed them passing him in the buff. He stared at them in shock until they all got inside their black van and drove off. "Boy, this is some good shit," he babbled to himself as he turned the bottle over to read its ingredients through bloodshot eyes.

As he went back to enjoying his morning cocktail, the sound of an explosion nearby startled him and caused him to drop the liquor bottle as it exploded in pieces and expended its contents as it hit the ground. "Shit!" the man yelled out as he struggled to get to his feet. His buddy, concealed by a blanket over him, slowly came to as he shook him awake.

"What the hell was that Mo?" his mutually inebriated friend asked.

"I think that is the old Piper warehouse that just went up in flames down the street," he answered.

The Rolls Royce Phantom cruised down a stretch of Chicago's highway with a noticeable dent on the driver's side that no one would have ever guessed was put there by a seven-foot Lycan werewolf-like creature. No one except its occupants.

"I sure am going to miss that place," Jonathan said as he set the detonator aside on a tray inside his car next to a glass of cognac.

"Do you think the shapeshifters were still inside the warehouse sir," Iman asked, at the wheel of the big luxury car that probably cost more than the median price of a decent home in Illinois.

"Probably not," Jonathan said as he clipped the end of a Gurkha Black Dragon Cigar, lit it, and took a long puff.

"But I hope they get the message," he said, with a grin on his face.

"Where too?" Iman asked.

"Where no one can find us," Jonathan said.

* * *

The explosion was powerful enough to cause the black van to vibrate as it came to a screeching halt, including the three Harleys that flanked it ridden by some of Luna's crew. She looked behind her in the passenger's side mirror at the smoke and flames rising from Jonathan Piper's warehouse. "I guess that is what happens when you overstay your welcome," she said, as she finished buttoning up a western-style shirt she just put on.

"Check this out, boss," Wiz said as he handed Luna his cell phone.

Luna looked at the red moving dot pulsating against a map and route of intersection on the screen.

"Good job Wiz," she said as she tried to figure out during the brawl with the vampire specters when he had time to place a tracker on Piper's car. Not that it matters when? It only mattered that he did.

She handed Wiz back his cell phone. "Maybe after we are done in Harper Creek, we can pay our Dear friend Jonathan Piper another surprise visit," she said.

"Yes, I think he would like that very much," she added, as she displayed that one-hundred-watt smile of hers again, as the sound of sirens blaring from approaching fire engines resonated in the air. The black van took off again, creating as much distance from itself and now a five-alarm fire at Jonathan Piper's warehouse·

CHAPTER TWENTY-NINE

Needy listened as acutely as she could to every noise around her in the woods. It was no longer about preserving or getting out with the money that she and now most of her deceased crew members had robbed from the bank earlier. Her only and main concern now was survival and getting through this madness, and keeping herself and Hallie alive, as they made their way towards the main road.

"There is something in those bushes?" Hallie said as she got a glimpse of something reflecting back at her.

"What?" Needy responded as she raised her H&K, ready to unload it into anything that moved in front of them.

"Over there," moaned Hallie as she pointed in the direction where she was sure she had heard something.

"Are you okay?" Needy asked as she then watched Hallie bend over and grab her stomach in pain. "Fuck, I'll make it. Just a bad muscle cramp," Hallie answered as she gathered her composure.

"Holy shit!" Needy yelled out in excitement as they came upon what Hallie had seen hidden in the bush.

"How do you think it got down here?" Hallie asked as Needy began taking off the camouflage tarp that had also helped conceal the ATV except for part of its light bar that was left exposed and had given off the illumination when Hallie's flashlight had hit it, thus exposing itself to them.

"That's the million-dollar question, but at this point, who gives a shit Hallie, what you are looking at is our ticket out of this hellhole," Needy said, exuberated at what she thought was nothing short of a godsend.

"You are right; who gives a fuck? Let's see if this thing will start up," Hallie said, as she then began excessively coughing until blood came out of her mouth.

"What in the hell?" Needy said. She went over to Hallie and lifted her shirt to reveal a gaping wound in Hallie's stomach.

"We got to get you to a hospital," Needy said worriedly.

"Fuck that shit! Prison clothes doesn't look good on me," Hallie objected.

"Death doesn't either," Needy said as she proceeded to help Hallie get on the two-seater ATV.

"We are taking a vacation after this shit," Hallie said, coughing up blood.

"Sounds good to me. Where do you want to go?" Needy asked.

"Cancun," Hallie mumbled with her head leaned back on the headrest.

"Cancun, here we come," Needy said, as she said a little prayer in her head before she turned the key in the ignition to the ATV. The all-terrain vehicle rumbled to life to her relief. As she took off down the muddy dirt road, she had one thing on her mind: how to get around the checkpoint that she was sure that the local sheriff department had set up ahead.

"It's going to be okay; just hold on, Hallie," Needy said as she grabbed hold of Hallie's hand to comfort her. But somewhere in the back of Needy's mind, although she may have spoken those words of reassurance to Hallie. She knew that it would never be okay again. Besides the two knapsacks of money left, what did she really have to show for all the tragedy that had befallen them? But four of her team members dead. She thought - all of them which she felt personally and profoundly responsible for causing their deaths.

As the rain beat down on her face, she struggled to see ahead of herself in the dark as she bobbed and weaved down the road in the ATV to miss hazardous obstacles below and ahead. Needy wiped the rain from her face as she came to a smoother patch of road. She looked over to check on Hallie, who seemed to be teetering between semi-consciousness and unconsciousness.

Needy shook her arm. "Stay awake, Hallie, do not go to sleep on me," she said, worried, as she gripped the ATV steering wheel firmly. A prominent dark figure suddenly emerged from the clearance. It moved so quickly that Needy was barely able to comprehend what she saw. She swerved to avoid it, but it ran straight towards the ATV with no fear with a large, spiked club in its hand. As it closed in on the ATV, it took a swing at Hallie before she could react and draw her weapon and decapitated her with one blow as her severed head felled aimlessly to the ground. Needy looked over in shock at Hallie's convulsing headless body and began screaming and pushed the rest of her out of the ATV.

Needy looked behind her quickly. She could see the thing now closing in on her again, although she was doing close to 40mph. "Eat this motherfucker!" she screamed out as she let go of the steering wheel, grabbed her H&K, stood up, and began rapidly firing in the man-beast direction. A cry of pain erupted from the creature as one of the bullets pierced its shoulder. As Hallie turned back around to get back control of the all-terrain vehicle, it was too late as the vehicle not steered went over a muddy embankment flipping; she was ejected from the ATV and went rolling down the embankment. Needy tried to slow down the momentum of her descent as she heard the sound of rushing water below. Her nails bit into the hard mud, breaking and bloody as she attempted to anchor herself to something as she continued her descent into the river below. Needy hit the cold, muddy river below with force, knocking her unconscious as she was swept up in its strong currents. El, the man-beast, watched her from above with cold eyes as her motionless body floated downriver. He lifted the spiked club in his big hairy hand and admired Hallie's bloody eyeball embedded on one of the metal spikes.

CHAPTER THIRTY

The sound of the H&K being fired cracked the night air and echoed throughout the woods. "Did you hear that?" said Alvarez. "Yes, sounds like gunshots nearby," Shannon said.

"Turn down this road," Alvarez said, pointing to a dark patch of road ahead of them.

"All units, we got gunfire in this area, proceed with caution," Alvarez said into the mic.

"Stop!" Alvarez yelled out. As Shannon drove up to the edge of the cliff, almost going over.

"Fuck Chief, I am sorry I did not see that drop-off," she said, wiping her forehead nervously.

"No problem, I barely saw it myself," Alvarez said, to Shannon who responded with a shocked look on her face as they both exited the vehicle. She did not know if Alvarez was bullshitting or serious, but she did know if she had driven a few more feet, that would have been the endgame for the both of them.

Alvarez walked to the edge of the peak and shined his flashlight down the embankment as it illuminated part of the yellow Toyota 4 runner, mangled at the base of its drop-off.

"That's the car," Alvarez said.

Shannon quickly spun around, drawing her weapon at the sound of what she thought was something moving behind them in the thick of some trees nearby. "Who's there?" she shouted out, while shining her Maglite held above her weapon in the direction of those trees.

Alvarez followed suit, covering Shannon as he drew his weapon out behind her.

"This is Sheriff Alvarez; if there is anybody out there, come out with your hands up," he ordered as he shined his flashlight in the dense tree line ahead of them.

The beam of light from Deputy Shannon's flashlight hit and lit up the dead body ten meters in front of her instantaneously, sending a jolt of adrenaline to her fight and flight response. "Shit! Chief, we got a body over there!" Shannon yelled out.

She and Alvarez quickly rushed over to the body that appeared to be a female lying on her side with her back facing them. Alvarez leaned down and checked for a pulse. There was none. He then rolled the body towards him to see the victim's face causing her head that was not attached to separate from the body startling him and Shannon as they both looked on in horror, their eyes fixated on the headless body.

"Chief, what in the holy name of God could have done this?" Shannon asked.

"This is not done in the name of God. I can assure you also this is not holy," Alvarez answered.

"That's not what I meant, Chief," Shannon said.

"I know," Alvarez said as he inspected Hallie's headless body, her attire and the weapon still stuffed in the waist band of her pants. "I think we have one of the suspects that we were looking for," he said glumly, as he shines her flashlight at the ground to see if there were still fresh tracks made by the person that killed and decapitated her and left her at this spot. His flashlight hit and illuminated boot impressions in the mud next to a blood trail away from the body.

"Shannon, we got something here," he said as he stood up. They then followed the tracks and blood with his flashlight ten yards down, until he came to another body, this time a male that had been badly mutilated and appeared to be dead much longer than the first body that they had discovered by its state of rigor mortis.

"We got another one," he said.

"What in the hell is going on, Chief?" Shannon said nervously and wide-eyed as she took in the second dead body.

No, this cannot be happening again, Alvarez thought, as he stared at the second dead body, blocking out his deputy's question. Did something happen amongst the bank robbers, and they had turned on each other, and they were now thinning the herd, or was something else more ominous at play? He thought like his first suspicion. No, Elwood Holmes was dead, and the possibility of another Serial Killer in his town had to be highly unlikely and statistically improbable, he concluded.

"Chief, did you hear me?" Shannon said, breaking his train of thought.

"What?" Alvarez said.

"Do you know what the hell is going on here?" she asked.

"Maybe, no honor amongst thieves, I do not know," he said.

"You think one of their own did this?" Shannon asked.

Alvarez stroked his mustache. " Money makes people do strange things," he said.

Shannon looked back down at the body in front of her. "Well, this shit sure does fits the definition of strange," she said.

"Let's get this roped off; we need to get the Coroner's office out here as soon as this weather breaks, " Alvarez said.

"10-4 Chief," Shannon said as she went to go get the yellow crime scene tape out of the trunk of the truck as the sound of thunder cracked in the sky.

He looked back down at the mutilated deceased body in front of him and shook his head in anguish. "It wasn't worth it, was it?" he said to it sullenly.

CHAPTER THIRTY-ONE

amantha had not been gone more than an hour, and Brandon was already missing her presence, as he made his way over to their Minibar to fix himself a drink. He had no idea why it had been so damn crucial that Sam fly back home tonight to South Dakota other than what she had told him that it was about an urgent matter that she needed to address. Which was vague and ambiguous as far as he was concerned.

Brandon took a sip of the drink he made himself as he proceeded to answer the incoming phone call coming in on his cell phone.

"Hello, Detective Crust."

"Hey Brandon, are you interested in some overtime?"

"Sure, Lieutenant, what you got?" he said.

"Believe it or not, I just got a lady that just walked in our station and said she killed Jonathan Piper in self-defense."

"The heir to Piper Industries, you are bullshitting me," Brandon said.

"No, I am serious," Lt. Jamerson said dryly.

"Do you think she is a nutcase?" Brandon asked.

"If she is, she might be a pyromaniac also," Jamerson said.

"What do you mean by that?" Brandon replied.

'There was a five-alarm fire at one of Piper's local warehouses today," his lieutenant answered back.

"Shit," Brandon said.

"Yeah, "Shit" burned to the ground," Jamerson replied.

"Wow, I am on my way to the station," Brandon said as he sat down the drink, glad under the circumstances that he had not finished it.

"Do you need me to call Ty?" Brandon asked, referring to his longtime friend and colleague Detective Tyrone Johnson, his patrol partner.

"No, he is already en route," Jamerson answered.

"Okay, Lieutenant, I'll see you shortly," Brandon said, feeling somewhat jealous that Jamerson had called in Tyrone first on the case. He was now regulated to playing second fiddle on what might be the case of his life once the press got wind of the allegations against one of the most well-known up-and-coming businessmen in Chicago and multi-millionaire Jonathan Piper.

* * *

Brandon's precinct was bustling with activity from misdemeanor arrests to felony arrests. He walked in and greeted the evening desk sergeant and then made his way onto the secured elevator to Homicide, located on the building's third floor. There he was greeted by Lieutenant Jamerson and his partner Detective Johnson that had already done a pre-interview of the suspect that had entered the precinct voluntarily and confessed to killing Jonathan Piper.

"Johnson will fill you in, Brandon," Jamerson said after greeting him on the floor.

"You want one, Ty?" Brandon asked as he walked over to the hot beverages vending machine to get himself a vanilla latte.

"Yeah, thanks," Tyrone answered back.
Brandon stood in front of the vending machine patiently as he watched the tiny coffee cup drop and make him its programmed version of a vanilla latte at a discounted cost.

"What do we have here, partner?" he asked as he handed Tyrone off one of the cups.

"Something more complicated than I suspected," Tyrone answers.

"What do you mean?" Brandon asked as he sat down at his desk across from his colleague.

"The victim or offender, depending upon how you want to look at it, is Laura Pennington. A real estate agent that resides on the north side of Chicago. In the police report, she stated that she went on a blind date with Jonathan Piper a week ago. She also said that he not only sexually attacked her but attempted to kill her, but during the violent assaults, she ended up killing him instead in self-defense."

"So what's so complicated about that?" Brandon said, taking a sip of his latte.

Tyrone took a deep breath before he continued. "I'll be honest, Brandon, if Ms. Pennington did not tell me herself, I would not have known."

"Known what?" Brandon said.

"That she is a transgender person," Tyrone said.

"Well, what does that have to do with anything?" Brandon asked.

Tyrone cleared his throat before he spoke again. "Because she also claimed during her date with Mr. Piper she had been trying to tell him that information all evening to avoid any misunderstandings or hurt feelings when he displayed romantic interest in her."

"Interesting and understandable," Brandon replied.

"Yeah, but here when things get weird, she stated that after he expressed that interest, he already knew without her having to pursue the issue any further, so she agreed to go back with him to his place, and that's when she was attacked in one room in his warehouse that he had converted to a suite."

"Okay, and I am sure his story will be that he thought she was compliant, or why else would she go back to his place, etc.," Brandon said.

"Probably, but after she says he attacked her, he turned into a giant vampire bat monster and tried to kill her," Tyrone said.

Brandon spits out his coffee, causing Tyrone to jump back to avoid getting any of it on his clothes. "Sorry, I was not expecting that," Brandon said, wiping his mouth off and brushing the droplets from the coffee off his shirt and tie.

"You are fucking kidding me, right?" he asked, grabbing a tissue out of a nearby box to wipe his mouth off.

Tyrone chuckled as he pressed down his tie. "No, and this shit gets even weirder. She claims that he has some special room set up in the warehouse with numerous comatose victims he uses as his blood banks, recycling their blood through sophisticated IVs and tanks."

"Invasion of the Body Snatchers and a rapist Dracula all rolled up in one, that's a helluva blind date," Brandon said.

"Not my idea of a great date either," Tyrone said.

"But we were able to pull the tapes at Logan's and verify that the two of them were together the evening she mentioned."

"Yeah, I know the place. I'll see if I can make a couple of phone calls and get a hold of Mr. Piper to confirm if he is alive, dead, or missing in action," said Brandon.

Tyrone smiled. "Thanks, Brandon. I appreciate you putting your white privilege to use," he said sarcastically.

Brandon chuckled and gave Tyrone the middle finger. His best friend Tyrone knew he came from money and privilege, but he never got the impression once that their friendship was connected to that factor in any shape or form. And that was just one of the things that he loved about the guy who he felt like was a brother to him as well, that he would put his life on the line for if necessary. And he did not doubt in his mind, Tyrone would do the same for him without hesitation. See, there was one thing Brandon had learned early on in his life, being brought up in wealth and privilege and that is the one thing money was incapable of buying was real friendship and loyalty. No, that had to be earned through mutual respect and trust he felt.

White privilege or not though he knew the last name Crust alone opened doors for him that would typically be closed to the average person. "Yes, I would appreciate it if you could do that. Okay, thank you, he said to the person on the other end of the phone.

Brandon looked at Tyrone and shook his head sideways for No, then looked at his watch on his wrist. "What interview room is she in?" he asked.

Tyrone threw up two fingers.

"Okay, then let us not keep Ms. Pennington waiting any longer than we have to," Brandon said.

* * *

"Hi, I am Detective Crust. May I call you Laura," Brandon asked as he entered the interview room with Tyrone and introduced himself to the complainant Laura Pennington? "Sure," Laura said as she shook Brandon's extended hand. After going over her rights with her that Laura waived, Brandon got straight to the point.

"Laura, I know you are already familiar with Detective Johnson and that he has spoken with you about the incident that you say transpired on your date with Jonathan Piper. Is that correct?" He said, careful not to say anything yet about murder.

Laura nodded her head nervously in agreement as she sat in her chair across from Brandon with her hands folded in her lap.

Wow, Tyrone was right, Brandon thought. She was a gorgeous woman. It was nothing ambiguous about her that told the eye of the beholder otherwise.

He looked at his watch again before sitting down in one of the three chairs in the interview room. It was about that time now, he thought.

"So, it is our understanding that you stated, "Jonathan Piper attacked you at his warehouse." "No, he attempted to kill me," Laura said, interrupting.

"Kill you, and you fought back, killing him instead, in self-defense," Brandon said, correcting himself.

"Yes, that is correct. I stabbed that monster through the chest with a crowbar," Laura said, unwavering. As knocking on the outside of the door interrupting the interview. "Come in," Tyrone said.

"Brandon, you got a phone call," said a tall, middle-aged colleague of theirs.

"Thanks, Joe, excuse me for a minute Laura, while I take this call," he said.

"Can I get you another coffee or pop?" he asked.

"No, I am fine," Laura said, as she nervously cupped the can of diet pop on the table in front of her."

After a few minutes had passed by, Brandon returned, looked over at Tyrone, and nodded his head in affirmation of the phone call that he had just received as he sat back down in the chair to continue his interview with Laura.

"Laura, you say that you killed Jonathan Piper in self-defense a week ago, correct?"

"Yes, how many times do I have to say it," Laura answers, annoyed.

"Well, that phone call I just took was a video conference call from Mr. Piper himself, and I can assure you he is alive and well," Brandon said.

"Impossible," Laura said as she looked on in shock and awe.

"To be dead and alive at the same time, yes," Brandon answered.

"I can take you to the warehouse and show you the bodies that he has comatose and using as a fucking blood bank beehive!" Laura said.

"His warehouse burned down today, Laura, and we have received no reports so far of any bodies burned or recovered on his property," Tyrone said.

"What?" Laura said, almost unable to believe what she had just heard.

"If you want to pursue the sexual assault charges against Mr. Piper, we can turn that investigation over to Sex Crimes," Brandon said.

"Are you fucking kidding me? I see the way you two are looking at me like I am some mental case," Laura retorted.

"We never implied that," Brandon replied.

Laura hurriedly gathered up her things, keys, and coat. "Fuck this! I know what I did, and I know what I saw."

"You both are so fucking totally in the dark," she said.

"Maybe," Brandon said softly.

"Am I free to go?" Laura asked.

"You wouldn't have any information regarding his warehouse burning down today?" Tyrone asked.

"No, am I free to go?" she asked again.

"Yes, Ms. Pennington, unless you have something to add to what you have told us," Tyrone said.

"I do," Laura said.

"It was a mistake coming here thinking that the police could help."

As that statement sank in, Brandon and Tyrone escorted Laura out of the interview room and off the floor. "Wow, what in the hell was that all about?" Tyrone said. Brandon remained quiet as he contemplated that question himself.

* * *

The Boeing 747 that Sam was now on was a nonstop red-eye flight to South Dakota. Sam had a window seat next to a well-dressed passenger, her senior decked out in business attire with her head and thoughts buried in *The Economist* magazine's recent publication. Sam noticed that her fellow passenger did not appear all that interested in chitter chatter or making her acquaintance, which was fine by her. Frankly, all she wanted to do was take a nap and rest a little if that was possible before she arrived at her final destination.

Sam put a pair of earbuds in as she accessed her playlist on her iPhone. She scrolled down her playlist and tapped the song *Sailing* by Christopher Cross. As the song began to play, she turned her night light off and reclined her seat slightly back to get more comfortable. *"We are now cruising at an altitude of thirty-one thousand feet."* The pilot said over the plane's (PA system).

She looked over at her neighbor, who was now ordering a rum and coke from one of the flight attendants. Sam signaled no to the attendant when he asked if there was anything he could get her, some snacks, or beverages. Sam closed her eyes and attempted to get as comfortable as she could in her seat as her music shut out the aircraft's noise in the background.

The red-eye flight was dead silent now as Sam woke up inside an airplane cabinet that was a lot darker than when she had fallen asleep. She looked down at her watch and realized that it would not be that long before her plane should be touching down at Rapid City Regional Airport. Sam removed the earbuds and put them and her phone inside a small purse. She raised the shade on her window to get a night time view of the sky as she looked out the small window.

Within seconds of raising the shade, Sam thought she spotted something moving outside on the aircraft's wing. No, it cannot be, she thought. It must have been a trick of light or shadows. She thought as she looked back out the window again, only to see nothing there. Sam turned to her neighbor, who was reclined back with a sleep mask on her face and sleep dribble running down the corner of her mouth and her impeccably applied make-up.

Sam looked back out the side window again, and this time it was no mistaking what the thing was that was looking back at her with glowing amber eyes as it snarled at her revealing its black gums and dagger-like teeth. Sam recoiled back in horror as she tried to grasp what she had just seen.

She turned to wake up her neighbor but discovered that she was no longer there, just her sleep mask laying on her chair. What in the hell? Sam thought. Sam had not heard her neighbor get up out of the seat right next to her. Not only was she seeing things she thought but was she going deaf also she thought.

"Fuck!" Sam yelled out as she grasped the armrest to her seat tightly as the plane violently shook. A sense of overwhelming danger and fear that things were not right on the plane begins to creep over Sam as she tries to stay in control of her emotions. Sam hit the service button above her to summon a flight attendant to her seat.

The plane rumbled and shook violently again, almost throwing Sam out of her seat. The air pressure suddenly dropped rapidly in the cabin. Her oxygen mask and her neighbors dropped down in front of their faces. Screams of panic and shock erupted amongst her fellow passengers on the plane. As the Boeing 747 now appeared to be descending rapidly in a fatal nosedive.

Sam watched as a flight attendant made her way towards her that could barely stand on her feet. A primal growl erupted from behind the flight attendant as a massive creature behind her took one swipe at her neck and decapitated her head from her body, causing it to land on a nine-year-old passenger's lap. The young passenger began screaming in horror as she knocked the wide-eyed, gaping mouth head off her lap.

Sam spotted the businesswoman that was sitting next to her come out of the bathroom disheveled and confused. She yelled out at her to go back into the bathroom and lock herself inside. As the woman responded, fumbling haplessly with the bathroom door to get back inside, another creature savagely attacked her from behind, taking the door and her down at the same time, in a violent blur of feral rage.

The realization set in quickly with Sam that werewolves had now overtaken the plane as they savagely ripped into the passengers. Sam rushed towards and made her way to the cockpit where she found both pilots, the Captain and Co-pilot dead with their throats viciously ripped out. Sam picks up the captain's mic and begins trying to contact air traffic control.

"Mayday Flight: 1810 is in distress, Mayday, please respond."

"Air traffic control, Flight: 1810 I read you loud and clear what is the problem?"

Sam looked behind her nervously as she could now hear the creatures trying to breach the cockpit's security door that she had locked behind her.

"Air traffic control, Flight: 1810 I read you loud and clear what is the problem?"

The Captain suddenly sprung to life and grabbed the aviation headset off of Sam's head.

"We got Motherfucking werewolves on this Motherfucking plane!" he shouted into the headset's mic, before going unconscious again.

As the 747 plummeted down like a burning comet in the nighttime sky, Lycan (werewolf) like creatures covered the outside hull of the plane like a contagion as they attempted to breach its fiery hull.

"Dear, are you okay," her neighbor asked as she shook Sam awake.

"Yes, sorry, bad nightmare," Sam said, embarrassed.

CHAPTER THIRTY-TWO

Don Chumpski rolled into Mayor Mallowater's office on a customized motorized wheelchair that he had nicknamed "Sweet Ass." He even had the affable nickname stitched and personalized on his chair's back and painted on its wheel wells in flaming letters. It was a new lifestyle for Chumpski due to a vicious animal attack that he had suffered years ago on his property that had left him paraplegic and his handyman William Fletching dead.

"Hey, Ritchie boy, how it's going?" Chumpski said as he rolled into the empty spot in front of Mallowater's desk, reserved for the guest office chair that the mayor had removed to accommodate him. "Fine, Don and you?" Mallowater said with a fake smile on his face, pretending that he was looking forward to Chumpski's visit. He was not.

"Oh, just trying to get a leg up on things," Chumpski joked as he wheeled himself in front of Mallowater's desk.

Mallowater did not know if it was appropriate or not for him to laugh at his comment, so he just uncomfortably cracked a half-ass smile.

"It's okay, you stiff son of a bitch to laugh, it was a joke," Chumpski said, chuckling. Mallowater let out a short chuckle himself to please Don as he sat behind his desk. He leaned back in his chair, hands folded, as he thought about a million ways he could tell Don this new information that Sheriff Alvarez had just given him. And he concluded no matter how he told him. It was still going to come out well, shitty.

"Ritchie, you look like someone just stole your joy. What's up?" Chumpski asked.

"Don, you remember the shit this town went through four years ago?"

"How could I not? It put me in fucking this wheelchair," Chumpski answered.

"Oh, by the way, how do you like my new wheels?" Chumpski said, changing the subject as he rubbed the armrest to his new motorized chair.

"Nice," Mallowater said.

"You bet your sweet ass!" Chumpski said, grinning as he spun the chair around quickly with the toggle of a small joystick mounted on one of the armrests. The back of the chair and its nickname - Sweet Ass, facing Mallowater.

"How impressive," Mallowater said as he watched Don turn the chair just as quickly back around to its original position.

"Yeah, I was thinking about at first nicknaming it "Kiss my ass" as a tribute to you," Chumpski said, laughing. "What?" Mallowater retorted, not amused.

"Just fucking with you Ritchie, what's got your tighty whities all twisted?" Chumpski asked.

"Don, I just got information from Sheriff Alvarez that the trouble that we had four years ago might be coming back to pay us a visit, and we need to prepare ourselves and our town."

"What kind of craziness are you talking about, Ritchie boy?" Have you been snorting the fillings out of those jelly doughnuts again?"

Mallowater did not immediately respond as he looked over Don Chumpski. Yes, he was empathetic that Don's ability to walk had been taken away from him, and Don had almost lost his life in the process from the vicious attack he had suffered and endured from the beast that had visited and wreaked havoc on their small town. But after all was said and done about this matter, one thing he could not deny. His fair-weather friend Don Chumpski, after all these years and despite his disability, was still an ostentatious asshole. He was just an ostentatious asshole in a wheelchair now.

"Look, Don, I know you want to believe that you were just a victim of a wild animal attack that ripped your legs off and Midnight's head; if that makes you feel good, Hell, go with it."

"But that still does not explain all the other twisted shit that happened back then."

"Watch your cocoa butter-loving mouth about my dog Midnight, you asshole!" Chumpski barked out loudly and visibly upset. Mallowater stood up and walked away from behind the desk, closer to Chumpski, who was still upset by what he had said. He had not intentionally set out to hurt his feelings but damn if the asshole did not know all the right buttons to push when it came to him.

"Look, Don, I am sorry about what I said about your dog," he apologized – giving him a one-time pass on his bigotry and an apparent crude reference to his African American wife.

He had not noticed it before, but Chumpski was now shaking uncontrollably. What the hell was he having a stroke, Mallowater thought. "Don, are you okay?" Mallowater asked.

Chumpski looked up at Mallowater, slowly head-shaking, and motioned for him to come closer. "What the hell, Don? Are you okay?" he repeated himself as he leaned in closer to Chumpski. That's close enough; Don said to himself as he hauled back and punched Mallowater in his jaw, sending him sprawled out to the floor.

"You sonofabitch!" Mallowater said, holding his jaw.

Chumpski laughed. "That's for Midnight," he shot back. As he shook the soreness out of his hand that he just punched Mallowater in the face sneakily.

Mallowater rubbed his jaw as he got back on his feet. "I thought you were having a stroke, you old shit stain!"

"I don't need your empathy, you little prick," Chumpski said.

"I ought to kick your fat ass up out of that wheelchair," Mallowater threatened with a menacing look on his face.

Chumpski put his fingers under his tongue and let out a loud dog whistle.

Mallowater watched as a large white German shepherd pushed his unlocked door open and ran over to the side of the Chumpski. As he petted the dog on top of his head, the dog looked at Mallowater and started growling.

"If I were you, I would reconsider what you just said," Chumpski said, grinning.

"When you get him?" Mallowater said nervously, never taking his eyes off the dog, as he backed away from Chumpski.

"He is a her, and her name is Daytime," Chumpski answer. "Well, that is the stupidest goddamn name for a dog that I ever heard," replied Mallowater.

Chumpski dog rose from a sitting position and began growling again. "Down girl, down."

"Watch your mouth, Ritchie. Has anyone ever said that your last name Mallowater sounds like something you want to drink and piss right back out?"

"I don't give a shit about your dog - Daytime, Afternoon, Evening, or whatever time of the stupid fucking day you want to name it! But I do give a shit about our town," Mallowater shouted out angrily and red-faced.

Daytime growled. "Shut up, mutt!" Mallowater said. Which seemed to do the trick as Daytime let out a whimper and sat back down.

Chumpski looked at Mallowater, surprised with his mouth agape. "Mine, mine, look who just grew a pair," he said. " You are going to have to get big boy pants now, Ritchie."

"Don, look - I did not invite you to my office to blow smoke up your ass. Trouble is on its way, and if we are not ready this time, we might not have a town left this time when it leaves." A knock on the door interrupted them. "Come in," Mallowater said.

Chumpski's mouth dropped as Jay Fletching entered the room.

CHAPTER THIRTY-THREE

"**H**i Don," Jay said to his longtime friend that he had not seen in years. Chumpski continues to stare at him as if he had seen a ghost. Not that it mattered to Jay because he already knew what was going through Don's mind. When did they let him out of the loony bin? *Greenwood Psychiatric Hospital.*

"Jay, it's been a long time, huh, Bud?" Chumpski said. "Yes, a very long time, Don," Jay answered.

"Well, are you going to come over here and give me a fucking hug or what? As you can see, I ain't exactly as mobile as I used to be," Chumpski said.

"No, all I see is you sitting there on your sweet ass," Jay countered. Chumpski laughed. "Yeah, she's a beauty, isn't she?" he said, patting his wheelchair.

"Jay looked at Chumpski's dog, whose full attention he had. He looked back at Chumpski.

"Oh' relax, girl," Chumpski ordered his dog, Daytime.

Jay walked over to Chumpski and leaned over, and embraced his old friend.

"It's been a long time Jay," Chumpski said.

"Too damn long, you old redneck," Jay said, smiling.

"Why in the hell did you not tell me Jay would be here?" Chumpski asked Mallowater angrily.

"What in the hell gave you the impression that I knew," Mallowater shot back.

Chumpski looked back at Jay, confused. "He is right. He did not know," Jay responded.

"What in the hell is going on?" Chumpski asked.

"What Richard is telling you is the truth Don," Jay said, as Mallowater placed him a chair to sit in that came from out of the corner of his office. "Thank you," Jay said as he sat down.

Mallowater reached inside his desk and pulled out a Manilla envelope, and handed it over to Chumpski. "Please look at these," he asked.

Chumpski took the mayor's envelope, took the pictures out inside, and began attentively flipping through them. "What in the hell happened to him?" He said, holding one of the pictures up that showed a man sprawled out on the floor of a gas station ripped apart by what looked like a wild animal of some kind.

"The same thing that happens to you, but only worse, he's dead," Mallowater answered solemnly.

"Can I see those pictures," Jay asked. "Sure," Mallowater said. Chumpski handed Jay over the pictures.

"I wonder when did wild bears or wolves start visiting gas stations causing this kind of carnage," Jay said as he flipped through the gruesome pics as well.

"Never," Mallowater bluntly answered. "Exactly," Jay agreed.

"Mayor, as much as I miss my friend sweet ass over here, I take it that this is not business as usual," Jay said, looking over at Chumpski that was still looking at him like he was looking at a ghost.

"Years ago, this town said you were bat shit crazy, Jay, but you were right!" Mallowater said.

"How so?" Jay said, loving every bit of this, even if it was a half-assed apology from the Mayor himself.

"This town had a werewolf problem, and now from what credible sources told me, that problem may be coming back to haunt us again soon."

"That's not the only problem we had in case you have forgotten," Chumpski said.

" Don, If you are talking about our own local grown "serial killer" Elwood Holmes, that asshole is dead!" Mallowater said with a huff.

"Yeah, so I hear, but they never did recover his body in that river, did they?" Jay asked, skeptical.

"Yes, but that doesn't make him no less dead!" Mallowater said defensively.

"So, what's the plan?" Jay asked, getting back on the subject of the werewolf issue at hand.

"We protect our goddamn town by any means necessary," said another voice that did not belong to any of the three men that had been conversing.

Jay turned around in his chair and smiled at Cody, who had just entered the room.

"Sounds like a plan to me," Jay said.

"How did you know?" Mallowater asked Cody.

"Alvarez told me I might want to get my shit kickers over here so that I can be in the loop."

"We got a…. "A werewolf problem, I already heard," Cody said, cutting Mallowater off in mid-sentence.

"Ritchie boy, anything you need, I am here for you," Chumpski said, this time with not a hint of sarcasm or contempt in his voice to Mallowater's surprise.

"I appreciate that, Don," he responded. Daytime, Don's dog whined his approval as well.

CHAPTER THIRTY-FOUR

Luna and her crew, the Bone Squad, now roared ominously down the highway in a convoy formation inside a black van and on motorcycles headed to South Dakota. Final destination: Harper Creek. She wanted fucking answers from this little shit of a town that had somehow conspired with her ex-lover Solo Chase and had managed to her humiliation, capture her, and ship her off to Romania to the bloodsuckers for a life of imprisonment and servitude. But they, like everybody else, had underestimated her, she thought. And for that Faux Pas, she had decided, Harper Creek would now pay the ultimate price.

Luna leaned back on the headrest as she watched the scenic landscape quickly being chopped up in only momentary glances and flashes as they barreled down the highway. She closed her eyes and reflected on Solo Chase's past and how she had not seen the Hansel & Gretel traps that he had set in place for her at Harper Creek. Why him? She thought. Why him? As she begins to drift off to sleep to the sound of the van's wheels humming on the tar paved highway. As she begins to drift off for the first time, she lays eyes on him again at Stone Hill Manor.

* * *

The antiquities and rare art exhibit were a function held annually for the serious collectors, buyers, and connoisseurs of those hard-to-find pieces of artifacts that were all brought together to be put on display or auctioned off.

This year the black-tie affair was being kicked off in Shreveport, Louisiana, at a Victorian estate called Stone Hill Manor.

The gala was now in full function and attendance. The champagne was flowing, and the deals were being made, not necessarily in that order. The young and dapper dressed gentleman conversed with some like-minded associates about a piece that he had seen earlier when he noticed the young woman by herself across the room from him at the cocktail bar. It wasn't so much her he had noticed if he were to confess, but it was the red dress she wore. That dress appeared to cling to every curve of her body like it was painted on her. He was captivated by her. And as he continued to observe her from a distance, it became apparent he wasn't the only admirer in the room that had made this consensus.

Within a few seconds of her catching his eye, he attempted to be discreet about his interest as he curiously observed more than one hawk approach her at the bar. The way they left after their brief encounter with her told him that she was nice enough to let them depart with most of their pride intact. How benevolent of her, he thought. It wasn't just the red dress he found captivating, but the woman that wore it as well. She was a natural beauty already with dark hair that was put up in a sophisticated French Twist, with tendrils of flowing hair along the side of her face. Sure, the red dress was a break from the norm that the other women were wearing at the function, but her distant admirer noticed no one at the gala seemed to mind.

He glances over at her again to only see that she was gone from the cocktail bar. Oh? Well, he thought. At least he still had his pride intact.

As a waiter came by, he set his empty champagne glass on a silver tray; the waiter held prop up in one hand and was given a refill by the waiter in return. When he looked, the lady in the red dress was now just several feet in front of him, conversing with some of the other attendees.

She was just as lovely close up, he thought, as she was far away, and he could not help wondering what she looked like out of that red dress.

He suddenly felt more than a tinge of guilt for objectifying her in his mind, but it was just a tinge. She felt his presence and looked at him and smiled. That is when their eyes met. He smiled back nervously, not sure if her smile was intended for him or some other lucky bastard in the room. Sure, he was tall, handsome, and quite dapper in his tux. But so were the other men that she had rejected at the bar. Thus, he wonders if she was out of his league.

He was new to this business of buying and selling unusual antiquities and art. And even newer to women like the one in the red dress.

The young man suddenly felt an urge to get a confirmation of that smile. He cordially excused himself from his entourage and made his way over to the mysterious woman in the red dress before he lost sight of her again. It would be easy to do. He figures in a large guest room such as this.

"Here goes nothing," He says to himself as he takes a sip of his refill and walks over to introduce himself to the mysterious woman. "Hello, forgive me for staring, but I felt compelled to come over to you and introduce myself. The young man stated with a newfound air of confidence.

My name is Chase, Solo Chase, and yours?"

The stunning young lady smiles in the red dress, revealing a set of pretty white teeth, lips trimmed with a lipstick shade that matches her dress. She extends her one free hand in greeting; the other is holding the champagne.

"Please to meet you, Mr. Chase; my name is Luna Dye, and what's your pleasure?"

"You at the moment," smartly he said, as he takes her extended hand and kisses the top of it.

Luna smiles again, revealing those almost perfect white teeth of hers, and it is then when Solo notices her canines are almost vampiric in appearance. He assumes she's unlikely a vegetarian with a set of choppers like that.

"Wow, what an amazing smile you have," Solo said.

"It's the mutt in me," Luna said with a wink.

"What can I say? I like my meat."

Solo assumed correctly.

"Unlike these skinny vegetarian bitches, walking around here," she added.

Solo laughs.

A waiter comes by with a platter of sushi and offers them some. Luna declines as Solo takes one of the delectable little morsels from the waiter's platter.

"I take it you're not a big fan of sushi?" Solo asks.

"Only when it's stuffed with prime rib," Luna responds.

"A true carnivore, huh?"

"In ways, you couldn't imagine," she answered as she took a sip of her champagne.

"And what brings you to this event?" Solo asks, still inquisitive with the questions.

"The same thing that brings you to this event, Mr. Chase."

"And what's that exactly if you don't mind me asking Ms. Dye?"

"Let's just say I am a collector of hard-to-find things," Luna said. As she then took a sip of her champagne.

A voice coming over the guest room's installed loudspeakers suddenly interrupted their conversation.

"The next auction on the Mandarin collection will start in five minutes. All guests willing to participate, please be present and seated in room A."

Solo thinks to himself hard to find things, although he wasn't quite sure what Luna meant by that.

If he had known now what he would eventually discover later, he would have left his curiosity with a simple glance and a smile at her doorstep.

But truth be told, his reality didn't work that way. Luna Dye's influence over men didn't work that way.

"Here's a toast too hard to find things," Solo said with a grin as his glass clanged with Luna's.

"And moonlight specials," she added.

"And moonlight specials," he repeated as they took a sip of their champagne.

As Solo stared into her eyes, he now notices that Luna's eyes appeared to have an almost amber glow to them with flickers of yellow light around the irises, or was it too much champagne?

* * *

The red dress fell slowly to the floor, revealing a curvaceous body underneath it. Luna's skin was soft and supple and her nipples hard as she leaned against his muscular naked body.

She unpinned her French twist as her long locks cascaded to her shoulders.

Luna had the most beautiful body he had ever laid eyes on and legs that wouldn't quit. Solo wanted those legs wrapped around his back while he explored her with his mouth.

"Are you okay?" a voice asks, breaking him from a dream-like state.

He was back in the guest room as the sound of other people talking came flooding back to his senses; he was not alone with her, although it had all seemed so real.

"What the hell had happened? Solo wondered. It was as if he had momentarily blacked out.

The familiar voice from earlier before came back over the loudspeakers. *"All guests that have chosen to participate in the next auction, will you please proceed to room A."*

Luna looked at Solo and extended her arm. "Shall we?" she said.

Solo nodded and smiled and locked his arm with hers. He could feel the eyes on his back.

"How the hell did he get her?" The other men were probably whispering amongst themselves, he thought.

"Heck," truth be told, if he were on the outside looking in, he probably would have asked himself the same damn question? Why had she chosen him? A beautiful and sophisticated woman with the shapeliest ass and body, all tucked neatly in a red dress.

"Hell," did it matter? Solo concluded. This evening, he was the luckiest man alive at Stone Hill Manor. The other male guest's envy was evident, and the female guest's jealousy was equal.

Though in reality and unknown to Solo. The red dress had been studying him and watching him from afar all night.

Yes, suffice to say, she had been watching him like wolves watch their prey before the slaughter.

Because in reality, it was not Solo that had chosen her, but Luna who had chosen him.

Luna, unknown to him, had already implanted herself in his psyche the minute Solo had laid eyes on her. He will do well, she thought. After all, she was herself, a collector of things that were hard to find, including humans.

Later that night, after the gala was over, both would retreat to one of the many reserved rooms for guests in the manor and make passionate love to each other all night long.

Her fantasies that she had implanted in Solo's mind she would fulfill many times over and more. Luna would soon become like an addictive drug to Solo as their relationship progressed. The more he had of her, the more he would want.

Only when Luna knew that she had him lock, stock and barrel would she then turn him.

Unfortunately for Solo, as far as Luna was concerned, that decision was not his to make either. She was like a pathogen, one that would spread throughout his body and mind.

Meanwhile, not too far from Stone Hill Manor, as they embrace in the throes of sensual intimacy, howling erupted in the distance of the night.

Solo abruptly awakened by something that sounded like an animal, or was it a human? He could not tell. As he laid on the satin sheets, he instinctively reached over for Luna, and that's when he discovered she wasn't there with him. He called out her name but no answer.

Solo got up out of bed and began getting dressed; that is when he noticed that the red dress she was wearing was no longer on the bedroom floor either. He left the Manor's guest suite and went looking for Luna throughout the estate but could not find her to any avail. It was as if she had disappeared altogether after giving him the most mind-blowing and stimulating experience on an intimate level that Solo had ever shared with any woman. As much as he hated to admit it, he doubted that he had pleased her sexually as much as she had satisfied his desires. It was almost as if she were insatiable, and Solo could not help wondering what other secrets she had? While searching for her throughout the Manor. Had he bitten off more than he could chew? Solo looked at his watch on his wrist; it was now 4:00 am: even the staff had retired to their quarters, and the mansion was deathly quiet now, almost too silent. Solo started to feel strange about creeping around the estate at this time of the hour and did not want to gain a reputation as a house guest if caught prowling and snooping around at this ungodly hour on someone else's property.

He decided it was best now to retreat to his guest room. Solo wondered now if he had made too much out of his encounter with the mysterious women? Maybe he was just a one-night fling to the red dress, and she left, he thought. As he enters his suite, all the previous thoughts that he had in his head begin to disappear, as the first thing he notices is Luna sprawled out on the bed between the satin sheets asleep.

He notices that the bedroom window is now open as the sheer curtains flutter from the cool breeze. The red dress is now also lying where it had fallen earlier on the floor.

Had he overlooked it? He wondered and missed her passing him in one of the corridors, he thought. But how could that be? Solo walked over to the window and closed it. Luna did not stir and appeared to be sound to sleep.

The third thing he noticed made his heart beat a little faster and his mouth go dry. Solo eyes followed the dirty footprints on the floor from the window to the bed where Luna laid. He slowly walked over to Luna, where she slept.

Solo pulled the satin sheets off her feet. They were, as he suspected, covered with dirt as if she had been walking on the outside breeches of Stone Hill Manor. Could she be sleepwalking, he presumed. But that still did not explain the footprints from the open window leading back to the bed? It was as if that had been her port of entry back into the room. But how could that be, he thought? How could she climb in such a short time that he was gone three stories back up to the room? Impossible, he thought, or was it? He ponders as he looks back at Luna suspiciously on the bed.

* * *

Louisiana was notorious for its torrential rainfalls and the following day was no exception to that kind of day in the bayou.

The guest that offered overnight accommodations had all but left and were now on their way home by whatever form of transportation they took to get there. Those were the guests that would be returning to the repetitiously mundane aspects of their lives. One of them would not be that fortunate, though.

The groundskeeper was the first to discover the badly mutilated body as if it had been mauled and eaten by a wild animal. Later on, that day on the estate's property after the rainfall had let up. After the police had done their investigation, they determined that the victim had indeed been one of the many attendees and an overnight guest at Stone Hill Manor.

It was also determined and concluded; that the guest had most likely become intoxicated, wandered, and strayed too far away from the Mansion near the woods' swampy area. Most likely became disoriented and ended up near the swamp.

The local police summed up when the guest foolishly decided to take a skinny nighttime dip in the bayou, the guest became alligator food unwittingly. Suffice to say, the auction and its representatives were found not liable for the death as well as the wealthy inhabitants of Stone Hill Manor.

A healthy donation to the local police fund from the organization was made and discreetly looked upon as a thank you note and not a determining factor in the investigation outcome. The victim had a closed casket funeral. That is, what was left of her and the black dress she wore. And business went on as usual.

The news of the death came, of course, after Solo had long left Stone Hill Manor. But he did not find out about the other guest's death until a week later, after he had flown back into Casper, Wyoming. During that time, the only thing that had been of concern to him was his purchases at the manor and the fact his financial backers were happy with those investments.

* * *

He concluded that the mysterious woman he had met named Luna Dye was just a sweet bonus to that deal. The memory of those dirty footprints would soon fade from his mind, only to be replaced by the memory of how good Luna now felt in his embrace and how sweet she smelled.

He would long for her presence, and his heart would beat faster at just the mere thought of her. You could say he was living and breathing her, and as far as Solo was concerned, Luna was like no other woman he had ever met before or would probably meet again.

The latter of this belief, he would no doubt eventually come to appreciate more. One-night stands were usually not his thing, but he sincerely felt that his night with Luna had been different. Maybe that's why he reasoned he had felt compelled to go searching for this beautiful creature that night in Stone Hill Manor. Of course, any insecurity he had felt quickly dissipated when he had returned to his suite that night to find that she hadn't left for good after all.

Solo could not help but find himself reflecting on the intimacy that followed that morning. To him, it had been just as hot as the passion that they had shared the night before. Luna now finally had him under her spell, and it would be hard for him to break its binding hold.

As time passed, Solo soon became a rising star in the game of purchasing and acquiring antiquities and works of art. As his career progressed, so did his relationship with Luna. Their weeks together quickly turned into months and their months into years, and one day when Luna thought Solo was ready, she made good on a promise she had made to herself from day one. Maybe more of a vow than a promise. It was a *"savage attack"* that he never saw coming, as Luna turned him against his will in the darkness of the Wyoming mountains under the pretense of a hiking and camping trip, into something he could never go back again to being - *human*. As Luna's eyes met his, she could see only one other thing than fear in his eyes. The question that she would not be capable of answering in her bestial savagery. "Why me, why me?" he asked, barely above a whisper of his voice.

* * *

Luna woke up from her dream staring back out at the now dark landscape. She looked over at her driver Wiz who looked like he could use a break.

"Pull over at the next exit, and I'll take over," she said.

"You sure about that boss," Wiz said.

"Yeah, it looks like you can use some rest," she answered.

"By the way, how far out are we?" she asked.

Wiz yawned, "A few hours, give or take," he replied. He had heard Luna utter Solo's name in her sleep, but he was too scared to ask her why? Some questions he learned were best left unanswered.

"You want to know why I was calling out my ex-lover's name in my sleep, don't you?" Luna said as she lit up a cigarette.

"It's not my business, boss," Wiz answered nervously. Damn, did nothing ever get by her, he thought.

"No, it's not, but if you were calling out some bitches name in your sleep, I cannot say I would not be curious as to why?" Luna said with a grin.

"Fair enough," Wiz responded.

"Those four years I spent down in Romania was nothing short of a living hell, and I never want to forget the bitch who was responsible for putting me there," Luna said.

"So, if he creeps or enters into my dreams occasionally, that to me is a small price to pay for me, not forgetting wouldn't you agree," Luna concluded as she lit herself up a smoke.

"Make sense," Wiz said, keeping his eyes on the road for the next exit.

"You are damn right it does, by the way, don't miss the exit; it's coming up," Luna pointed out.

"Shit!" Wiz mumbled. How could he not see the exit ramp coming up as he quickly merges over, followed by the band of Harleys behind him? As he thought, she never misses anything.

Omar seated behind Luna, and Wiz woke up yawning. "Damn, I am hungry. I sure can use some Waffle House," he said.

"The guest or the food?" Wiz asked.

"Both," Omar said, grinning.

"What's up, sleeping beauty? I think it's one at the next exit we are coming up?" Luna said.

"Road whores and a breakfast of pork chops and eggs, how can life get any better?" Omar said.

"Probably if you only ate one," Luna shot back.

"Good point!" Omar said, laughing.

CHAPTER THIRTY-FIVE

Gina had not seen her daughter in months as she nervously waited for her curbside at Arrivals for her at Rapid City Regional Airport. She had mixed feelings about her coming home under these dangerous circumstances that she wrestled with on her drive to the airport to pick her up. But she knew how stubborn Sam was and that she would not be able to talk her out of coming back home to help them deal with the danger ahead no matter how hard she tried.

Gina's face lit up as she saw Sam coming out one of the terminal's numerous front doors with her luggage in tow. Gina popped her trunk open from the inside as she then exited the vehicle and greeted her daughter with as much of a smile she could muster up under the circumstances.

"Hi baby," she said as they both embraced.

"Hi Mom," Sam replied, glad to see her mother again, only now realizing how much she had missed being in her company.

They both proceeded to put her luggage in the trunk of the car.

"How was your flight in?" Gina asked as they both made their way inside of the SUV.

"Fine," Sam said, buckling up her seat belt as she watched the other travelers greet their loved ones and friends outside of the airport.

"Wow, thanks," Sam said as she noticed the second cup of Starbucks pumpkin spice latte in front of her that she had overlooked in the SUV's cup holder.

"You are welcome. I thought you could use that," Gina said.

"Oh boy, could I," Sam said, as she removed the plastic lid off and took a sip of the whipped cream on top.

Gina looked over at Sam and her now whip cream mustache, laughing.

"What?" Sam said, smiling.

"You got whipped cream on your top lip," Gina said.

"Oh, thanks," Sam said, laughing as well. It felt good to laugh, especially under the circumstances that they were now facing.

"Have you heard anything else from Solo?" Sam asked.

"No, not yet. But he should be arriving here shortly," Gina answers.

"How do you feel about that?" Sam asks as she takes another sip of the coffee.

"Ambivalent at best," Gina said, shrugging.

"I understand," Sam said. "But we need his help."

"I wish we did not," Gina replied.

"I wish we did not either, but it is going to be alright mom," Sam said, as she took her Mom's free hand into hers and kissed the back of it.

"I hope so, baby," Gina said.

"I know so," Sam responded assuredly.

"How is Sheriff Alvarez doing?" Sam asked.

"I hope well. The last time we talked, Al was out looking for some suspects that robbed one of our local banks."

"Shit, Mom! You have been holding out on me; when did this happen?" Sam asked.

" Relax, a few days ago, but they are probably long gone by now and in another town counting their loot," Gina said.

"Anyone get hurt?" Sam asked.

"Not to my knowledge, but since you brought that up, I will give Al a call as soon as we get back," Gina said.

"You have an incoming call?" The artificial voice said on her SUV's Bluetooth center.

"Yes, I'll take it," Gina answered back.

"Hi Gina, Sheriff Alvarez."

"Yes, speaking of the devil," Gina said.

"I hope not," Alvarez replied sullenly.

"Good Morning Sheriff, any news on those suspects that robbed our bank? Gina asked, sure he would tell her the same thing that she had just told Sam that they were probably hundreds of miles away now from their town on to their next robbery.

"Well, we found two of them dead by Bent Lake, and I suspect there might be more victims; we just ain't found them yet, " the sheriff answered with a sense of grim finality in his voice.

"Were they animal attacks?" Sam interjected.

"Who's that?" Alvarez asked before answering back.

"Hi sheriff, it's Sam."

"Hey Sam, I did not know you were back," Alvarez said.

"Yes, I am back to do what I can," she said.

"Good, we need all the help we can get," Alvarez said.

"Were they animal attacks?" Sam asked again, although something told her she already knew what the answer would be to that question.

"Off the record, Sam."

"Sure, Sheriff."

"It sure looks like it to me, the way the two deceased were ripped apart," Alvarez answered.

"I'll get forensics out there, and I am on my way," Gina said.

"Be careful. The back roads are shit!" Alvarez said.

"The call is now disconnected," said her SUV's voice command.

Gina looked over at her daughter Sam. She been wrong, she thought about the bank robbers. They had not gotten one hundred miles away from their crime scene. Something or someone had made sure that never occurred. Now it was their job to find out who or what it was? That had stopped them. Gina now begins to dread what she may have brought her daughter back into now and what carnage they would see when they made it to Bent Lake.

Sam turned to her and uttered the words that she knew might be true but were the last words she wanted to hear. "It's happening again, isn't it?" She said.

"I hope not, baby, I hope not," Gina replied softly.

Then Sam said something that completely caught her mom off guard.

"They never did find his body, did they?"

"Whose body? Sam."

"Elwood Holmes," she answers.

"No, we never did," Gina said. "What are you trying to say, Sam."

"I always wonder if he was actually dead," Sam said with a sense of foreboding in her voice.

"Let's hope so; we got a shitload of problems already," Gina said as they shot past the road sign that said *Welcome to Harper Creek.*

CHAPTER THIRTY-SIX

It would be daylight soon, and Elwood knew that he could not stay hidden in the shadows forever as he watched the police activity from afar. He had changed back physically to his human form and now had to find clothes and shelter without being discovered while he did. He knew these woods now would be crawling with police activity as soon as the sun came up. Which left him with only one option, and that was to create as much distance as possible between him and the search party that would soon come hunting for his head.

He has survived all these years because of his ability to be invisible and live out in conditions that were not fit for man or beast. Which he was now ironically both. He scarcely remembered how many people he had killed before he had made the change back. But if the copious amount of dried up blood on his huge hands up to his elbows were a reminder, he would have to say - plenty. He looked back down at those large hands and back up at the police personnel between the cover of the trees and brush.

"What am I?" he said, his deep voice cracking with disdain.

* * *

The black truck driven by Gina pulled up outside the tape-off crime scene as it arrived at Bent Lake. She and Sam quickly exited the vehicle and made their way over to Sheriff Alvarez, who was sipping on some coffee out of a stainless steel mug he was holding in one hand.

"Glad you could make it, Doc," he said to Gina as he saw them approaching.

"It's been a long time Sam," he said, greeting her with a friendly hug.

"I know," Sam said.

"Wow, look at you all grown up and a big-time reporter," Alvarez said.

"Well, I don't know about the big-time reporter part," Sam replied.

"And humble too," Alvarez said.

He looked at Gina. "Good job with this one."

"Are you going to report this?" Alvarez asked Sam.

" I would not be doing my job if I did not, right?"

Alvarez smiled and took another sip of his coffee. "Like I said, good job with this one."

"What do we have here, sheriff?" Gina asked as they made their way over to the first dead body.

"Carnage," Alvarez answered bluntly.

Gina looked over Hallie's headless corpse. "Where is her head?" she asked.

"Over there," Alvarez answered, as he pointed to Hallie's head a few feet away that had a look of shock on her face.

"She looks like she never saw it coming," Sam said.

"Something tells me it would not have mattered if she did," Gina said.

"Can you do me a favor, Sam, and hold off on this story before you submit it to your editor," Alvarez said.

"How long?" Sam asked.

"A few days, Sam, or at least until we find out what in the hell is going on around here?" Alvarez asked.

"I'll see what I can do, sheriff," Sam said, reluctant to make promises, as they then made their way over to the second body or at least what was left of its mutilated corpse. They watched as Smith now arrived on the scene with one of his officers accompanying him.

"Morning folks," Smith said as he made his way over to them.

"Jesus Sam, is that you?" he said.

"Yes, it's me, Cap," Sam said.

"How long have you been back?" He said.

"I just arrived this morning," Sam answers, hoping that Cap was the last of the home welcoming committee. Shit! This situation wasn't about her; she thought it was all about as far as she was concerned what they would soon be up against as a town that would be leaving bodies in its wake like the ones that laid on the ground amongst them.

"Something happen here," Sam said.

Smith looked at the body on the ground in pieces. "And by the looks of it too, nothing nice." "Nasty," he said, grimacing, as he took his hat off and crouched down by the second body.

"What do you think Doc," he asked, looking up at Gina.

"Too familiar, that's what I think," Gina answered.

Cap stood up and let out a sigh. "I agree, this is too savage to be human, too organized to be an animal.

"Goddammit! Cap, you are beginning to sound just like Doogen," Alvarez said, referring to their friend Carl Doogen. A Cryptozoologist who had been instrumental in assisting them the last time Harper Creek had a rash of suspicious murders in their town and searching for the culprits.

Smith laughed. "Good, cause I was a hard-headed sonofabitch last time."

"I can't argue with that one," Alvarez said.

"Speaking of Doogen, when was the last time you spoke with him, Cap?" Sam asked.

"It's been a while, Sam. Why?" Smith asked.

"Luna's not here, but we have killings similar to the ones that she committed four years ago, that's why?" Sam responded agitated.

"I am still not getting it?" Smith said, shaking his head.

"If Doogen was here, I guess my first question to him would be, is it possible that she left someone or something behind in our town?" Sam answers.

"Are you saying that she bit someone and infected them, and now they are on a rampage after four years of remaining dormant?" Alvarez asked, skeptical.

" Well, look around here, sheriff. There are plenty of other things to eat out here," Sam replied.

"She got a good point there, Al," Cap agreed.

"Well, that would sure explain why the pack is coming," Alvarez said.

"Maybe, I am going to get these bodies back to my lab for further examination after we gather up all the pertinent forensics evidence on scene," Gina said.

"Sounds like a good start to me, Doc." *"Chief, we got a situation here,"* his deputy said on his radio, interrupting them.

"This is the sheriff. Go ahead," he said into his radio mic.

"I think we just discovered another dead body over here five miles away from Anderson's place."

"You think?" Alvarez said.

"Yeah, it's hard to tell, it doesn't even look human," the deputy responded nervously.

CHAPTER THIRTY-SEVEN

As Solo checked into the Bed & Breakfast, he noticed that he had not run into one single person that had recognized him back again in town. Maybe he had not left the undeniable impression that he thought he did after all in this town. And if so, Solo thought. Perhaps he could feel less guilty about the events associated with him after arriving four years and many moons ago to set up shop as he now observed that the people of this good town appeared to have moved past those tragic events as they tried to live their best lives. But seriously, who was Solo bullshitting, he thought. Because here he was back again, after being warned never to return. Back again, ironically fighting those same demons that he had fought four years ago.

"I think the bed has fresh sheets on it, Frank. But if not, just call up at the desk, and I'll bring you down a fresh set," Arnie said, referring to Solo by the alias that he had given him.

"Sure," Solo answered as he took the room keys out of Arnie's hands.

"Have a pleasant stay, Mr. Frank," Ernie said as he watched Solo trying to remember where he had seen him before. He sure looked familiar, he thought. But he just could not recall meeting anybody that looked like him named Frank. Oh! Maybe he was mistaken, he thought, as he jotted down his new guest name in the logbook.

Solo responded softly with a "Thanks" as he walked away with his room key in hand. He had felt the older man's gaze on him and how he was studying his face for a sense of what he perceived as recognition. And although Solo knew damn well who the desk attendant was and his wife who ran this Bed & Breakfast. It was best for their safety that they knew as little about him as possible. He was their guest, "Frank" and that's all they needed to know, he concluded as he stuck the key into the door's keyhole and unlocked the door to a place where Solo could hopefully rest his head for a few hours before he got down to the business at hand.

* * *

His deputies had discovered the other body had appeared to fare no better than its two predecessors as Alvarez studied its gruesome remains. "Someone or something has been very busy," he said.

"Appears so," responded Gina as she examined the remains. "What do you think, Cap?" she asked.

"It looks like the leftovers from a Grizzly Bear's meal," he answers.

"Or a werewolf," Sam interjected as she cut Cap a glance.

"Or a werewolf, Cap agreed." More open mind than before.

Alvarez took off his Stetson and scratched his head in aggravation, and plopped the hat back on his head. "Shit!" he said.

"Well, look at it from the bright side, Al. We only have to look for two suspects now," Smith said.

"You are all heart, Cap," Alvarez said.

"I try to be," Cap quipped.

"Well, one thing for sure, let's not forget. If we do not have one here already, werewolf, we got one on the way," Sam said.

"How can I forget that?' Alvarez said.

"Sam's right, Al, we need to get prepared for what's headed our way," Gina said.

Cody looked at Al and nodded his head in agreement.

"Okay, then let's get this wrap-up; we do not need any more surprises," Al said to his deputies.

"I'll get this last body or at least what's left of it back to the Coroner's office," Gina said.

"Doc, you might be jumping the gun on that one," Alvarez replied.

"What do you mean?" she answered.

"What makes you think this is the last body?" he asked.

Gina said nothing as her eyes drifted off into the denseness of the surrounding woodland.

CHAPTER THIRTY-EIGHT

The sound of a helicopter hovering above abruptly woke El up out of his sleep as he quickly sprung up to a sitting position and looked up in the sky while covering his ears from the noise of the helicopter blades as he watched the aircraft circling from above. He knew now that his only chance to avoid being captured was to destroy the temporary debris hut shelter he had built and get to one of the numerous underground camouflaged bunkers he had constructed to provide him with complete anonymity from the activity above. He estimated that the nearest bunker was less than a quarter-mile away. He had at least enough food rations stored inside to last him for two weeks, maybe more. As soon as the helicopter disappeared, El quickly destroyed any traces of the hut and its existence.

* * *

The only thing that John wanted to do was put all the shit that happened to him and his family with the bank robbers behind him as if it never occurred. Go back to his old life as he made his way to a barn-like garage. As John entered through a service door, he turned on the dark garage lights with a faint light coming in when its double doors were down. He walked over to a tool cabinet in the garage's center to retrieve a wrench set when he felt something wet drip on his face from above. John wiped his face and looked at his fingers which were now stained red. His eyes went slowly up towards his rafters at the bloody body hanging lifeless on a tow hook. John stumbled backward in fear and then ran out of the garage, yelling for his family to call the sheriff's department.

But unknown to him, Sheriff Alvarez had already put his place under surveillance. And he was being watched and observed by two of Alvarez deputies as he ran screaming in anguish from the garage. Deena and Jason bolted out of the house when they heard John's screams for help.

The deputies sprang into action and met him before he made it to his house, catching him off guard. "What the hell are you doing on my property?" he asked, bug-eyed, forgetting that he was just screaming for his family to call the police.

"Just rack it up to quick service," Deputy Snyder said.

"What the hell were you screaming your lungs out about John?" Deputy Cannon asked.

"You don't have to answer any of their questions, Pops, unless they got a search warrant," barked Jason.

Deputy Cannon took the search warrant out of his pocket and handed it to John.

"Shut the fuck up, Jason!" John said, after looking at their warrant.

"You got blood on your face. Did you hurt yourself?" asked Cannon.

"It's not my blood," John answers, still shaken and in shock.

"Not yours, then who the hell is it?" Cannon asked him.

John turned nervously around and pointed towards the garage. At this point, the realization set in that he would never be able to put what he and his family had done behind him. The gift in his garage from a killer was evident to that harsh fact. The two deputies proceeded cautiously towards his garage slowly with both of their weapons drawn and ready.

"Jesus, how the hell did he get up there?" Cannon asked as they entered the garage, and he looked up at Dez's lifeless body hanging by the towhead from the rafters.

Both deputies walked around to the back of Dez's body, and that is when they could see that he had been impaled through the back by the towing hook as he hung there like a large slab of frozen meat in a meat processing facility on a butcher's hook.

"I have no idea; that's how I found him," John answers, as his wife Deena cupped her mouth as the smell of death hit her nostrils.

"107 to 111," Cannon said into his walkie-talkie.

"Go ahead 107," Alvarez responded.

"We got a 10-54 out at the Andersons place."

"Secure the scene 107. I am en route," Alvarez replied.

"10-4 Chief."

"Anderson's place. What's going on, Al?" Gina asked after overhearing Alvarez's conversation with his deputy.

"I think we just found number four D.O.S.," he said bluntly.

(Dead on scene).

"Shit!" Sam interjected.

"Yep, and it keeps piling up sky high," Alvarez said.

CHAPTER THIRTY-NINE

A gauntlet of Alvarez and Cody's patrol cars with roof lamps flashing red and blue strobes of light now blocked the road and entry point into Harper Creek. But what stood out amongst them all was the tactical armored BearCat that set like a beast amongst the other vehicles equipped with the latest tactical technology and equipment to get the most dangerous jobs involving law enforcement done. Chumpski had informed Alvarez that he had a contribution to make to their defense. But shit! He sure was not expecting the beast that's parked out on his roadway right now.

Alvarez only hoped that he had assembled all the resources armed with high-power weapons with no reluctance to use them. Conveyed one message like the BearCat that towered over the other vehicles to Luna Dye and her crew or whatever troublemakers that were now en route that "Harper Creek" would not go down without a fight no matter what element they were up against, supernatural or natural.

* * *

Alvarez could now see and hear the sound of motorcycles and a van approaching the border and entry point into their town. The morning sun created a hazy mist in the distance that floated in front of the approaching entourage like a bad omen. His officers and Cody waited with weapons at the ready for the mysterious convoy. Alvarez wonders if this were Luna and her crew, would he even remember what she looked like when she arrived if he saw her. After all, it had been four years since the last time Alvarez had laid eyes on her. Who was he kidding, he thought? He would remember that damn face from anywhere. Yes, she may have been a "wolf in sheep's clothing" but he had to admit you would never know that from her striking appearance that was nothing short of attractive, even, or maybe captivating.

The three Harleys stopped about twenty-five yards from them in front of the van that flanked them. Alvarez instructed his personnel to stand down as he proceeded to identify who the cyclist and van occupants were? Alvarez put the binoculars to his eyes and zoomed in on the three helmetless riders. It was no mistaking who the middle rider was... Luna Dye.

"It's them," Alvarez said, his AR -15 rifle in front of him locked and loaded. Sam and Gina had both been deputized earlier by Alvarez, and both carried equal stopping power. Game Warden Smith was also armed and present. They all stood their ground together as a formidable team against the opposition in front of them as they advanced towards Luna and her crew.

"My, my, my, do you always roll out the red carpet like this for your guest?" Luna said to Alvarez with a wide grin on her face as she stood between Mako and Omar as three of her other members exited the van behind them, Riley, Wiz, and Dean.

"Only for you," Alvarez answered dryly.

Luna laughed. "Well, ain't I something special," she quipped to the laughter of her crew. Her eyes lit up as she looked over at Gina and Sam.

"Hi ladies, I remember you two," she said.

"Really? We tried to forget you," Gina replied, not batting an eye.

Luna laughed again. "I do understand. I cannot say I was the best house guest, was I?" she asked.

"No, you were not. In fact, you were an absolute bitch!" Sam answered back.

"Come to think of it. I guess I was," Luna chuckled. "Maybe I did not like the head Alvarez's deputy gave me," she said, harshly referring to one of Alvarez's deputies that she had murdered by snapping his neck right in front of Gina four years ago.

Sam raised her assault rifle at Luna's face. "You fucking bitch!" she growled, ready to blow her brains out.

"Sam No!" Alvarez said, putting his hand out in front of Sam to stop. As he observed the look in Luna's crew eyes like they were ready to pounce on them at the sound of a dog whistle by her to attack. He did not want any bloodshed and carnage if he could avoid it. But if that's what Luna and her crew had arrived in his town to accomplish. He was ready to hand them their hairy asses back to them on a platter if he had to.

Smith remained silent as he sized up which one of her people he would take out first. It was pissing him off that not only did he have a fresh bottle of Jack Daniel's at home he could be enjoying right now, but he could be enjoying it while on the other end of a fishing pole at the lake.

"What do you want, Luna?" Alvarez asked, cutting to the point of her visit.

"Four years in that dungeon that you fucks help imprison me in, and you dare to ask me, Sheriff, what do I want?" Luna shouted out loudly.

"You lucky I have not taken your head off where you stand!" she threatens.

Alvarez cut Luna a steely glance. "I have a suggestion for you, Luna."

"What?" she answered back.

"Do not write a check with that pretty mouth of yours that your narrow ass can't cash," he said.

Luna cracked that one-hundred-watt smile of hers, right before her eyes began to change color as Alvarez watched in awe as her facial features started to change. "Is that a fact?" she asked in a deeper and more guttural voice.

"Yep, that's a fact!" shouted out someone from behind Alvarez and his group.

Gina recognized that voice and who it belongs to immediately - Solo.

CHAPTER FORTY

Alvarez ordered his man to stand down as Solo made his way towards them and Luna. "He's on our side," he said.

"Solo," Gina murmured as his eyes met hers and Sam.

"When in the hell did he get here?" Smith asked.

"Does it matter?" Sam responded.

"I know what you are here for, Luna, but it is not going to go well for you," Solo said. "None of you!" he said, looking into the eyes of her crew.

"I made you," Luna said defiantly.

Solo looked Luna dead in her eyes with a look and snarl on his face that she had never seen before. "That was your first mistake!" he replied, quickly bursting out of his clothes, transforming into something that was more than a match for the beast inside of Luna or her pack. Alvarez and the rest of them watched on in uninterrupted horror and awe.

"Is he still on our side," asked Cody?

"I hope so," answered Alvarez.

"I told you I was not crazy," Jay said to Chumpski as they both watched, with weapons also at the ready.

"This is going to be one helluva dog fight!" Smith said, as he raised his weapon at Mako, who had now shape-shifted into the seven-foot snarling and growling beast that stood before him.

The sound of growling, screams, and gunfire now filled the morning air as Alvarez and the others made sure that the check that Luna had written did not bounce.

Sam stopped shooting and slung her AR-15 over her shoulder as she looked at Luna and Solo engaged in a gruesome battle. Luna's intense amber eyes met hers as she growled at her with a mouth full of teeth that could now rip her throat out as the drool rolled down Luna's black Lycan gums. Growllll. Sam unsheathed the silver dagger and looked back over at Luna, her eyes widening. This time she would not be held back until the blade she wielded finally met its proper resting place, and that place was Luna's Dye's cold dark heart.

EPILOGUE

The river's current had carried Needy's body downstream, where she had finally washed up on an isolated patch of river beach almost three miles down from where she had initially fallen off into the river. As she began coughing, she spewed the water up onto the dirty sand as she felt the warm rays of the sun beating down on her face. Needy slowly begins to come to as she attempts to orientate herself to her surroundings through squinted eyes as they adjust to the shimmering daylight. Needy immediately begins patting her body down for any broken bones or injuries that she might have sustained in the fall. Other than feeling like she had just ridden a bull. Needy quickly determined she had been unnaturally lucky and would survive.

Needy took off the wet backpack that was still strapped on her back. She looked at the damn thing that was soaking wet. Needy suspected somehow that this thing had miraculously saved her life and acted as a flotation device when she had fallen off into the river. Needy shook the bag off, opened it up, and looked inside at the remaining ten-thousand dollars in wet cash still inside the bag. She zipped the bag back up and threw it off in the river. The money was cursed as far as she was concerned, and she would be damn if she spent a dime of it towards her niece's care, she had decided.

Needy looked across the river and up at the morning sky, not knowing why her life had been spared. But at that moment, she swore to herself from this day forth she would be retiring from pulling another bank heist. After all, she was of better use to her niece Hannah alive; she concluded then dead. There had to be another way she further thought to finance Hannah's treatments. And if there was? She also swore she would find out. Or at least die trying, as a pair of intense amber eyes concealed in the thick of some nearby trees followed her off the beach. Grrrrr…

DISCO CLUB OF BLOOD

THE NOVEL

Lee J. Minter

ISBN: 978-1-7340930-4-9 (e)

Dedicated to all of those who have a love of the unknown and seek the truth.

PROLOGUE

The city of Pontiac had now fallen on hard times when its main factory and job producer General Motors finally shut its doors, and thousands of jobs that Pontiac's residents held were now gone. First, the Pontiac Silverdome was the home to major sports teams The Detroit Lions, Pistons, and Detroit Mechanix. It had also served as a venue for concerts and motocross that had bit the dust after Its retractable roof problems. Other building maintenance issues followed and became too expensive to fix and maintain by its owners.

What was now left in the aftermath of all of this was a city on the verge of economic bankruptcy and vast unemployment. In the place of that long-gone prosperity came a proliferation of drugs and other social malfeasances that was more than happy to take its place.

Despite its social and economic ills though its young people still wanted to party inside and outside of the city that was now trying to re-establish itself as a venue with thriving nightclubs and a vibrant social scene.

One of those places to go and party was an old Cathedral building, formerly a church located on Saginaw Street

in Pontiac, Michigan. Decommissioned and sold by owners First Church Of Pontiac three years ago and converted
into a nightclub called Tentacles, a popular hot spot, and
hangout for young adults on the weekends.

In contrast, its closest neighbor across the street was a
recovery and rehabilitation center for men, women, and
children addicted or homeless. First Steps to Recovery and
Hope. Which also happen to be owned, connected, and
run by the First Church Of Pontiac.

Tentacles was a spacious nightclub, thirty thousand
square feet with three floors and a sanctuary with a balcony
that seated up to six hundred and fifty people. That included
an overflow space for an additional; one hundred people and
a bar situated on each floor for its thirsty patrons who wanted
to cool their palettes with something wet after twerking,
bumping, and grinding. The main floor was house music,
techno, and disco. The second floor was "urban music," and
the third floor was reserved for hip hop.

Although there were three other nightspots close by in
Pontiac, none of them had the allure that Tentacles did on
the young college crowd on the weekends and "Thirsty Thurs-
days," as the club's promoter billed that day before the week-
end for extra revenue. The club's consistent advertising on the
local radio stations and one of the local stations broadcasting
live from the club on weekends also help to hype up its reputation even more as the place to party and be on the weekends.
That and the scantily clad young women even on the colder
nights in Pontiac, Michigan. That attracted the young studs
with dreams of scoring a one-night stand or maybe some mys-

tery head from one of what they called bobbleheads in one of the club's numerous skanky bathrooms. Or if they wanted to be more discreet inside their ride out in the building's sixty car capacity parking lot, which every frequent flyer to the club knew that if you did not get to the club by at least 10:00 pm, the small lot for a building that size would be full, and you would have to use the adjacent overflow lot across the street at the rehab center that cost you five dollars to park, which most of the young crowd did not want to pay because it was cutting into their weed and beer money.

Community rumors now flowed that the church was now cursed after they had converted to a nightclub. Talk that the building was a haven for demonic activity and haunted. All of these subjective rumors did nothing, though, to curtail its customers from patronizing its new establishment. In fact, it seemed to have just the opposite effect and made it an even more popular destination and hangout spot due to its association with these creepy allegations. The church turned nightclub had a giant "Kraken-like" Squid adorning its outside brick wall with its appendages stretched out widely with the name Tentacles in colorful letters above it. This unofficial mascot was also painted and illustrated over the entrance in another position which gave it the appearance of staring down at the patrons with outstretched and welcoming arms (tentacles) as they entered the nightspot.

* * *

Javon brushed the waves in his hair and sipped from a rolling rock beer he held in the other as he stood in front of the bathroom mirror with a shower towel wrapped around his waist. "Hey roomies, where are we hanging out tonight?' he yelled out at his two best friends Marty and Scott, engaged in the video game "Call Of Duty" on a nearby sofa.

Scott took a toke on the blunt between his fingers. "Man, I heard about this new place called Tentacles; we should check it out," he said as he exhaled out the vapors.

"Is that right? Where is it at?" Javon asked.

"Pontiac," Scott answered. "Goddammit, he just got me," he yelled out in frustration, referring to just being killed in the game.

"Fella's the party is up here; what are we fucking around down there for?" Marty said.

"Man, I am tired of these stuck-up bitches around here. I just want to meet some down-to-earth girls for a change," Javon replied as he finished drying himself off with the towel.

"You mean some girls that are dumber than you," Marty said sarcastically, grinning.

"Fuck you, man," Javon said, laughing.

Javon walked out of the bathroom towards Scott and Marty with the towel still wrapped around his lean and muscular body.

"Let me hit that blunt," he said to Scott.

"Why don't you put some clothes on your ass and stop walking around here butt ass naked," Scott said as he passed Javon the joint.

Javon took a long drag of the blunt himself and then passed it back to Scott. "Why? Your Mother never complains," he shot back smiling.

Scott laughed. "Really, she said you came up short last night, Peewee."

Marty burst out laughing, spitting out some of his beer. "That's cold. He got you there, bro."

"Man, whatever," Javon said, walking back towards the bathroom.

"Don't get mad, homie, cuz you got your junk posted all over social media, we warned you about dating that crazy-ass Juanita from that sorority," Marty said.

"Yeah, that was cold, but I did do her dirty by sleeping with her cousin."

"Which one was better?" Marty asked.

Javon takes another swig of his beer and smiles. "Their Aunt!" he answers.

Marty and Scott both exploded in laughter. "Homie, you out cold," Marty said, still chuckling.

Javon stepped back out of the bathroom, this time with a tank top on and a pair of lounge pants. He walked over to their fridge and grabbed three rolling rock beers out of it, and popped the tops off all three. "So what's the game plan fella's for tonight?" he asked, as he passed his boys off the other two bottles.

"Fucking Tentacles!" Marty shouted out enthusiastically as they all raised their cheap green bottles of beers in a mutual toast of agreement.

CHAPTER ONE

Farmington Hills, Michigan. "I see you, girl, you going to have those nigga's thirsting tonight," Gabriella said to her friend Crystal, who had FaceTime her to show herself off in a new dress that she was wearing for their girls night out that evening.

Crystal twirled back and forth, smiling, flipping her hair up as she held her iPhone out in front of her on a selfie stick. The hot pink dress did indeed complement her svelte hourglass figure.

"Crystal, you better have the right hoe shoes to go with that dress, girl."

"You know it," she answered as she put the camera on her diamond and studded encrusted heels. "Oh my god bitch I hate you. Now I gotta go dig deep in my closet tonight," Gabriella said, with envy.

"I love you too, Gabby," Crystal said, laughing.

"Hold on, I got an incoming call," she said.

"Hey Ms. Thing, it looks like you are ready to party," Pepper said, smiling as Crystal three-way her on FaceTime.

Crystal pumped her hands in the air, smiling. "Girl, you know it."

"Hey Pepper, what's up?" Gabriella said as Pepper entered the video chat.

"Hey Gabby, I am babysitting my little brother Juno until my parents get back."

"Say hello, to my bitches - Crystal and Gabby," Pepper said as she brought her cute five-year-old little brother Juno onto the chat. "Hey bitches," he said in a small voice, causing them all to burst out in laughter.

"Oh my god, no, he didn't," said Gabriella with her hand over her mouth.

"Juno, bad word, do not use that word," Crystal said. "Okay," Juno replied.

"Are you going to tell Mom?" he asked.

"No, I am not going to tell her shit, now go play," Pepper said.

"Ooooooo – you said shit! That's a bad word," he said.

"Boy, I am grown, I am allowed to curse," his sister responded, smacking her lips.

"No you not, you're a child like me," he said.

"You little smart ass, I said go play," Pepper said, frowning her face up, causing her little brother to run off.

"Oh, he is so adorable," Gabriella gushed.

"Please, girl, do not let his cute face fool y'all. He's Chucky in disguise; that's why I hide all the damn kitchen knives in the house," Pepper said.

"For real?" Crystal asked.

"Naw, I am just fucking with y'all," Pepper answers. "He's more like Damien 3.0," she said, laughing.

"Pepper, you off the chain girl," Gabriella said, grinning.

"Hey guys, I gotta go. I think I hear my parents pulling up," Crystal said.

"Okay, Pepper, don't stand us up tonight," Crystal said.

"No way, I've been holed up in this house for a week, and it's time to get out and get some fresh air," she said.

"And some fresh dickkkkkk," Gabby shouted out.

"Girl, you so nasty, bye," Crystal said, laughing.

" Oh, by the way, before I let you go, where are we hanging out at tonight? So that I can let my parents know," asked Pepper.

"Pepper, are you serious? You're still telling your parents your every freaking move?" Crystal asked, making Pepper feel instantly guilty and immature.

"No, that's not it at all," she answered back defensively.

"Good, then be ready by 9:00 pm to roll out," Crystal said. Not accustomed to hearing the word no, in her shelter and privilege world that her parents' money and influence provided for her lifestyle, that she flaunted on Facebook and Twitter that had amassed Crystal a vast social media following in return.

"Bitch," Pepper said underneath her breath as she disconnected from the call.

"Dad and Mommy back!" she heard her little brother Juno scream out excitedly downstairs.

"I am coming," Pepper yelled back down to her little brother before heading downstairs to greet her parents as she thought up a lie to tell them regarding where she would be hanging out tonight. And although she hated lying to her parents, she hated losing face and looking weak in her friend Crystal's eyes even more.

In fact, in many ways, she wished she could be more like Crystal, who seemed able to speak her mind no matter the consequences and who she was interacting with socially. And if you were her friend and someone crossed you, Crystal was always the first to speak up and come to your defense fiercely. On the contrary, her other friend Gabriella was more of a laid-back go-with-the-flow person. But at the same time very observative and intelligent in her own right and did not take any shit off anybody either, including their friend Crystal, something Pepper wished she could do more often, instead of being so passive-aggressive.

"Hey guys," Pepper said, greeting her parents as they entered the house.

"Hey honey, thanks for watching your little brother. By the way, how was he?" her father asked.

Pepper looked at Juno and smiled. "Like a little angel," she said, smiling. Juno stuck his thumbs in his ears, wiggling his fingers while making a funny face at his big sister as he stood behind their father's leg for cover and protection.

"Archangel," Pepper truthfully thought, frowning quickly before bringing her face back into a fake smile.

"How was that new Chinese restaurant?" Pepper asked.

"Dear, don't ask," her mom said as she removed her heels.

"Yeah, I have never seen egg foo young made like Quiche," her father answered.

"Yes, and that fried rice was horrendous, taste like they recycled it off another guest's plate," her mom added.

"Gross," Pepper said, sticking her tongue out as well.

"You should Yelp them," Pepper said.

"Yelp, pretty damn nasty," her father quipped, causing her to laugh.

"That's not what I mean, dad." She said.

"I am still hungry; let's order a pizza and put a good movie on," her mom suggested.

"Pizza!" Juno yelled out! Jumping up and down ecstatically.

"That sounds good, Mom, but I already made plans to hang out with Crystal and Gabby tonight."

"Dear, it's okay. Where are you going, and what time will you be back?" her mom asked.

Shit! Pepper thought. Here come the lies.

CHAPTER TWO

The Lexus pulled up in front of Pepper's house with horn honking as its two occupants giggled. "Tell Crystal to lay off the horn she is going to wake up the whole damn neighborhood!" her father said, annoyed.

"Dad, it's only nine o'clock," Pepper said.

"The only thing that goes to bed that early is old people and puppies," she said sarcastically.

"Funny," her father said as he bit into his slice of pizza.

"Be safe baby," her mother said, kissing her on the cheek.

"I will love you," Pepper said.

Pepper looked over at her dad with that look on his face, tapping his watch. " Don't forget Pepper," he said.

"I gotta go. Love you too, dad," she said.

As he watched his daughter leave, he shook his head sideways in disapproval. "That kid is going to be the death of us," he said.

"Don't be a grouch. She's young; let her have some fun," her mom said, coming to her daughter's defense.

"You do remember what it was like when you were younger, don't you?" his wife asked.

"Nope, my youth went away with my hair, the birth of our second child, and baby shark," he replied. As he went to his bay window and watched his daughter and her friends pull off. He recognized Crystal's car, which brought him some relief. Maybe he was too strict on Pepper, he thought. After all, she had never done anything not to warrant his and her mother's complete trust. Maybe he would loosen the reins. He felt, after all, Pepper would soon be turning eighteen years old next month.

"Bowling?" he said to his wife, sitting on the sofa with their son between them watching an animated movie.

"Yes, Shady Green Oaks Bowling Alley, " answered his wife. About where Pepper told them she would be hanging out tonight with her girlfriends.

"Bowling outfits sure has changed since I was a kid," he said.

"Yes, dear, this ain't "Happy Days," his wife shot back condescendingly.

He looked down at their son Juno ruffling his hair as he ate his pizza.

"Don't grow up too quick, kid," he said.

"I won't" his son surprisingly replied.

CHAPTER THREE

Tentacles had three deejays providing the music for Friday's night party. But the headliner was Deejay Reptile, a deejay that wore a human-like lizard face mask with tail included. The club owners thought his act was a bit over the top, but his presence and abilities seemed to bring in the crowds and the money. Therefore if his fantasy was to be a lizard that spin turntables and mix music, more power to him they thought as long as the cash flowed in behind his eccentric deejay persona. The other two deejays were residents and knew the music scene quite well at the club and how to keep the party going until 2:00 am – closing time.

* * *

The crowd was already starting to gather and build up outside the club in the cold November weather. That did not stop the young women from wearing their skimpiest and tightest outfits with high heels included. Most of them had not dressed for the weather and were only concerned about how cute they would look amongst their friends in their latest and hip outfits. The cheap rum and vodka flowing through their bloodstream made some oblivious to just how chilly the November weather was, while others felt the cold bite of the wind and could not wait to get inside, to get warm, and get drunk.

"Man, this joint is off the hook!" Javon said excitedly as he and his friends made their way towards the club's front doors as they eyeballed the groups of young women headed in the same direction as them.

"The female to male ratio must be at least 10 to 1, he added."

"I don't know about that, but so far, not bad," Scott said, as an attractive young lady met eyes with him and smiled.

"You tripping roomie, I saw that eye play you just got," Javon said, grinning.

"Don't hate the player, hate the game," Scott said, puffing his shirt out, smiling.

Javon laughed. "See, I taught him well," he said, to their friend Marty who laughed as well.

"Man, check out that eye candy over there," he said, pointing to the three girls ahead of them in the line. One of the young women in the group looked over at them and smiled.

"Shit! It's cold as hell out here," Marty said, clenching his teeth together.

"Hey, I got an idea. Let's go over there and pretend we are with them so that we can get ahead of the line," Javon suggested.

"Man, you are joking," Scott said.

"Naw, man, we are going to be out here forever with the rest of these noobs. Let's do it."

Marty looked around at the line building up. He blew in the air, watching vapors form in the cold air. "Man, I can see my breath," he said.

"Then why don't you give it a Tic Tac," Javon jokes.

"Ha, ha, ha, good one," Marty said.

Marty turned to Scott. "He's right, Scott, what we got to lose."

Scott thought about it for a minute. He looked back over the girls who were still staring in their direction, talking amongst themselves. "What the hell, roomies, if y'all game I am game," he said.

"My man," Javon said, wrapping his arm around Scott's shoulder pulling him in.

Javon looked at his friend Marty. "Damn, homey. Can you think of warm thoughts? We can't walk over there while you're shaking like a chicken at a meat processing plant."

"Fuck you, homey; it's colder than polar bear shit out here," Marty said. "But I got this," he said, straightening out his posture and puffing out his chest.

Javon laughed. "Warm thoughts' bro," he reiterated.

"Man, I can barely feel my nuts," Marty said.

"Nobody told you to wear those nut huggers," Scott said, referring to Marty's tight slim leg jeans.

"No, I think they accentuate his tight ass," Javon said in an effeminate voice.

"Fuck you both, let's see who gets more action," Marty said.

"Relax, bro, we just fucking with you," Javon said, wrapping his arm around Marty and kissing him on his forehead as they made their way over to the group of young women.

"Hey, ladies, what's up? I'm Javon, and these are my homies, Marty and Scott."

"Hi, I am Crystal, and these are my homies Gabby and Pepper," Pepper said, mimicking Javon.

Javon laughed. "Oh, okay, okay, that's what's up," he said.

"We were wondering if we could join you Queens, and buy y'all a drink when we get inside," Scott said.

"Are you sure y'all are not just trying to cut in line?" Crystal asked.

Scott threw his hands out at them. "Naw, baby, we could never jump in front of royalty like that with that type of disrespect."

Crystal and her girls laughed. Scott was a smooth talker, she thought, and not too bad on the eyes either.

"Listen to him. The white boy got game," Gabby said, looking Scott up and down with a smile on her face.

"Like Mike and Kobe," Scott said as he shot an imaginary basketball in an imaginary hoop.

"I hear you, I hear you," Gabby said, smiling. She was an attractive girl with long wavy black hair and a bright, engaging smile.

"Whatever," Javon said, rolling his eyes at Scott's remark, slightly jealous.

"It's cool but don't try to dip on us once we get inside the club," Pepper said.

"No, no, it's not like that, I promise," Javon said, laughing.

"So where y'all from?" Crystal asked as she took a hit off her passion fruit-flavored vape pen and passed it to Gabby.

"Ann Arbor," Javon answered.

"College boys?"

"U of M," Marty responded.

"Where are you guys from?" Scott asked Crystal and her friends.

"Detroit," Crystal lied.

"Oh yeah, what part ?" Javon asked.

"Eastside," Gabby said, continuing the lie that Crystal started.

"Man, y'all don't look like no girls from Detroit's eastside," Javon said skeptically.

"What the hell does an eastside girl from Detroit supposed to look like?" Gabby said, sounding offended.

"He didn't mean anything by it," Scott said, coming to his friend's defense.

Javon interrupted. "No, actually, I did. Like you know the eastside," he said. He leans over and sniffs Crystal, who pulls back.

"What the hell are you doing?" she said, confused.

"You don't even smell like the eastside!" he said, causing Crystal and her friends to burst out laughing.

"Okay, okay, you got us; we are actually from Farmington Hills," Crystal admitted.

"I knew it!" Javon said, laughing as well.

Scott let out a sigh of relief as the tension immediately left the cold night air between them.

"But don't get it twisted. It doesn't make us no less dangerous," Gabby said, shaking her head and finger for emphasis at the same time.

"Hey, we're all friends here," Marty said, laughing nervously.

"ID's out," they all heard a loud booming voice say as they all made their way to the front door. Upon giving entrance into the building, each one of their identification cards was scanned. As they entered the atrium, they were met by another muscular security guard who swept a security wand over them for weapons. Crystal noticed the coat check was to their immediate right and did not look all that secure, so she and her friends removed anything of value from their coat pockets and put it in their purses. Loud Disco music booming from the first floor level of the club. KC and the Sunshine band's - Do you wanna go party echoed off the walls.

Javon and his two friends watched as Crystal and her girls checked their coats in at the club's coat check.

"Damn! Dawg, look at the jolly rancher on her," Javon said to his boys as Crystal took off her coat, revealing her tight-fitting hot pink mini dress.

"Bootylicious!" Marty said, rubbing his thin mustache.

"Hey, I think she likes you," Marty said.

"You think so?" Javon replied, grinning.

"No, I was referring to Scott," Marty said, laughing as he high-five Scott.

"Whatever," Javon said. "Chill fool, they're coming back this way."

"I see y'all still here," Crystal said, smiling.

"Yeah, we were about to bounce and get lost in the crowd, but… ouch," Javon said, as Scott elbowed him in the side. "Ignore him. He's just screwing around."

"Drinks on us ladies."

* * *

The six of them made their way through the crowd on the first floor over to the bar. "You want to do some shots?" Scott asked Crystal and her friends.

"Bring them on, handsome," Crystal said, flirting with Scott as Javon looked on with envy.

"Six shots of Jamerson," Scott ordered after he got the bartender's attention. "I need to see some ID," the bartender asked.

Scott pulled out his driver's license and handed it to the bartender, who looked it over quickly and handed it back to him. "Six shots, coming up," she said.

The bartender sat six shot glasses on the bar and filled each one with the bottle of Jamerson in her hand. "That will be eighteen dollars," she said. Scott handed her his credit card. "Keep the tab open," he requested as he passed everyone their shot off the bar. "Here's to new friends," he said, raising his shot glass in the air.

"To new friends, the rest of them repeated," as they all tossed back the shots.

"Aaaahhh! Damn, I can feel the heat coming back to my balls now," Marty said smiling.

As Scott locked eyes with Gabby, a nervous smile came across his face, damn she was beautiful, he thought. "Do you want to dance?" she asked him, taking him by surprise.

"Sure," he said as he took her hand, and she led him to the dance floor to the sounds of Peaches & Herbs. "Shake Your Groove Thing."

"Bartender another round," Javon said.

"Who's paying?" the bartender asked. "My boy got this," Javon said as he pointed to Scott out on the dance floor and gave him a thumbs up. Scott noticed him, smiled, and gave him the thumbs-up right back.

"See, I told you," Javon said back to the bartender with a mischievous smile on his face. "Attitude," Javon said smirking as the bartender walked off to get their drinks.

Pepper could feel Marty's eyes on her before he got up the nerve to speak. "Hey, would like to dance with the Marty man," he asked, smiling and dancing in place. She looked at Marty, who had a wide grin on his dimpled face. He was the shortest out of his two friends and the chubbiest. But Pepper got the impression that did not stop him from thinking he was a lady's man.

"Go Marty, Go," his friend Javon egged him on.

Marty licked his two fingers and rubbed his chest with them while swaying his hips.

Pepper laughed. "I'll dance with you, but please don't do that move on the floor."

"You got it!" Marty replied, grinning.

Crystal took a hit on her vape pen as she sized Javon up. He was tall with an athletic build and attractive and the most vocal of his small entourage. "So, what's your story?" she asked.

"What do you mean?" he answered as he looked off into the crowd of people and strangers on the dance floor.

"What do you think?" she asked coyly.

"Right now, I am just hanging out with my boys and enjoying the company of some beautiful women, but the night's still young and full of possibilities," he said flirtatiously, as the bartender finally poured their second round of shots at the bar.

Crystal smiled. "Okay, okay, I'll drink to that," she said. As she observes their friends coming off the dance floor and headed back over to the bar. They all pick up their shots.

"What are we toasting now?" Scott asked.

"To the creepiest club in Pontiac, maybe in the world!" Crystal said.

"Wait, what in the world are you talking about?" Javon said.

"Come on. You did not hear about this club?" Crystal asked, surprised.

"Hear what?" Scott interceded.

Crystal went silent as the bartender began wiping the bar off in front of them with a towel. "Can I get y'all anything else?" she asked.

"No, we're good for now, thanks," Javon answered back.

He looked back at Crystal. "You were saying?"

"Are you first-timers here?" Crystal asked.

"Yeah, so what," Marty answered.

Crystal and her girlfriends laughed.

"Let me give you guys a little history on this place," Crystal said.

"Please do," Javon said.

"This club use to be a church that was closed down due to numerous allegations of sexual abuse by the clergy as well as satanic rituals and blood sacrifices."

"Get the fuck out of here!" Javon laughed.

"No, seriously, there are people that say that their friends visited this club and were never heard from or seen again," Gabby stated.

"Well, wouldn't the police look into something like this?" Marty asked.

Crystal laughed. "Sure, but no evidence, no case, right."

"Bottoms up!" Gabby said as they all threw back their shots.

Crystal took out her iPhone and typed in mysterious disappearances associated with Nightclub. "Look at this," she said, showing Javon and his friends the news report and other stories related to the same nightclub that they were now occupying.

"This is some crazy shit!" Javon said.

"Yeah, but it also could be a publicity stunt orchestrated by the owner of this club to generate more business," Marty said, skeptical.

"True that," Scott said.

"Man, I gotta pee; anybody else has to go?" Marty asked.

"What? You scared to go to the restroom alone now, Marty?" Javon teased.

"Of course not," Marty responded sheepishly. "I was just asking, that's all."

Pepper grabbed Marty by the hand. "I'll show you where it's located. Javon, don't be an asshole," she said.

" What? I was just joking," Javon replied.

"Man, Pepper in rare form tonight, she ain't never been this outspoken before," Gabby said, as she took a sip of the beer they just ordered poured in clear plastic cups.

"Don't be an asshole," Javon said, mocking Pepper in a silly effeminate voice.

Scott patted Javon on the back. "Relax, dude, you are an asshole," Scott said, laughing.

Javon looked behind them at the bartender. She was smiling at him weirdly, but what was up with her eyes, he thought? They look all black with no hint of the sclera. "What the fuck?" he mumbled.

"What's wrong?" Scott asked.

Javon pointed at the bartender. " Man, her fucking eyes are zombie out."

"What?"

"Bro, her eyes were all fucking black! Eyeballs and all." He insisted.

"Dude, whatever you are smoking, I want some of that shit," Gabby interjected.

"Here she comes," Javon said with panic in his voice as he noticed the bartender headed over to a small booth with a table that they were now sitting at in the corner.

"You forgot this," she said, handing Scott his credit card.

"Thanks," Scott replied.

"Anything else," she said, as she made eye contact with everyone that was at the booth.

"No thanks, we're good," Scott said.

"You too?" she asked Javon.

Javon swallowed the lump in his throat. "Yea…Yeah… thanks," he stammered. He watched her intensely as she walked away from the table.

Scott took a sip of his beer and shrugged his shoulder. "She looked normal to me," he said.

"Bro, don't you think that was weird that she turned to me and said you too?" Javon asked.

"Yeah, that was weird," Crystal answered before Scott did.

"Maybe she likes you, roomie, I don't know," Scott said.

"Man, where in the hell is Marty, and your girl? Did they get lost?" Javon asked.

"You right; they have been gone for a while," Crystal responded, looking at her cell phone.

A commotion suddenly broke out on the dance floor, directing all their attention to what was going on in that area of the club. All they could see was two large bouncers rush in and pull two guys apart fighting on the floor over only God knows what. One of the combatants looks worse for the wear than the other with a black eye and a busted lip.

"Wow, First fight for tonight," Gabby said.

After the two patrons were removed from the dance floor and most likely the club itself, the other clubbers filtered back out on the dance floor and began dancing again to the music as if nothing ever occurred.

"Hey, did you see that dude get his ass kick?" Marty asked as he and Pepper returned to the table.

"What did you do fall through the toilet?" Javon asked.

"No, Pepper and I were just getting to know each other better," he said, winking at Pepper, who blushed.

"Whatever," Javon said. "This beer tastes like warm piss."

"Javon saw one of the black-eyed kids," Gabby said.

"No shit! Who?" asked Pepper.

"The bartender," Gabby answered, nodding towards the bar.

"What the fuck is a black-eyed kid?" Javon asked, agitated.

"They are paranormal creatures that disguise themselves as children that appear to people at their homes or parking lots, and their eyes are completely black, including the whites of their eyes," Gabby answers.

Javon took the last sip of his warm piss beer and crumpled the plastic cup in his hand. "Man, y'all weird as shit!" he said.

"What are you scared of?" Crystal asked.

"I ain't scared of shit!" Javon replied defensively.

"Then I have a proposal," Crystal said, gushing with delight.

"What's that?" Javon asked.

Crystal's face lit up. "Let's hideout in the club after it closes and everybody leaves."

"That's trespassing. Can't we get arrested for that if we get caught?' Marty stated, concerned.

"Not if no one knows we are here," Crystal answered.

"I am in," Gabby said. "Me too," said Pepper.

Scott laughed. "That's crazy, but why not?" he said.

Pepper walked over to Marty and gave him a soft peck on the lips. "Okay, I am in," he said, grinning.

"What the fuck! Seriously?" Javon said, flustered. He grabbed Scott by the arm. "Bro, we need to talk," he said as he escorted Scott away from the booth and the listening distance of Crystal and her friends.

"What's up, Roomie?" Scott asked.

"Are you kidding me, bro? We barely know these Halloween bitches, and you all are talking about hiding out in this nightclub with them after it closes. For all, we know they could be part of a cult and setting us up as sacrificial fucking lambs, for a black mass or some shit!"

Scott busted out laughing. "Come on, are you fucking serious, bro? These girls are just trying to punk us."

"What?" Javon replied.

"Javon, you don't think they are fucking serious, do you?"

Javon looked at Scott, still confused. Was it something that he had missed? Or maybe his friends had been hexed, by these broads he thought.

"Look, bro, we are all getting laid tonight and our pipes wet if we play our cards right, including Marty, who probably haven't had a piece of ass since he broke up with his girlfriend, Carly."

"That would be about three months ago," Javon said.

Scott placed his hand on Javon's shoulder. "Exactly, if he keeps jerking off, he is going to have arms like Popeye and carpet palms like Bigfoot," Scott said.

Javon laughed. " Ha, ha, ha, that's funny, roomie."

"Bro just play along, and the next thing you know, you will have Crystal moaning in your ears. Oh,' Javon, Javon," Scott said, leaning into his friend's ear.

Javon grinned. "Yeah, I would like to tap that ass."

Scott laughed. "Get to work, then pimping and stop acting like a Chump."

"Bro, you keep talking like that, and your Wasp ass parents are going to disown your ass," Javon said.

"Yeah, right," Scott replied, smiling.

Crystal walked over to Javon and put her hand on his chest. "So, what's up?" she asked softly.

"I am in," he said. Crystal smiled and took Javon's face into her hands, and began kissing him. He felt himself getting hard as her tongue entered his mouth.

"I knew you'd come around," she said.

"Wow, that was hot!" Pepper said, giggling.

"Our turn," Gabby said to Scott.

Marty jumped up and raised his drink. "Let's get this fucking party started now!" He shouted out excitedly.

Javon looked back over at the bartender. Was it just his imagination, or did she just nod at him with a mischievous smile on her face?

"I knew you would come around," Crystal's voice echoed in his head. But had he made the right decision? His voice asked back in his head.

ACKNOWLEDGMENTS

Special thanks, to editor Mark Strange, for his invaluable expertise and taking this book to another level.

All contributors to this edition.
And last but not least the fans of this genre that keeps it alive.

~ Lee J. Minter May 2021 ~

Thank you for purchasing this novel. If you enjoyed this novel and found some benefit in reading this, we would like to hear from you and hope that you can post a review of this novel on Amazon. Your feedback and support will help this author significantly improve his writing craft for future projects and make this book even better.

~ Thanks, from TCP. ~

ALSO BY THIS AUTHOR ARE THESE NOVELS ONLINE AND IN SELECT BOOKSTORES

Follow me on Twitter **@LJMHorror4u**
Follow me on Instagram **@mintboogie**
Visit me @ my web page at **LJMHorrorTales4u.com**

LEE J. MINTER is back again, this time with the long awaited sequel to "In Sheep's Clothing" Never Cry Wolf proves worth the wait and is a worthy addition to its predecessor. Make a hole and make it wide for the new master and self-proclaimed rock star of horror, aka mintboogie. Horror will never be the same. Stay tuned.